D1237267

NELSON ALGREN'S
OWN BOOK OF
LONESOME MONSTERS

Books by Nelson Algren

The Neon Wilderness

The Man with the Golden Arm

A Walk on the Wild Side

Who Lost an American?

Nelson Algren's

OWN BOOK OF

Lonesome

Monsters

PUBLISHED BY

BERNARD GEIS ASSOCIATES

DISTRIBUTED BY RANDOM HOUSE

Hum
PZ
1
A412 Ne

ADDRESS BY GOOLEY MacDOWELL TO THE HASBEENS CLUB OF CHICAGO by Saul Bellow, Hudson Review; © 1951 by the Hudson Review

AMONG THE DANGS by George P. Elliott; © 1958 by George P. Elliott

THE CLOSING OF THIS DOOR MUST BE OH, SO GENTLE by Chandler Brossard, The Dial—1962; © 1962 by the Dial Press, Inc.

DAY OF THE ALLIGATOR by James Blake; © Paris Review #17 (1957)

ENTROPY by Thomas Pynchon, Kenyon Review; © 1960 by Thomas Pynchon

THE HOUSE OF THE HUNDRED GRASSFIRES, from A WALK ON THE WILD SIDE by Nelson Algren; © 1956 by Nelson Algren, F, S&C

HUNDRED DOLLAR EYES by Bernard Farbar; © 1962 by Bernard Farbar

THE MAN WHO KNEW WHAT ETHIOPIA SHOULD DO ABOUT HER WATER-TABLE by H. E. F. Donohue; © 1961 by Carleton College, Carleton Miscellany

PEACETIME by Brock Brower, NWW #19; © 1961 by J. B. Lippincott Company

THE SHORES OF SCHIZOPHRENIA by Hughes Rudd; © 1961 by J. B. Lippincott Company

SHOW BIZ CONNECTIONS by Bruce Jay Friedman; © 1962 by Bruce Jay Friedman

THE SLEEP OF BABY FILBERTSON by James Leo Herlihy; © 1953 by James Leo Herlihy

SOUTH'S SUMMER IDYLL by Terry Southern; © 1957 by the Paris Review

TALK TO ME, TALK TO ME by Joan Kerckhoff; © 1962 by Joan Kerckhoff

WORLD FULL OF GREAT CITIES by Joseph Heller; © 1955 by Manvis Publications, Inc.

All rights reserved under International and Pan American Conventions. Published by Bernard Geis Associates; distributed by Random House, Incorporated, in New York and simultaneously in Canada by Random House of Canada, Limited.

Some of these stories previously appeared in a collection edited by Nelson Algren and published by Lancer Books.

Library of Congress Catalog Card Number: 63-18453

Manufactured in the United States of America

First Printing

LIBRARY
FLORIDA STATE UNIVERSITY
TALLAHASSEE, FLORIDA

FOR CANDIDA

not an agent—a possession

Contents

Contents

NELSON ALGREN'S
OWN BOOK OF
LONESOME MONSTERS

Introduction

O<small>N A JUNE</small> afternoon in 1959 a three-and-a-half-year-old girl was murdered in the basement of a Philadelphia home.

The murderer was an honor student, a gentle boy of fifteen from an exemplary home, who had always given an excellent formal presentation of himself; who after the crime was described as "seldom or never a bother to his parents, very clean and basically unexpressive."

How can such promise yield such ill result? In the phrase "basically unexpressive" we already have been told: Nothing human is unexpressive—basically.

"I didn't know I was alive in this world until I felt things hard enough to kill for them—I feel all right when I look at it that way"—Bigger Thomas felt all right, in the final chapter of Wright's *Native Son*, when he looked at it that way. Because it was better, he now knew, to be admitted to the company of men as a murderer than not to be admitted at all.

"My work shall not be an utter failure because it is not an endless analysis of affected sentiments but in its essence it is action, nothing but action—action observed, felt and interpreted with an absolute truth to my sensations, action of human beings that will bleed to a prick, and are moving in a visible world" an English seaman named Joseph Conrad wrote in 1902.

Like Bigger Thomas when confronted by a void where his life should have been, Conrad filled it by a creative act. That his was an act of love while Bigger Thomas' was an act of hate is irrelevant: whenever you shut a human being out of the world, he will, for better or for worse, build one of his own.

"He was uninterested in this boring yet threatening world from which he hardly knew what to ask. He was offered activities, responsibilities and honors—nothing, no simple venture interested or excited him. He wished to be both a public figure whose acts are ordained by convention and routine, and a live human being as well," Simone de Beauvoir writes of the Marquis de Sade.

A common tie unites the strangler of a child, the creative artist, the classic eroticist and the murderer of fiction; upon which the father of the slain girl, writing to the people of Philadelphia a few hours after the crime, throws a white light:

"This comes from a profound lack of comprehension, a failure of admission of the full range of human emotion which is our common heritage," he wrote, "and which, for convention's sake, we are so fond of denying. It ought to be openly recognized that every human being must, by his nature, express hostility, rage, fear and destructiveness as well as love, creativeness and joy.

"Let no feeling of vengeance influence us. Let us rather help him who did so human a thing."

So *human* a thing!

The implications of the victimized father's letter are startling. He is not here simply reminding us of Goethe's confession— "I have never heard of a crime of which I am not myself capable" —but he is saying that if all men are good (as Bruno Bettelheim has pointed out) that there never was an Auschwitz. There never was a Belsen. He is saying that if Adolf Eichmann was a being different from the rest of us, now that he has been put out of the way, the world is a better place. If the conventional image we keep of ourselves *is* our true image.

He is saying that the pitiful figure of Eichmann dangling from a gallows has no meaning beyond the gratification of the urge to punish. Unless it can bring us the understanding that in each of us an Eichmann only waits for the proper circumstance to start giving orders.

He is saying that the question before mankind is not merely whether he shall survive, but whether he will then remain the wildest beast that still roams free. He is saying that conventional fatuity is denying us understanding of what we really are. That while we fancy the gates of Auschwitz shut forever, Auschwitz has been extended to North Africa and the S.S. extended to the O.A.S.

And as the S.S. destroyed the image of what it once meant to be a German and the O.A.S. has undercut the image of France as a civilized nation, we must recognize that, in the eyes of the world, the C.I.A. is now reversing the meaning of what it once meant to be an American.

"If you don't know my name," the Negro novelist James Baldwin cut in close, "you don't know your own."

In order to make Man free we must first understand what Man is.

And at St.-Paul-de-Vence a schoolmaster who once replaced a code of blind obedience, for seven-year-old pupils, by one appealing to their friendship, received two direct results. The children's painting and writing became as original and lively as possible—and the villagers stoned his windows.

Pacifists, one New England summer, sculled up to the Harvard-Yale crew races, uninvited, with a huge balloon, also uninvited, upon which they had emblazoned LET MANKIND LIVE, sailing above their scull. Somebody brought it down with a police pistol amid the cheers of thousands.

Yet the fact that freedom is an inexhaustible source of discovery remains.

The stories that follow have the common hope that every man, no matter how lonesome nor what a monster, is deserving of understanding by us other lonesome monsters.

The two stories I found of most interest here are not the most skillfully written. Neither is the work of a craftsman.

Yet, in James Blake's *Day of the Alligator* one feels human beings "that will bleed to a prick, and are moving in a visible world."

And behind the preposterous tears of the whimpering bride-groom of Joan Kerckhoff's *Talk to Me, Talk to Me* I heard the grave voice of a slain child's father saying over and over—

"Who did so *human* a thing."

—NELSON ALGREN

JOSEPH HELLER

World Full of Great Cities

THE BOY left his last telegram with the receptionist in the lawyer's office and walked down Beekman Place to the apartment house. He rode the elevator to the sixth floor, found the door he wanted, rang the bell, and waited. After a few seconds the door opened, and a blonde woman looked out at him. She opened the door wide when she saw him. She remained motionless in the doorway, studying him coldly from head to foot. She was a beautiful woman, and the boy felt his face color as he lowered his eyes and waited for her to speak.

"Where'd you park your bicycle?" she asked finally.

"We don't have bicycles," the boy said. "I had to walk."

"Is that why you got here so fast?"

"I came as soon as I could," the boy said. "I had to make four stops before I came here."

"I wasn't being sarcastic. You came sooner than we expected. Can you wait a few minutes? My husband is busy."

"I can wait," the boy said.

"Come inside then." The woman stepped back and he followed her into the apartment. As he moved inside, he noted immediately how expensively decorated the room was. He stared about him with wondrous respect at the large room and at the rich furnishings that met his gaze wherever he looked. There were several photographs about the room, and behind her he noticed a cigarette burning in a silver ash tray.

"How do you like it?" the woman asked caustically.

"I'm sorry," the boy said. "I was just looking around."

"Don't be sorry. You can look around all you want. It's a privilege we extend to the proletariat."

She walked across the room, picked up the cigarette, and crushed it out. She turned slowly and looked at him.

"I bet it's just like your own home."

The boy remained silent. He stood in the center of the room, feeling warm and uncomfortable, and moved his cap slowly in his hands.

"Isn't it?" the woman persisted.

"No," the boy answered softly.

"Why isn't it? I suppose your home is nicer."

The boy didn't speak.

"Is it?"

"My home isn't as nice as this," the boy said.

The woman turned from him and picked a cigarette from an ivory box. On the table there were some glasses, a bottle of whiskey, and a bottle of club soda. She lighted her cigarette and turned, exhaling smoke through the side of her mouth.

"It's a beautiful place, isn't it?" she asked in a softer tone.

"Yes," he said. "It's very beautiful."

"I suppose you think anybody can be happy living here." When he didn't answer, she asked, "Don't you?"

"I don't know." The boy looked down at the floor.

"Don't rationalize. You know damn well they can. Don't you realize the power of money?"

The boy looked up and met her eyes. "Why are you picking on me?" he asked. "I didn't do anything to you."

The woman raised her hand and rubbed it across her cheek, leaving a pallid mark that disappeared instantly, and she pursed her lips together in a nervous expression of regret. "I'm sorry.

I didn't mean to pick on you. I'm upset. I have to talk to you until my husband comes and I don't know what to say."

The boy smiled apologetically, realizing she was under some strain. She was very beautiful and he was sorry for her.

"What's your name?" she asked.

"Sidney."

A man called from another room, "Who is it?"

"It's the messenger," the woman answered.

"How does he look?"

The woman looked at the boy. He stood without moving, turning his cap slowly in his hands and wondering what they wanted of him.

"He's pretty," the woman said. "But he's very young."

There was the sound of footsteps on tile, and a thin middle-aged man entered the room, wearing a deep blue dressing gown with a towel around his neck and holding an electric shaver in his hands. He nodded coldly to the boy as he studied him. The woman sat down in a corner of the sofa. She kicked off her shoes and tucked her legs up behind her.

The man frowned. "He looks effeminate."

"That would be just my luck," the woman said bitterly.

"I'll send him back." The man stepped toward the boy and smiled. "Look, go back to the office and tell them to send an older boy. We have a special errand and we need an older boy. Do you understand?"

The boy nodded and turned to go.

"Let him stay," the woman said. "I think it will be better with him. I think I'll feel a little safer."

"Do you really think so?"

The woman nodded.

"All right." He turned to the boy. "I'll be with you in a few minutes. Sit down and wait. Give him a drink," he said to the woman and left the room.

"Sit down, Sidney." The boy walked across the room and sat down in a chair facing her. "And don't look so uncomfortable. No one is going to hurt you."

He placed his cap on a table near the chair and looked about the room self-consciously. There was a photograph of a good-

looking boy in a football uniform, and he wondered if he was
her son. She looked too young to be his mother.

"What's the matter?" the woman asked.

"Nothing," the boy said.

"Don't be afraid of me. Do you want a drink?"

He shook his head.

"I didn't think so. You're too young to drink."

"I drink," the boy said.

"Whiskey?"

"Sometimes," he lied. "I like beer, though."

"I have some in the kitchen. Do you want a bottle?"

"No, thanks. We're not allowed to drink when we're working."

"Do you smoke?"

"We're not allowed to smoke either."

"You go ahead and smoke," the woman said. "Do they pay
you well?"

"Pretty well."

"How much do you make a week?"

"I don't make so much," the boy explained. "I only work
after school. The ones that work all week make a lot."

"You're going to make a lot today," the woman said, sitting
up as she crushed her cigarette out. She poured some whiskey
into a glass and added a bit of soda. She stared soberly into the
glass for a few seconds as she swirled it around in quick circles.
Then she raised the glass and emptied it. The boy watched her
face. She swallowed without expression.

"Sidney," she said, setting the glass down, "you're a very
pretty boy. I'll bet the girls in school go wild over you."

The boy turned away, flushing with embarrassment.

"Do you go with girls?"

He nodded.

"I'll bet you have a lot of them."

"I have a few," the boy answered. He felt good because she
thought so.

"Do you get much?"

The boy thought he had misunderstood her and turned to
her questioningly.

"Do you get much?" she said again.

The boy's face burned with shame, and he stared down at a patch of rug between the legs of a round table that stood before the large window.

"You don't have to answer if you don't want to."

"I don't want to."

"All right, don't. If you're still a virgin, it's your own fault. The girls in school are wild about you."

"No, they aren't," the boy said, smiling shyly.

"Yes, they are. You look around and you'll see. You're a very pretty boy, Sidney. I'd like to see you on a cold day. I bet your lips and cheeks turn crimson when it's cold."

Sidney grinned with guilt. He had already noticed how red his lips and cheeks became on cold days and how good-looking he was compared to other boys his age. He had been kept close to home while his father was alive. Now he was forced to work in the city, and the world about him was beginning to unfold slowly in a vast and puzzling panorama, delighting him with each new revelation. He pointed to the picture of the boy in the football uniform.

"Is that your son?" he asked.

"No," the woman said. "It's Mr. Ingall's son." When he looked puzzled, she explained, "I'm his second wife."

"Oh."

"He used to stay here six months during the year, but now he's away at college. He hasn't been here for almost six years."

She reached forward and took another cigarette, tapping it nervously against the back of her hand. She picked up the lighter and turned to him, hesitating, and her face became really soft for the first time.

"You're a nice boy, Sidney," she said slowly. "The girls are crazy about you. I was your age once and I know. Get as many as you can before it's too late. That's what they're here for. Take them while you can and you'll never regret it. Neither will they." She stopped speaking when she saw how distressed he looked. "What's the matter?"

"I don't know," he mumbled.

"Are you always afraid to talk to girls?"

"No," he answered.

"Then what is it? Don't you ever discuss such things with them?"

"No grown-up woman ever talked to me about it before."

"Is it because I'm older or because I'm so nice looking?"

"Both, I guess."

"Do you think I'm nice looking?" she asked.

He nodded, blushing.

"Beautiful?"

He nodded again. He looked toward the foyer, wondering when the man would return.

"What do you like about me?"

"Everything, I guess."

"There must be something special you like. Is it my face, or my breasts, or the way you imagine my thighs are shaped?"

The boy felt himself perspiring and looked away at a table in the corner.

"Well? Which is it?"

"I wish you wouldn't talk like that," he said.

"All right," the woman said. "I won't talk like that. How would you like to go to bed with me?"

He turned to her with surprise, angry now and afraid, because he remembered her husband was in the next room. "I have to go," he said, and stood up. "I have to get back to the office."

"All right, Sidney," she said, with a shrug. "Sit down. I won't bother you." He sat down slowly, watching her suspiciously. "What's the matter?" she asked. "Don't I appeal to you?"

"Not that way," the boy answered in a low voice.

"Why not? If you saw me walking on the street, I'd appeal to you. Wouldn't I?"

He turned away. She was the most beautiful woman he had ever spoken to, and he knew that if he ever did see her walking on the street, he would stop and stare after her until she disappeared from sight.

"I guess I just don't interest you," the woman said wearily.

A silence fell, and the boy sat with his hands in his lap, trying not to stare at her pretty face or the full curves of her body. The man entered briskly with a nervous smile.

"Well, how's it going?" he asked.

"I don't think Sidney likes me," the woman said.

"Of course he likes you. You're probably just scaring him to death. Go inside and get ready. And hurry up. We can't keep him here all day."

She handed him her cigarette and walked from the room. The man turned to Sidney and smiled. He was somewhere in his late forties, with deep serious eyes, and his face, clean shaven now, was marked with deep lines running down from the sides of his nostrils to the corners of his mouth. His voice was soft and smooth, calm and serious. He led Sidney to the center of the room and they sat down facing each other.

"Do they mind if you stay out long on an errand?" he asked.

"I can't stay too long," Sidney said.

"Can you fix it up someway if we keep you?"

"I don't know," the boy answered.

The man reached into the pocket of his dressing gown and removed two bills. He held one out. Sidney took it hesitantly and put it away, noting, as he folded it, that it was a ten-dollar bill.

"That's for waiting so long," the man said. "I'll give you the other one when you do what we want."

"What do you want me to do?" the boy asked suspiciously.

"Didn't she tell you?"

"No."

"Well, don't worry about it. It isn't anything much." He poured a drink. "Do you want one?"

"No, thanks," the boy said. "What do you want me to do?"

"We'll tell you when she comes in." He swallowed the whiskey, making a wry face, and set the glass down. "What do you think of her?"

"She's very pretty," the boy answered.

"She's beautiful," the man said. "Beautiful. Do you like her?"

The boy nodded cautiously.

"She's beautiful," the man repeated. He seemed very depressed, very tired. He started to pour another drink, stopped himself, and set the bottle down. "She's an actress," he said.

The boy was thrilled. It was a new experience talking to an actress. "Are you an actor?"

"I work in television," the man said. He stared thoughtfully before him for several moments. "She's very unhappy," he said, slowly looking up. "We're both very unhappy."

The boy listened with interest.

"That's why we called you. It's an experiment. Would you want to help us?"

"I'd like to if I can," the boy said.

"All right. Maybe you can. How old are you?"

"I was just sixteen."

"Christ, you're just a kid. A happy, oblivious kid. You're a good-looking boy. I'll bet you make out all right with the girls, don't you?"

The boy didn't answer.

"You can talk to me," the man said. "I'm not a woman. Have you had much experience with girls?"

"I go with them a lot," the boy admitted.

"Are they fast?"

"Some of them are," Sidney answered. "Some aren't."

"Do you like the fast ones?"

Sidney grinned sheepishly. "What do you think?"

"Are they pretty?"

"A few are. Most of them aren't."

"You'll find that all through life. Are any of them as pretty as her?"

"No," the boy said. "None are that pretty."

The man leaned forward. "She's really a beautiful girl, isn't she?" he asked, watching the boy closely.

"Yes," he answered. "She is."

"How would you like to make love to her?" the man asked.

The boy turned away quickly. There was a strong under-current of desperation in the man's manner. It was strange and intense, and the boy was afraid because it was new to him and he did not know what it meant. The man's eyes were fixed upon him as he waited for a reply.

"I'd like a girl as pretty as her," the boy admitted, in a low, hesitant voice.

The man started to say something but fell silent and watched him for a while. He leaned back in the chair, drumming his fingers slowly on his knee.

"Do you ever get lost when you're working?" he asked.

"I used to at first," Sidney said. "I still do sometimes when they send me uptown."

"It's a hell of a feeling, isn't it?"

"It isn't so bad. The first time I was a little scared. Now I just ask somebody. It sure is a big city."

"It's a hell of a feeling being lost in a great city," the man said slowly. "And the world is full of great cities." His voice was deep and solemn. He spoke slowly, staring straight ahead, and his words seemed to emanate from a trance. "The human mind is a great city in which a guy is always lost. He spends his lifetime groping, trying to locate himself."

The boy listened solemnly, too impressed to reply.

"We're still strangers when we die," the man continued, "lost in a great big city."

He stood up and walked slowly to the window. He stared out at the afternoon without moving, and the boy felt that he had forgotten his presence. The man said quietly:

"It's a horrible picture when you think of it that way. A naked arm in every brain groping its way through a great black city. Can't you just see a world full of naked, groping arms?"

He turned and looked at the boy. He had his hand to his forehead, running his fingers slowly around his temple. "I can feel the arm in my own head. I get headaches. I can almost feel the fingers probing through the tissues." He looked at the boy with surprise, as though just discovering he was there. "Do you know what I'm talking about?"

"I think so," the boy said.

"No you don't. You're too young. And it's just as well." He walked into the foyer. "Goddammit, Helen," he called out, "hurry up. The kid doesn't have all day."

He walked across the room and seated himself in a chair facing the sofa. He poured some whiskey into a glass and held it between his legs, staring down at the floor. After a few seconds the woman returned. The boy sat up with surprise when he saw her. She had changed into a blue dressing gown and slippers, and when she walked across the room and sat down on the sofa, he could see the lithe round lines of her body rippling beneath the shiny film of material.

"Well?" she asked, looking at the man.

"Tell him," he said. "This is your idea."

"I thought you were going to."

"Do you want me to?"

The woman nodded. The man raised the glass to his lips and drained it. The boy watched his face curl into an expression of distaste. He waited fearfully. The man set the glass on a table and turned to the woman.

"You do it," he said.

"All right," the woman said, and turned to Sidney. "Have you ever seen a naked woman before?"

The boy gasped and looked away quickly. He felt the silence grow in the room and start to tingle and then ring in his ears.

"For chrisakes, don't be coy. Have you or haven't you?"

"No," the boy answered faintly.

"Would you like to see one now?"

Through the corner of his eye the boy watched the folds of her gown, terrified, not knowing what she was going to do. He shook his head. He felt panic rise within him, and the seconds crawled ominously.

"All right, Helen," the man said, "I'll do it. You sure as hell have no tact." He turned and looked at the boy. "Here's what we want you to do. We want you to make believe that Helen is one of your girl friends. Okay?"

The boy's breath caught in his throat. "What do you mean?"

"You know what I mean. Sit down and neck with her. We want you to make believe she's one of your fast girl friends."

The boy leaped to his feet violently, shaking his head again. His face was hot and damp, his body cold with terror. "No!" he said, blurting the word out. "I won't do it. Here." He groped in his pocket. "Here's your money back."

"Forget the damned money," the man said. "That's yours. Why won't you do it?"

"Because it isn't right, that's why."

The man shook his head slowly and forced a laugh. "You don't understand. It isn't anything wrong." He pointed to the photograph of the boy in football clothes. "You see that boy?" he asked. Sidney nodded. "That's our son. Mine and Helen's. He's dead now. She misses him. You know how mothers are. We just want you to kiss her, to sort of take his place."

The boy remembered what the woman had told him and knew the man was lying, but the fear left him slowly. He remembered how pathetically the man had turned from the window with his fingers on his forehead.

"You mean you want me to kiss her like she was my mother?" he asked.

"No. Just make believe she's one of your girl friends, the one you like best. That's all."

Sidney glanced at the woman. She was watching him with a tight, hopeful, pleading expression. The boy suddenly felt sorry for her. The man leaned forward, waiting for the boy to decide.

"All right," the boy said. "I'll kiss her if she says it's all right."

The woman smiled weakly and nodded. "It's all right."

The man stood up and walked to the liquor tray. The woman rose, beckoning the boy to approach, and he walked to her slowly. Behind him he heard the light splash of whiskey spilling into the glass. He came to a stop before her. She was an inch or two taller, and he looked up at her, trembling with fear and uncertainty. She held up her arms.

"Don't be afraid," she murmured tenderly, with a strange, sad smile.

The man stood to the side, motionless, watching with rigid attention. "Go ahead," he said, when the boy glanced his way. "It's all right."

The boy swallowed nervously. He leaned forward and kissed her on the mouth. The woman slid her arms around him. The boy raised his hands slowly to her shoulders. As he felt his fingers touch her, he pulled his face away quickly and stepped back with alarm.

"What's the matter?" the man demanded.

"He's afraid," the woman said.

"No wonder. You look like you're gonna scratch his eyes out. Smile at him."

The woman turned to the boy and smiled again. Her face grew soft and appealing, and deeply sorrowful. The boy felt a tide of affection grow, and he smiled back slowly. He stepped near her. She took his arms and placed them around her. She pulled his face against her own and slid her arms around him in a tight grip. Then she began kissing him about his mouth. The boy was too frightened to move. Her lips moved about his face more and more rapidly and then left him entirely.

"He's not doing anything!" the woman cried, tearing her face away for a moment and then throwing it back against his neck. Her shoulders shook and the boy knew she was crying. He heard and felt the giant sobs rolling through the body in his arms.

The man ran up behind him and began beating his hands on his back, shouting, "Kiss her! God damn you! Kiss her! Kiss her!"

He pushed him hard with both hands, and the boy and the woman tumbled to the sofa. The woman was weeping loudly. The boy stared and saw that her face was wracked with despair. Suddenly, she put her hands on his shoulders and shoved him away violently. He fell to the floor on his knees. He rose quickly and scampered across the room in panic, away from the man, who was glaring down at the woman with a wild, fiery expression, his fists clenched.

"It's no use!" she cried. "He's too young."

The man whirled upon the boy. "Go back to the office," he shouted angrily. "Tell them to send an older boy. Do you understand? An older boy. We want an older boy."

The boy nodded. He ran to the table and grabbed his cap, glancing quickly at the woman, whose loud, hysterical cries were tearing through the apartment. The man caught him when he started to the door.

"Wait a minute. Don't tell anybody anything. Forget what happened. Do you understand?"

"Tell them!" the woman cried. "Tell everybody!"

"Shut up, Helen. For Godsake, shut up."

The woman rose and ran to the boy, her face haggard with hysteria. "Tell everybody, Sidney," she sobbed. "Tell the whole damned world."

"Helen, shut up," the man pleaded, catching her shoulders. "Please shut up."

The boy watched her, unable to move. Her face was like chalk, shaking and cruelly distorted as she fought to break away.

The man raised his hand and slapped her across the face. She was stunned and stopped struggling. He backed her up slowly and set her down gently in a chair. He watched her sadly for a moment. Then he turned to the boy and walked him slowly to the door.

"Don't tell anyone a thing," he said quietly. He pushed the other ten-dollar bill into the boy's hand. "Forget all about it. Do you understand?"

The boy could hear the woman sobbing softly. Behind the man he could see her shoulders shaking in the chair.

"Remember now. Don't tell anyone. Okay?"

The boy nodded.

The man opened the door. "You'll forget all about it, won't you?"

The boy nodded again and stepped into the hall.

The door slammed shut.

JOAN KERCKHOFF

Talk to Me, Talk to Me

October 5, 1956

Dear Susan,

I met this kid named Marvin Karp, Jr., about three weeks ago. He's nuts. He's rich. And I'm going to marry him. There are probably a number of reasons why I shouldn't but I can't think of any of them. I can think of one big reason why I should. MONEY. I moved in with him last week. He thinks I did it because I couldn't bear being away from him for two seconds. Actually, I didn't have my rent money, as usual, and I didn't think it was a good idea to hit on him for any at this time. It could scare him. And enough people are telling him about me. You remember that dumb Bob I got $700.00 from for a fake abortion? Well he happens to be a friend of Marvin's, and when he found out I was living with Marvin, he told him all about it. Can you imagine anybody telling how they'd been taken? I told Marvin it was all a lousy lie. He believes anything I tell him. Marvin and this Bob go to the same shrink. He says he talks a lot about me to the doctor and Bob did too. I wonder if old Dr. Dedicated will know I'm one and the same? A few people in the area where I used to hang out are making bets on whether the kid will marry me or not. He gambles a lot.

Maybe I should tell him about it and he can win something for the first time in his life. I could tell him, "Okay, Marvin, here's a chance to win a lot of money. All you have to do is marry me." He's stupid enough to go for it. But he wouldn't like it that way. I'll have to go through some big dramatic scene with him. He's really going to have to go through a big dramatic scene with his parents when he tells them about me. I don't think they are going to approve of me. Difference in religion could be one reason. I could tell the senior Karps that some of the Junior's best friends are gentiles. How about that for a sound argument, Doctor? How about that for a sound basis for marriage?

Paula

October 18, 1956

Dear Susan,

I'm going to marry the kid in about ten days. I thought I might as well get it over with as soon as possible. I knew I'd have to go through a lot of bullshit.

About a week ago we were sitting around the apartment and I told him I wanted to marry him. I thought it would sound more dramatic if I just said it out of the blue. He hedged for about five minutes with dumb remarks like, "I'll have to think about it, you know marriage is really serious, you love me don't you?" I told him I was going to my sister Jane's house while he thought about it. "You need to be alone while you make your decision, Marvin. If you don't marry me though, I'm going to move. If I'm not good enough for you to marry, then I'm not good enough to stay with you." "Incidentally, I love you so goddamn much I couldn't bear it if you didn't feel the same way about me. And I know you don't love me if you don't marry me." I even cried a little bit for realism. I almost broke myself up though, I was getting so romantic. Jesus, wouldn't that have been rotten of me to laugh after telling him all that nonsense? I left and he picked me up at Jane's a couple of hours later. He walked in with a, "Hi, Jane, did Paula tell you we're getting married?" He looked at me and winked and I honestly thought he was going to do the old elbow in the ribs number and say, "Got that, I'm really going to marry you." I guess that was his way of letting me in on it. I had already told Jane he was going to marry me so she wasn't too taken aback by all of his silliness. I just smiled a dumb smile and felt like saying, "You won't be sorry, Old Man. You're doing the right thing." He wanted to get laid, I guess to sort of clinch the deal, so we left Jane's right away.

On the way home he asked if he could name the date for the ceremony. I told him, "Sure, if it's two weeks from this Saturday." He said, "Oh, that's really a perfect date, Honey."

He told a lot of people, including his parents, about us. None of them like the idea. People are even calling his father, Marvin told me. "Don't marry that girl, she just wants your money" seems to be the big line these days.

Marvin doesn't want to hear that. It doesn't make any difference to him what they say.

"I love you and I don't care what you've done in the past." I swear, his dialogue sounds like a Grade B movie or a page out of *True Confessions*.

All I can say is that when I get the divorce, the settlement better be worth my time and effort. By the way, his shrink does know I'm the same one that dumb Bob went with. He told Marvin maybe he should wait awhile before marrying me. He is too. Just about two more weeks.

Paula

November 1, 1956

Dear Susan,

Well, I just married the kid. He's definitely a lunatic. Really, I mean all you have to do is look at the expression in his eyes and you know immediately that he's totally nuts. The wedding was just only the silliest thing I've ever been in.

I was a smidge high and I had to act like I was nervous and wring my hands a lot. Marvin didn't have the foggiest notion what was going on. He ran around the apartment saying, "You love me don't you?" I think he was also nervous about a bet he had on a football game. I had the record player on, he had the television on, Jane was laughing, Marvin's brother (his parents couldn't make it), was on the verge of crying, and a lousy snob friend of Marvin's just sat around and shook his head. I guess in disgust. When I saw the wedding cake he brought us, I shook my head in disgust too. Or maybe it was disbelief. He told me, "Listen, Paula, you're going to have to go out of your way to win Marvin's friends over because they already have a bad taste in their mouth since you lived with him out of wedlock." I just said, "Uh huh, I'll do that." Jane said later on she thought I was really great in my role of nervous bride. I didn't laugh one time during the ceremony. Marvin still doesn't realize I married him only for his money. His parents do though. His father is also aware of his son's insanity, because after I met Mr. Karp, Sr., he told Marvin, "I thought that girl was marrying you for your money, but after meeting her I just think she's crazier than you are." I actually had to get drunk before I met them, I was so nervous about it. Marvin hit a car on his way to his parents' house that night, and we had to go to the police station and all kinds of nonsense. I thought the cops would put him away he was acting so nutty. The desk cop asked him for some identification and Marvin showed him a picture of his mother's poodles.

I was still laughing about it when we got to his parents'. I guess his father sort of had reason to think I was crazy. Besides being drunk and the accident, I think I did act a little peculiar. I can understand why they object to the kid marrying me though. Altogether different backgrounds and all. And I'm not exactly holding any good conduct certificates. Actually, I'm doing this kid the biggest favor that's ever been done him. He really needs help. He's twenty-six but more like a young fourteen. You know he got tears in his eyes at the police station? I started laughing and he looked at the cops and said, "Oh look, isn't she cute?" The cops shook their heads and let him go. Anyway, I now have tons of money and a charge account everywhere. I intend to put it to use immediately.

Paula

November 29, 1956

Dear Susan,

I've been married to this basket case for almost a month now. He refuses to see his shrink any more. I told him one time (I think before I married him) that I could help him but

I didn't want him to stop seeing his doctor. Jesus, with his problems he needs about three doctors and me. He's really peculiar. He's starting to do an awful lot of crying. Literally. I mean he cries over the dumbest things imaginable. Like, "This Is Your Life" on television or when I tell him I can't stand his guts. He doesn't know if I'm serious or not is why he cries I suppose. It's sort of sad, but I don't think I can stand much more of his weeping.

When I said he was a young fourteen, he had me snowed. He's more like an infant that needs a pacifier of some sort. I told him tonight that the next time he started crying I would put him in the closet. The one without the light. That should pacify him. I mean you have to understand that I'm not dealing with a sane, adult man here but a goddamn nut in diapers. There's not really many ways of communicating with him. He lies constantly about his job. He doesn't do anything there but listen to his father, who happens to be intelligent enough not to let that kid near anything that's of the smallest importance. He usually comes home from work and tells me, "Well, I made $50,000 today." Now I don't have to have a very high I.Q. to know that this is sheer fantasy on his part. If he could make fifty cents all on his very own, I'd be amazed. He also does a great deal of winning in card games. I've been through the checkbook and there are stubs in it for $450.00, $300.00, $125.00, etc., made out to everyone of his friends, "for bridge games." I'd just love to hear all the things he's told his shrink in the past. I wonder how a wife goes about having her husband committed.

Paula

December 5, 1956

Dear Susan,

Mr. Sob-ass had me so nervous tonight I had to put him in the closet. I can't feel guilty about it because I had warned him I would. We were having this little argument over whether I was going to go on reading or sit on the goddamn couch with him and watch "Lassie" on television.

The long and the short of it was he went into this stupid crying act of his, and I just told him, "O.K., you have to get in the closet now." He just sat on the couch and continued crying and I told him, "I mean it, get in there until you can stop that lousy crying." So he did. He stayed in there for what seemed to me too short of a time but he had dried his eyes so I had to let him out. He was fine the rest of the evening. Thinking that he might listen to me, I tried to talk to him and I asked him what was bothering him, but he wouldn't talk about it. I don't know if he's getting better or worse. I think I'll send him back to the shrink. He's too much of a burden for me to handle alone. You know how I've been amusing myself lately? I ask him dumb questions and get even dumber answers just to see how stupid he is. Then I explain to him how stupid his answers are, and he falls for it every time I do it. He turned out to be a lot sillier than I imagined. He's really fond of my sister Jane. If he doesn't understand a joke or something, he calls her. Last Sunday we were having breakfast (that's the only time I've cooked since we've been married), and it was really dull see, so I told him his food was poisoned and he had about one hour until he would be in his last agonies. He ran to the bathroom and stuck his finger down his throat, and when I told him, "That won't do any good, it's too late now, Old Man," he ran to the phone and called Jane (who's beginning to get a little irked at both Marvin and my jokes) and told her I had poisoned his food. She consoled him and told him I was only kidding. Christ, you'd think a person would know a joke when they heard one.

He wants to go on a belated honeymoon trip to Florida for a couple of weeks. I mentioned that I wanted Jane to go with us, but I couldn't tell how he felt about it because he just started muttering a lot. I'm not going to try to handle that kid alone away from home and everything. If he gets too unruly, I'll just put him back in the closet. I'm sure they have closets in Florida too.

Paula

December 16, 1956

Dear Susan,

We just got back from that unbelievable belated honeymoon trip to Miami. Jane went with us and I have her to thank for getting me through it. I knew it was going to be awful. I had never liked Miami and never will. Jane also hates it. You know

how most of the places, people, etc., are there anyway, well add
a frenzied, dotty, reasonless kid, a lot of rain, a hotel room that
cost $104.00 a day (plus Jane's which was $40.00 a day), and
you can just imagine how rotten it was. It was raining when we
got there and kept raining the whole two days we were there.
I thought it might be a good idea to stay inside while it was
raining and I could also just sit around and try to appreciate a
$104.00 a day room. Jane agreed because she wanted to make
a couple hundred telephone calls to her boy friend. I think her
room, plus calls, plus B & B's, sandwiches, etc., amounted to
around $150.00 per day, so she wasn't left out of the finer things
of life either.

As soon as we got settled in our room, Mr. Unhinged called
room service. We ordered three coffees, one corned-beef sandwich and one dish of ice cream. Jane got hysterical instantly
after they brought up our order. I didn't know what the hell was
happening and I could just see Marvin getting paranoid over it,
so I asked her, "What the hell's wrong?" She said, "I got a
look at the bill for our little snack and it was $12.00." I broke up
too but Marvin didn't at all. I don't know but maybe that's the
difference with people who are used to money and ones who
aren't. He didn't blink an eyelash over it, and Jane and I were
roaring. Actually, he was probably right because any simple son
of a bitch that would pay $104.00 a day for a hotel room
couldn't possibly get a laugh out of a $12.00 dish of ice cream.
We woke up the next day and it was still raining. So we just
had breakfast in our room. (I still hadn't fully appreciated that
dreary room.) I suggested something about going to Jane's
room, but he wanted to get a little sex in. So we went in the
toilet and he got laid and I got depressed. I suppose I was out
of line in my thinking then. After all, it was supposed to be a
honeymoon thing. The whole sex thing with him is pretty
pukey. It sort of leaves a rotten taste in my mouth. "One
never gets something for nothing" is what I have to keep in
mind. But then it was lunch time and that cost about $40.00 so
he was pretty happy. We went over to Jane's room after lunch.
I just wanted to sit and relax and talk to Jane. I was so tired of
being with the moron and not being able to talk talk that made
any sense.

He fell on the bed and started making a lot of noises like he was gagging or something, and Jane and I started giggling. I asked him if he felt ill or did he just feel like making gagging noises. Then we had this very intelligent conversation. He said, "I don't know what to do." I asked him, "About what?" He said, "I don't know about what." After that I thought I had had all the talk I could handle for that afternoon. We got dressed for dinner that night and we were on our way out the door and he glanced in the mirror and asked his usual question, "You love me don't you, I don't look Jewish do I?" I said, "Jesus, Marvin, no you don't look *very* Jewish and yeah, I love you." "Christ." Since all I could think about was getting home, I told Marvin I was going to make reservations to go the next day. He had lost any grip on sanity that he ever had anyway so it didn't make any difference to him. We were supposed to stay there two weeks but I just couldn't stand it. Don't ever marry an idiot, Susan, and if you do, don't go to Florida with him.

Paula

December 28, 1956

Dear Susan,

Man am I down today. I think it's about time to get out of this damned marriage. Marvin saw his father after we got back from that dumb Florida trip. The senior asked him why we came back so soon and Marvin told him because it was raining. He woke me up to tell me this and also to tell me his father wanted him to get a divorce.

He said his father told him the trip didn't sound like much fun but Mr. Deranged told him it couldn't have been more delightful. Except for the rain. I wonder how parents feel when they know they have an idiot son. These parents work pretty well with theirs. They say, "Oh, yes?" and "Really?" all in the right places. They seem to work this way with everybody else though, come to think of it. The kid is really beginning to grate. Actually, I'm scared of him. The other night he was pretending to be asleep so he could say things that he doesn't have nerve enough to say to me while he's awake. "I love her but I'm going to kill her," he said a couple of times. I couldn't sleep for about a week and it was driving me crazy. He did start seeing

his shrink again. Three times a week. I think he's goofier than
ever. Even when I tell him I don't love him he doesn't believe
it. I suppose he can't believe it right now. I don't make it with
him any more. He asked me why I wouldn't and I told him he
was too repulsive and I couldn't fake it any more. You know
what he said? "What am I going to do?!" I told him to drink a
lot of juices and make a few bets. Then go see his mother. He
can buy somebody if he wants to, I told him, but he thought
I was kidding. I think it would be easier to have him committed
than get a divorce. I feel that I've earned anything that I can
get from this rotten affair, though, so I might as well divorce
him.

                                                        Paula

                                                January 5, 1957
Dear Susan,
   This kid won't let me read, watch television, paint, sleep, or
anything. He keeps saying, "Talk to me, talk to me."
   When I try, he won't say anything. He's also being obvious
with his sickness with other people. We were out the other night
and some people I knew came in the bar so I introduced him
and the first thing he said to them was, "You like me don't you,
huh?" I can't seem to blank the kid out like I thought I could.
I really believe I've helped him though. Before he met me he
was completely stupid about people and the world. This marriage will give him something to think and talk about for the
rest of his life. He still won't believe I married him for his
money, and it's all right with me that he feels this way, because
like everybody else he likes to think he's loved. Boy I think I'd
really like to be out scuffling again. Not really, I wouldn't. I just
need a Sicilian bandit to do away with this kid so I can have
all the money.

                                                        Paula

                                                January 30, 1957
Dear Susan,
   I finally decided to see an attorney to get the divorce over
with. I sort of goofed though. I went shopping every day of the
week and bought $7,000.00 worth of clothes. I had everything

sent to Jane's so he wouldn't know about it. I started this on a Monday and by Friday I put my plan to work. He came home and I was pretty hostile towards him so he'd get upset. I told him I thought it best that we separate for a while. What I wanted to do, see, was to get him to leave me, then I could tell the lawyer he had deserted me. He cried after I told him about the separation thing, but he left, so I went to the lawyer the next day and he started a separate maintenance suit immediately. I mentioned that I had gone on a small shopping trip and my lawyer told me it was a big mistake because that would seem like I really didn't like Marvin.

I moved and the day before I moved Marvin and his lawyers came up to see what condition I was leaving the apartment in. It was in awful condition. I accidentally spilled paint on his "beautiful, white, four-inch wall-to-wall carpeting." The paint was spilled wall to wall too. I had called Mr. Out of His Mind and told him I was going to move, and he said, "Take anything you want but leave my Lester Lanin records." He sure is wild about Lester. Maybe he could marry him next time. I had painted Nuts' portrait, and his attorney said, "It certainly looks like you," to him. I had painted tears in his eyes, as it was the usual look on his face. I suppose his lawyers must have caught his crying act once or twice too. I asked Marvin for a hundred dollars for friendship's sake, and he gave it to me and said, "O.K. but just for friendship." He'll never learn. My lawyer told me Nuts left for Europe the day of the divorce. I hope he isn't bitter about anything. I really got a good settlement. I think I earned it though. Don't you?

Paula

BRUCE JAY FRIEDMAN

Show Biz Connections

Oℕᴇ ᴅᴀʏ Mr. Kreevy, a shambling, Lincolnesque man
of thirty, took a thorn out of a distinguished stranger's foot and
got himself a wonderful deal involving girls. Until the thorn
extraction, Mr. Kreevy had never done well with women. His
only satisfactory memory in that direction was of a masseuse
in Tokyo who worked with her feet and had given him a few
extra minutes of seductive toe digs about the lower back. A
dance critic by profession, he exercised little finesse in his handling of the ladies; at lunch once, an aging member of a touring
Yemenite folk troupe suggested she found his shambling, Lincolnesque qualities attractive, but he had frightened her off with
a loud, yellowed, whinnying horselaugh.

One night, after dashing off a cynical critique of the pach-
onga, Mr. Kreevy left his cramped dance critic's office atop a
Manhattan skyscraper and headed for his favorite place of all—
the elevator. Somber when entering elevators, Mr. Kreevy, once
he saw he was to be alone in one, would strike mid-floor ballet
poses, straightening up as he approached possible stops and
then falling into others when he was in the clear. He would
then emerge on the ground floor wearing a guardedly funereal
expression. On this particular evening Mr. Kreevy, anxious to

test out a newly styled *grand jeté* he'd gotten wind of, rang the down button with a certain giddiness; when the doors opened, he was disappointed to see seated on the floor a distinguished-looking old gentleman with Edwardian whiskers stroking one bare foot.

"Get that button on 'hold,' will you," said the man. "I've got a thorn in here and I've been going up and down with it. It isn't my first. I've had others, but this one is a lulu. Deep. I think they come in through my spats."

Mr. Kreevy, self-conscious when meeting new people, let fly his bellowing, toothy horselaugh, and the old gentleman said, "What in hell do we need that for. Look, do you think you can get 'er out of there? Just poke around and she'll slide out. I never can do them myself."

"I never went for feet," said Mr. Kreevy, falling into a suspicious, defensive crouch, and the old gentleman said, "They're sweet-smelling if that's what you're on guard about. Get moving will you. I have an inkling this one's a deepie and they can be murder."

Suspiciously, Mr. Kreevy knelt down, and in several seconds his craggy, Lincolnesque fingers had plucked out the thorn.

"Done with class," said the old gentleman. "I timed you on it and you're one of the swiftest. It *was* a deepie, too. Now look, I don't stand around pumping your hand in gratitude if that's what you're after. I *really* pay off. For an ordinary extraction I generally pass along your pick of any American compact car, whitewalls, service and parts for a year. But this one really *was* a deepie, and wait till you hear what you're getting."

"I'll settle for the car right now," said Mr. Kreevy, throwing up a defensive smoke-screen of surliness.

"You'll take what I give you," said the old gentleman. "Be at my lavishly furnished office at six tomorrow afternoon." He shook Mr. Kreevy's long, hairy, Lincolnesque fingers, gave him his card, and when the elevator reached the lobby, disappeared into a midnight crowd.

The next afternoon Mr. Kreevy, in shaggy, Lincolnesque clothes, appeared at the old gentleman's exquisitely paneled, secretary-less office and threw his bony legs up on the man's huge, bare desk in a manner that had always offended girls. The sign on the door had said, "Irving's Suite," and Mr. Kreevy, in what he considered earthy, log-cabin directness, asked "What's the Irving bit?"

"My wife wants me to change it to Brad for class," said the old gentleman, "but I'm hanging onto it. I figure you need one show biz touch to make your classiness all the more authentic. You're going to be glad you passed up the car. What I've got for you involves women, and from what I've seen of those charming little ways of yours, and those socks you wear, you need this like life itself."

Mr. Kreevy felt for his socks and pulled them out of his shoes. They were a strange swamplike color with beige stripes. He had several dozen pairs of them, having bought them in job lots, and they were the only kind he wore. Behind his back, office mates referred to them as "Lats," implying they were the kind of socks worn by newly arrived refugees from Latvia.

"I'll still take the car," said Mr. Kreevy, his great teeth horsy and sly.

"What I do," said the old gentleman, "is throw you in among women who are finished. They're in disasters of various kinds and they have, say, twenty minutes to live. You appear to them and suddenly they don't mind these cute little ways of yours the way they would if they met you under different circumstances. You're the last man they'll ever have a shot at. Are you getting the picture? You show up, they know it's all over, and *bam*, you're all set. As soon as you finish up, I whisk you out of there. *You* don't die, just them."

Mr. Kreevy threw his head back in what was to be a contemptuous horselaugh, but no sound came forth, and in spite of himself, he began to perspire. He tugged nervously at his swamp-colored "Lats" and, embarrassed over his own words, croaked, "How do I get started on one of these?"

"Funny how everyone wants a fancy way to do them. All right, Irving will fix you up. Tell you what. I'll start you off on them right from this office. When you come in here, maybe I'll be present, maybe I won't. Anyway, just lie down on that couch over there, holler out . . . Oh, I don't know . . . holler out 'What are Shelley Winters?' and close your eyes. I'll set it up that way. Let's do one now to get you rolling."

"I'm not so sure I go for this whole thing," said Mr. Kreevy, but as he said it, he was backing his way to the couch. "I don't con so easily," he said, but then he settled back on the couch, loafers smudging up the fabric, whispered the Winters line, and found himself on the deck of a flaming yacht, its bow beneath the surface.

"Am I visible to everyone or just the girl?" he tried to holler back, but by the time he got it out, a tall, high-cheekboned young woman with dirt-begrimed face was making her way toward him. "We're going down, but I'll be damned if I'll panic," she said. "Who are you, you vile man?"

"I show up on these," said Mr. Kreevy, not really sure what manner to assume.

"You're certainly a dreadful-looking person. I didn't notice you before. Keep your damned distance and don't get any vile ideas just because we're on our way down. Did I ever meet you at the Garretts in Southampton?"

"I don't know any Garretts," said Mr. Kreevy, wondering how much time he had.

"Isn't this a chore," said the woman, dragging deep on a cigarette as the flames came nearer and more of the yacht went under. "I suppose you're to become demented or something, but I'll be damned if I'm giving in to any of that. Look at those asses over there, shouting and carrying on as if it made any damned difference. If you can't wind it all up with a little reserve, what good is the whole business? God, you're a frightening-looking creature."

"Yes," said Mr. Kreevy, uncertainly, "but I'm the last man you'll ever see."

"Yes, and quite a specimen you are, too. At least if you weren't so wretched looking. You keep your distance or you're getting one right in your gizzard. Whoever thought you up must have had some joke in mind."

The water came up to both their waists then; they were the only ones who seemed not to have been washed overboard.

"Well, I suppose this is it," the girl said. "God, you're a beast. At least if you were *interesting* looking . . . Oh, heaven help me," she said with a little shiver and at the same time shut her eyes, reached over and tweaked Mr. Kreevy's buttocks, then

went under. Mr. Kreevy at that very instant being whisked back
to the couch.

"The answer's no, no one but the girl can see you," said the
old gentleman. "I'm sorry I couldn't get through to you. How'd
you do? I stood by to find out how the first one went."

"It was no bargain," said Mr. Kreevy, running two fingers
over his great horselike teeth. "I'm not so sure it worked out at
all. I got a little grab out of the whole deal."

"I'm not going along to hold your hand if that's what you're
after," said the bewhiskered gentleman. "I think the others
ought to go smoother. You're no Paul Newman, you know, and
those cute little ways don't help. All right, out you go. You can
do as many of these as you want, but I've found that one a day
works out best. Besides, I've got another man coming in and
need the office."

Affecting a scowl that had no real conviction behind it, Mr.
Kreevy shambled out of the office and later, upon returning
home, found parked in front of his building a new red compact
car with this note under the windshield wiper:

I'm tossing in the car. You either run a class operation
or you don't.

Irving

That night, in his bleakly furnished room, Mr. Kreevy had
trouble sleeping and writhed about in his simple Lincolnesque
bed till dawn. At his office the following day he was unable to
concentrate on a tango knock piece and finally laid it aside,
setting out for the old gentleman's office. There had been no
whitewalls on the compact and Mr. Kreevy was all prepared to
needle the distinguished duffer about the omission. But the
office was empty. On the old gentleman's desk was a note which
said:

If it's you, Kreevy, I forgot one thing. I wouldn't use Shelley
Winters again. Try another name, anyone as long as it's
show biz. Hollering out Dean Rusk will get you nowhere.

Irving here

Grumbling with hollow irritation, Mr. Kreevy settled back on
the couch, hollered, "What are Joannie Sommers?" and ap-

peared instantly in a small cabin that had a Japanese smell to it. The floor was tilted at a violent angle, and the furniture was all poured together at one end as though a giant had seized the cabin and was holding it up for inspection. Thrown in among the furniture was a plump woman in gaping negligee, a yellow-haired fairy princess who'd been married several years and failed to mind her calories.

"The earth just opened up and down I went into it," she said. "They'd been talking earthquake around here awhile, but we never thought we'd really be *in* one, not when you're a tourist. I didn't know you were in here, too. You're not Japanese, are you, although I suppose your teeth could be. You're sort of a Japanese Great Emancipator type. God, how I'm babbling. We're all washed up, you know. We're about 1,000 feet down, and as soon as whatever we're in closes together, that's it. God, you're probably the last man I'll ever see. Not that I'd ever sell out Milt."

Unable to suppress a great, gloating whinny, Mr. Kreevy shoved aside a bamboo breakfront and hauled her forth, her legs plump and princess-like as she came out of the furniture. "The last thing I'm going to do is sell out Milt," she said, "not while he's innocently putting over a transistor deal in Tokyo. But hold me close, will you. Didn't anyone ever tell you about those beauty salons for men they have back in Newark? I'm sorry I said that. It wouldn't make any difference if you were a doll. I don't sell out husbands."

The cabin tilted once again as though the inspection were continuing. "What have I got, maybe three or four lousy minutes to live," she said, pressing her fragrant head against Mr. Kreevy's hollow chest. "I'm selling out Milt. Here's a suggestion as long as we're on a limited time schedule. Bite my ear lobe as softly as you can. It puts me right in the mood."

With a great cynical whinny of triumph, Mr. Kreevy put his molars to work, and as great shock waves of sound split the air above them, the princess gasped, "You have your transistors, darling," and the two fell among some Japanese room dividers, mutually selling out the man in Tokyo. Minutes later the roof split apart, admitting tons of Oriental soil, Mr. Kreevy slipping back to the couch as the first dirt clump entered the cabin.

"I was out grabbing a coffee and Danish," said the bewhisk-ered gentleman. "Sorry I missed you. How'd she go? Better this trip, eh?"

"It was okay," said Mr. Kreevy cautiously, certain there were some grains of fertilizer in his Latvian socks, but feeling around and finding none.

"Cagey rascal, aren't you," said the Edwardian oldster. "Look, I'm not stopping these if that's what you're worked up about. They just go on and on. And it isn't one of those deals in which you have tons and tons of pleasure and find out that too much pleasure is a bore. This just stays good. Now tell me, how was it? Sometimes I really wish I could get out in the field."

"It was all right," said Mr. Kreevy, still wary, hunched over on the couch like Neanderthal man guarding a triceratops cut-let.

On subsequent days, without missing a single session, Mr. Kreevy appeared to a celebrated fashion model on a doomed El-Al airliner, a robust Kiev tractor girl about to hang for black marketeering, and a weekending French governess caught aloft in a defective cable car. Each of these and dozens of others followed the same pattern. The fashion model dubbed him "King of the Uglies" but then slipped out of her jumper when a wing fell away; the tractor girl grunted with displeasure, then peeked at the scaffold outside her cell and fell earthily at his knees; the governess screamed "*cochon*," but capitulated with Bardot eagerness when the cable began to snap.

One afternoon, a month after the extraction, Mr. Kreevy, his confidence at a peak, no longer shambling along in Lin-colnesque humility, walked briskly in for a session and took his place on the couch in a businesslike manner.

"How are they going?" asked the elderly gentleman, not look-ing up from his work.

"Very well, thank you," said Mr. Kreevy, all wariness gone.

"I told you," said the dapper Edwardian. "Remember how suspicious you were? I told you it was a class operation. Oh well, see you sometime."

Mr. Kreevy showed up this trip in a thickly humid thatched hut, the tropical air so foul and thick he was barely able to breathe. Animal skins covered the dirt floor and outside there was a pound of drums, the beat uneven and somewhat amateur-ish. Huddled in a corner, her hand shaking as she sipped a cock-tail, was a woman of about thirty-five, with blinding red hair and theatrical make-up on her face. She had on khaki bermudas and her hips flowered out so brazenly from her spare waist that Mr. Kreevy had to look down at the skins.

"Do you mind if I tell you something?" she said, walking toward Mr. Kreevy. "You're terribly attractive."

"I am not," he said, afraid to check her hips again.

"Don't even *ask* what I'm doing here," she said, emptying her glass with a crimson hair toss that made Mr. Kreevy's back-woods knees go soft. "No one'd believe it in a thousand years. I'm part of a goddamned movie company. We could've shot the damned thing on Hollywood and Vine, but Nudelman wanted authenticity. A Grade Z film and he's after authenticity. We're getting it all right. We got here on a goddamned re-ligious holiday and they've killed all the leads and the whole production crew. They'll be in here any second now. I'm just a lousy extra on the thing."

She seemed to notice Mr. Kreevy for the first time all over again and said, *"Oh, my God."*

"What?" he asked.

"Nothing," she said, hanging her head. "It's just when you smiled, I got a funny feeling inside. Hasn't happened since high school. I'm crazy about your kind of smile."

There was no triumphant gloating in the barely perceptible whinny that came from Mr. Kreevy's throat. It was a sweet, modest, grateful sound and no sooner had it issued forth than the girl clutched his wrist and said, "Please don't do that. It's not fair. You're terribly appealing, you must know it, and I have enough to worry about now without becoming involved."

"Look," said Mr. Kreevy, "there are a few minutes. Just try to hold out if you can. I can't explain, but I think I can get us out of here. Are they coming?"

The girl peered outside the shack and Mr. Kreevy dared this time to look at her hips, surprised he did not turn to stone. "They just got Fowler in the neck with a spear," she reported. "He was our diction instructor. They're about seven huts down. I really needed authenticity."

"Maybe I can pull this off," said Mr. Kreevy. "I love you."

"I think I love you, too, you crazy beautiful nut, even though I didn't want to get involved."

Mr. Kreevy stood in the center of the shack and concentrated with all his might, getting into a crouch and squeezing hard until he trembled. When he opened his eyes, he found himself trembling on the couch. The mysterious gentleman was seated behind his desk, his great plumed pen flying across a sheet of paper.

"Something's come up," said Mr. Kreevy. "I want to get a girl out of one of them. I love her, and she's got to come out."

"Well you can just stop right there and forget it, because there's no getting them out. The idea is to go in there, watch them panic a little, enjoy them and that's that."

"Well I'm springing her," said Mr. Kreevy, "no matter what you say." He yanked the giant plumed pen out of the old gentleman's hand and held it against his distinguished throat. "Now you just come along with me and get us out. I'm a desperate man and even though I'm not sure I can handle people like you, I'm trying."

"You've just canceled out the thorn extraction," said the man softly. "All right, on the couch alongside me."

Mr. Kreevy took his place beside the old gentleman, continuing to hold the plumed pen in a threatening manner. They held hands, the senior citizen muttered something, and the pair reappeared inside the crude Congo hut. "You brought along your friend, lovie," said the girl. "Is he going to talk to them out there?"

"Thank God you're safe," said Mr. Kreevy, flying to her side. The cocktails had made her unsteady on her feet.

"All right, get us back," said Mr. Kreevy.

"Nothing doing," said the old gentleman. "I can't do it and even if I could, I don't like you any more and wouldn't."

Mr. Kreevy took the redhead's hand and led her to the center of the hut. "This worked before," he told her. "Let's do it together. Close your eyes, squat down a little and concentrate real hard."

"Funsy," the redhead said. "We did things like this at the Studio."

They held hands, mutually sealed their eyes, shook and trembled together, but to no avail.

"You're lying," said Mr. Kreevy, seizing the old gentleman by the throat. "You *can* get a girl out of one these."

"All right, you've got me," said the older man. "They do come out in certain situations."

Gratefully, Mr. Kreevy released his grip, only to hear the Edwardian add, "But somebody's got to stay behind." With that, the oldster shrieked, "What are Gracie Fields?" and soared aloft, the redhead at his side as though she'd been yanked upward on a string. Mr. Kreevy remained rooted to the dirt floor. The pair hesitated just a moment at the roof of the thatched hut, long enough for the old gentleman to issue his own triumphant old man's whinny.

"Help me," Mr. Kreevy pleaded to the redhead, her hips dazzling him at this new angle.

"He seems to know celebs," she said, stroking the Edwardian's bewhiskered chin. "And I'll do anything to get a break in show biz."

Then, as the first natives broke in, walking uncertainly to the beat of their amateurish drum, Mr. Kreevy watched the couple twinkle off into the sun.

BERNARD FARBAR

Hundred Dollar Eyes

Sure, with a build like yours, you'd do great."

"Yeah?"

"Look, would I kid you? You're always fighting anyway, so why not do it the right way and make some money besides?"

"I'd get killed."

"Ah, Buster, I'm surprised to hear you say that. Do you think if I thought that I'd let you fight? Jesus, you're more to me than just my nephew—I love you more than if you were my own son. You know that."

"I know, Ed, and it's not that I'm afraid . . . really I'm not. But I'd hate to do it and be a bum and no good at it."

"Look, I promise you. If you're no good, I won't even throw you in for one fight. The training'll keep you in shape anyway. Whaddya weigh now?"

"About 180."

"And strong as a horse. We'll get you down to 173 or so and fight you as a light heavy to start."

"I think I'm too small for that. I should really be a middle-weight."

"Too small? Because you're not six feet? Jesus, with legs and a back and arms like that he says he's too small. How old are you now, Buster, sixteen, seventeen?"

"Eighteen."

"Eighteen years old and look at him. When I was eighteen, I was the original ninety-seven-pound weakling, except I was tough, real tough. When I think what might have been if I'd had your body . . ."

"O.K., O.K., I'll leave it all in your hands. When do we start?"

"That's my boy Buster talking now. But one thing—don't tell your mother that I'm telling you to fight or anything—just say that you're working out. She'd be sore at me if she knew . . . I mean she'd think I talked you into it."

"I won't say anything."

"Good. Now we'll start right away. This afternoon."

"Today's Sunday."

"So what. You religious? There's no time like right away to do something."

"Well I thought the gym might be closed. Where are we going to train?"

"That's the best part of the whole deal. Who's the welterweight champ?"

"Sugar Ray."

"No, no, I mean like ex-champ."

"I don't know—Tommy Bell, Beau Jack, Pat DeCoco, that Cuban?"

"Hah, that's right! Patty DeCoco. The toughest billygoat there ever was. Now there was a guy who made it just on being a bull and a bully. Hard as nails, always charging—no fancy boxing for him. You ever see him fight?"

"Yeah, a couple of times."

"Well, whaddya think?"

"He was really rough."

"Yeah. Now he owes me a favor from Miami days and we're going to train at the All Souls Church gym, where he does, and I'm goin' to have him work with you. Great, huh?"

"Pat DeCoco. Where is this All Souls?"

"Down at 126 Montague Street in Brooklyn Heights. I'll meet

you there at three. If I'm late, you can change your clothes meanwhile."

"O.K. See you."

The old church had set aside its entire basement and part of the ground floor as a sort of good old-fashioned boxing club that has not survived the era of television. The ring was right in the center of the room, surrounded on all sides by wooden folding chairs bolted six or eight together. The place reeked with sweat and liniment and locker room odors, not at all like the clean, healthy, sweaty-young-men-working-hard smells that I knew at college. At the college sweat was part of a game; it was a result of having fun, doing something you usually wanted to do. This All Souls smell was of scared men torturing their bodies to earn them a living and every drop of sweat was forced and tinged with fear. (The gypsies in Spain believe they can smell fear or death on a man. It is reported that two days before the matador "Manolete" was killed, people could not sit near him in a café or walk with him, without smelling death.)

That first day and first week were rough: for almost two hours doing push-ups, sit-ups, jump-ups, "playing" medicine ball and endless jump-roping. This had all been preceded by a two and one-half mile run through a park that looked out over the river. In all that time I never once put on the gloves, and I was getting discouraged.

But then, in the second week, my strong body even firmer and feeling great, I started working out on the heavy bag. My weight was down to a solid seventy-four (I starting to talk like a boxer), I was full of confidence and eager to spar. And that week I met the Champ, as everybody called him.

He was short, stocky, thickly muscled and almost inarticulate, but he *was* a good friend of Eddie's and promised to work with me whenever he was in the gym. He also arranged for me to spar with some middleweights who were in his manager's stable.

How could I ever forget that first sparring session? Having my hands carefully taped, with extra-heavy bandages on my many-times broken right wrist, the big padded gloves being laced on, feeling my face flushed and hot as someone slipped a greasy, chewed-up head-guard around my ears and strapped it too securely on, having Ed slip an old, gray, rotten-tasting, smelly mouth-piece between my parched lips, stumbling through the ropes and hearing Ed and the Champ saying something to me as a bell rang and an eighteen-foot tall giant came dashing across the ring to meet me head on with a solid left that still makes my ear ring when I think about it. Hundreds of years later the bell rang and I was back in the calm noise of my corner, my refuge. Then suddenly, miraculously, my head cleared; I had weathered three minutes against a seasoned professional fighter and I was still intact and unhurt. It was like a switch being thrown, and I was anxious for the minute rest to be over so I could get out there and show these guys what it meant to be a fighter. I heard Eddie and the Champ clearly now.

"Hey, Buster, move around more. Go after him."

"Look, kid, save the right. You can knock this guy's head off with that left of yours. Use it."

Ring, bell, ring, I thought. And then it did.

I dashed across the ring and hammered two sharp lefts to the midsection of the surprised Italian and, as he bent over, straightened him up with a quick left uppercut followed by a right to the head that vibrated the bones in my arm and forced him back into the ropes. Now I was pounding him around the body and head with both hands when the bell sounded, a bit too soon it seemed to me.

"Jesus, kid, you're only sparring; you were trying to kill him."

"Let him alone, he's got the right idea," said Ed.

I was vaguely embarrassed and exalted with this tiger that had come out in me; I had seen it so often before that I should have expected it by now. Whenever I was down, beaten or frightened of anything, I always went completely overboard, almost berserk with the desire to excel, to succeed at whatever it was I was involved in. There was no real "killer instinct" here—I was merely afraid and conquered my fear the only way I knew how.

I went over to speak to the Italian who lay on a table with his head back to stop the flow of blood from his nose. I saw the bright red blotches all over his stomach and chest; he was quivering.

"Sorry I got carried away like that."

"You got to learn the difference between fighting and sparring kid," he gasped. His confidence was slowly coming back.
"You'll never do that to me again."

"Well, I'm sorry," and I walked away.

II

The weeks wore on and I was tired of boxing before I had
even had one real bout. One Wednesday, during the sixth or
seventh week, Ed came to me as I was deftly punching the
light bag.

"Well, I've got you a fight! They're going to have a few
fights here Monday night and you'll be fighting the second
prelim—four rounds."

"I don't know if I want it, Ed."

"Sure you do. This ain't the Garden, but you got to start
somewhere."

"Who will I fight?"

"Well, I won't kid you—he's a heavy, but he's light—
eighty-five or so. The guy that was supposed to fight him fell
down a flight of stairs and broke his arm—that's how Patty and
me got you in as substitute."

"Jesus, a heavyweight! How much money do I get?"

"Thirty-five to the winner."

"And if I lose?"

"You won't lose . . . you can't lose."

"How much if I lose?"

"Twenty. But I tell you it's in the bag. We're goin' to build
you up as the next champ."

Some champ. The next few days were nervous, uncomfortable
ones and the nights were sleepless. Each day I decided to tell
Ed I wouldn't go through with it, and once told him that my
wrist felt bad again and didn't he think I should have it
X-rayed? He gave me a withering look and walked away.

We had a very light workout Sunday morning and walked
miles home. I thought of Monday night. We had a big dinner
and I thought of Monday night. I remember trying to read
Madame Bovary and even though it was the second time I was
reading it, I found it difficult to be absorbed or interested.

Somehow, clearly in focus, my problem seemed more vital and important than Emma's. I went to bed early, thinking of Monday night, and awoke early on Monday, thinking of Monday night. The coming battle had pervaded and perverted my whole being. I was no longer a thinking, doing, living person—I was some sort of fighting machine going to its rendezvous with . . . what? That's what was bugging me—the what. What would I do? What would he do? WHAT WOULD HAPPEN TO ME?

I decided to see a movie to help kill the day: Flaubert and even Hemingway's *Green Hills of Africa* couldn't hold me. I think the film was *Battleground,* that war movie with Montgomery Clift and Ricardo Montalban, and it was a mistake for me to see it: I left the theater feeling gloomy and depressed.

I met Ed about 1:30 and we went to the Original Joe's in Brooklyn, where I had a huge, tasteless (only to me, I'm certain) steak. Then he took me to the apartment of one of his numerous girl friends, where I was to nap for a few hours.

I lay awake in the dim room listening to her protests against Eddie, who was trying to make love to her on the couch. Finally, I must have fallen asleep, as Ed came in to wake me.

"What time is it?"

"C'mon, it's 5:30. We fixed you some tea with honey and a couple of pieces of toast out here."

"I'm not very hungry."

"Eat it anyway."

"Why?"

"It'll give you energy."

It was 6:30 or 7:00 when we got over to the gym where I was to fight. I was so far gone that my fear and despondency seemed to have completely left me. I was almost gay in my bearing and actions as I started to dress.

"Look, Buster, I got you a new pair of trunks."

"Good. I hope they have a reinforced seat."

"Ha, ha. Some joke."

I hopped on the scale before stepping into the satiny-smooth black trunks with their regal purple stripe on each side, and jiggled the weights until they balanced at 174.

"Well, even if this man didn't eat much today, he still has at least eleven pounds on me." I started to lace on the high shoes.

"So what? You're twice as fast and stronger too."

"What's his name by the way?"

"Jamison. Alonzo Jamison."

"What else does he do?"

"He's a longshoreman."

"Oh."

The almost paralyzing fear came back as some trainer started to tape my hands. I could barely hear, speak, think or move.

"I said is that too tight on that hand?"

"Uh no, it's fine. They're both fine."

"Lemme get that wrist now."

"Yeah, O.K."

"Whyn't you warm up a little while I go get that guy with the gloves."

"Yeah, O.K."

I was still sitting there when he came back. He had the Champ with him.

"How ya feel, kid?"

"O.K. Good, good."

"Ya look O.K. I seen the other guy. A big stiff."

"Big, huh?"

"Big like fat. Ya know."

"C'mon let's get these on and you'll do some movin' around. It's eight o'clock now and you'll go on about eight-thirty," said Ed.

As I slipped my sweaty hands into the cool, animal-smelling gloves, I realized that these were not the big twelve-and-sixteen-ounce pillows I had been sparring with. They seemed half the size.

"Christ, these gloves are light," I said.

"Eight ounce."

"Eight ounce, huh?"

"Sure, it's all in your favor—you got faster hands."

I put on a sweat shirt and started moving lethargically around the small, steamy-hot room.

"C'mon. Show some pep. Get those hands up there."

"Let him save it for the spade."

Time passed too quickly and soon I was being wrapped in a nondescript terry cloth robe that was far too large for me. I lay down on the hard rubbing table.

"What time is it?" I croaked.

"I guess there won't be a knockout up there so you got about five minutes."

Almost at once a man shouted down the stairs.

"O.K., Landon. Get your tiger up here."

I could no longer speak, but I slid off the table to my feet at once and started toward the stairs with my head hanging very low. Ed pulled me aside.

"Don't worry, kid, I told you it's in the bag. You gonna beat him big."

I nodded and we started up the stairs: a frightened kid, his loving uncle, and a sadly disillusioned ex-champ.

The large room was filled with choking smoke, and as I climbed the rickety stairs to a corner of the ring, I saw my man for the first time. I realized then that there had been no commission doctor to examine us before the fight, nor had there been any weigh-in. Well, perhaps it was just an informal club affair.

My man was a husky, healthy, six-foot Negro with the chocolate-brown skin that is so smooth and attractive on young people . . . and gray and wrinkled when they pass forty. Alonzo Jamison was gray and wrinkled.

A man with a large megaphone (like a cheerleader, I thought) came to the center of the ring, announced our names, weights (174 for me; 190 for him), where we were from (Harlem and New York—some difference), the color of our trunks (mine black and purple; his dirty gray-white and faded gray-black . . . almost like his skin), and the number of rounds we were to fight (four).

The referee called us to the center of the ring, mumbled something about neutral corners and low blows while I looked at Alonzo's shoe tops and he looked at mine. Then I was back in my corner being helped out of the sleazy robe, had a mouth-

piece pushed into my worthless mouth and the bell rang as I
was shoved out toward the center of the ring.

I was powerless, but old Alonzo seemed to be so too. I remember him hitting me several times about the head and
body and feeling nothing. We must have moved in our own
private dazes for two minutes before I could hear Ed yelling
to me to keep my hands up. Then I noticed Alonzo's eyes.

The huge, soft brown, hound-like pupils were surrounded by
an enormous white area that was not merely lined, but actually
coated or tinged, not with red, but brown. His eyes were filled
with tears, not of pain certainly, nor fear I felt, but of defeat.
"It's in the bag," and I was the only one involved who didn't
know.

I lifted my hands very high, exposing my midsection . . .
Alonzo threw a few harmless blows high off my arms. I dropped
them low and he started to work around my body. I started a
counter to the head and his hands moved to give me an opening
for the tentative left I stuck in his face. He reeled back as the
bell sounded.

Back in the corner I was boiling with hate, anger and frustration at everybody, including myself.

"Why didn't you tell me it was going to be a tank job?"

"Sh, someone'll hear you."

"Yeah, someone'll hear. Jesus, that old guy wouldn't hit me
even if he could."

"Sh."

"Yeah, you bastards—you even lied about his weight—not
that it matters. C'mon, tell me—what round does he catch one?"

"I'll explain the whole thing to you later. Give him a few
good shots this round and it'll be all over."

The bell rang and I went out to knock out Alonzo Jamison
in round two of my professional debut. It was easy. We moved
around for a minute or so and then I gave him a left, left, right
combination to the body, followed by a short right, a solid left
and then a long looping right all to the head, the last one landing on his jaw. I will never forget his eyes during that brief
exchange; hoping to get it over with and not be hurt too badly,
yet worried about doing a good enough dive to collect his fifty
or hundred dollars. His big bleary cow-eyes looked up at me as

if to say thank you for helping make it easy as he went down. I turned and walked back to my corner as he was counted out.

I stepped through the ropes and could hear people shouting encouragement and praises to me.

"Way to go, kid."

"Christ, wotta left, huh?"

"Just a young guy too."

"Good fight, kid."

Anonymous hands patted me on the back.

I undressed at once and stepped into the shower before Eddie said anything. I was toweling myself before he spoke.

"Look, Buster—it happens every day."

"Not to me it doesn't," I interrupted.

"We wanna give you a good start and make some extra money besides and look how upset you get."

"What about him? What's he do now?"

"You worried about him? He's just a punchy old bum we'll throw sixty or seventy to. He never had it so good."

"Why didn't you tell me all this before?"

"We didn't want you to worry about the details and all. Besides, you might fight different if you knew."

"So you didn't think I could beat him alone?"

"Nah—sure we knew you would, but it's more spectacular this way. Besides, there's an extra hundred for you."

"An extra hundred."

I put on my jacket and started up the stairs.

"Aren't you gonna stay for the main event?"

I didn't answer as I walked up the steps, through the gym, out into the street, and into a bar on the corner.

I got drunk and thought of his eyes and my hundred dollars.

H. E. F. DONOHUE

The Man Who Knew What Ethiopia Should Do about Her Water-Table

I T TOOK HIM a little time to realize something in the bar was wrong because he was wondering what he was doing there and he had been thinking about the ticket agent and what she had said. "Sorry your stay was so short, Mr. Brian," she had said, banging the big stapler. Whuummp! "Your bus leaves for the field in fifty minutes, Mr. Brian," she had said, handing him a paper ticket pouch. And when Brian had asked where he could buy something to read, the girl had waggled her head, No. Add the flash of grin.

"A cup of coffee, then?" Brian had said.

"Much too late." Both had turned to the clock. Twelve-oh-ten. "But the bar is still open I believe," she had said.

Brian had turned to peer across the expanse of empty airline terminal. Concealed lights formed endless paths on the pretend marble floor that seemed the size of Madison Square Garden. But for those lights, and the tiny floods above the agent's head transforming her with her swept-back black hair into one round white brow, San Francisco's huge air terminal was dark and hollow, echoing, bare.

"But," he had told the brow, "it is all dark over there."

"You are the last to check out tonight," the brow had replied, nodding. "And on the last flight out."

"Great," Brian had said, hoisting his portable and his brief case, walking across the vast flat space past the empty curved benches and the hooded stands, beyond the shuttered stalls, hearing as he walked dim remote city sounds from outside somewhere, wondering why it was silly for such a city to have no snow on such a holiday, wondering why it mattered so much, or why it mattered at all. He had found the bar. After he had found it, after he had gone in, he had wondered why the ticket agent had bothered him and why he was in the bar, this bar, any bar, after not having been in one for more than three years.

"Yes, sir?" the bartender said.

"A tonic and lime," Brian told him. "And no gin."

"Right." But he stopped to think about it. Then he turned to his utensils on the little lighted shelf beneath the bar, while Brian looked about the bar, surprised to find anyone else there, at that time in that place, and then surprised, alerted by the sense that something was wrong.

It was a very small bar, a small square bar with three or four high cushioned stools on each of three sides. The fourth side was a mirrored wall stacked with glasses and bottles standing on glass shelves. Brian stood between two stools on the left side. Across from him, beyond the bending bartender, was a pretty girl with pretty hair listening to a man whisper her something. Brian could not see much of the man's face, nor could he hear what he was saying. Whatever it was, it was something she wanted to hear, for she was leaning on one elbow, her head close to his, her hand in her hair, smiling at him warily, happily, in complete disbelief.

The two others in the bar were not talking. They were facing the mirror. Their backs were to the door through which Brian had walked, and now he could see that one was a young man wearing rimless glasses, sitting up straight before a high-stemmed glass that sat on a coaster, and an ash tray. The other was an older man in a brown suit, who was smiling at the top of the bending bartender's head. Nothing was on the bar in front of him.

"Yes, sir," the bartender said again, wheeling before Brian with tight gracelessness to slap a small round white quilted paper coaster down, centering the moist drink upon it, grimacing once, giving Brian his tolerant grin. Brian nodded back, noting that the short bartender was about his age, in the mid-thirties, and that he looked it even with the blond crewcut and the sharp thin blond mustache. His nose had been broken and well repaired. And he had the Heidelberg scar in the right place, forming on the cheek the slanting dimple. He also had the widest set of shoulders Brian had ever seen. A tailored white shirt. Black string bow tie. No apron. Black flannels pressed sharp dropped straight down from his concrete gut. And from the way he moved inside the shirt, inside the bar, suddenly, swiftly, to flick off a speck of dust here, to rub away a glint of gloss there, Brian decided he had not got the dimple nor the nose at Heidelberg.

"I'll say," the bartender said, turning away, ignoring Brian, not noticing the dollar Brian had put upon the bar, turning to speak to the young man who sat stolidly beside the older one, exhaling too heavily, speaking to the young man as if they had not been interrupted, as if they were never going to be. "I'll say," he said again, shaking his head thoughtfully. "They can be real tough, I know. I remember being in a small scrape once, a real nothing, and the other driver claimed he hurt his back. Lordy."

"Yes," the young man said, massaging his cigarette into shreds with his rotating thumb, smiling, moving only the corners of his mouth.

"And for a few days there," the bartender said, "for two whole days I did not know whether or not my insurance covered me for that sort of thing."

"Yes," the young man said, "I know."

Then the older man spoke. "Actually," he told the bartender, "a mere five should suffice."

"For two whole days," the bartender told the young man, "I sweated, let me tell you."

"Same thing," the young man replied, "very same thing happened to me coming up from Palo Alto."

"Might need the five," the old man told the bartender, "for the chute, you know." He beamed. "The parachute."

"What happened?" the bartender asked the young man. "Tell me. Tell me."

"I was stopping for this light," the young man replied, "and my Jag hit a small stone. And that stone—it was more of a pebble really—that stone chipped into a store window nearby and the cop stopped me when the owner ran out screaming about how I was going to get sued."

"Yes," the bartender said.

"I wonder if I am covered for that," the young man said.

"Yes," the bartender said, concentrating on him..

"With that chute," the old man quietly told the bartender, "I am golden."

Brian had sipped his drink. Now he put it down. "Say," he said.

"Sir?" the bartender said.

"There's gin in this," Brian said. He pointed at his drink.

"But," the bartender began, "you ordered—" Then he said, "I am sorry, sir. I am very sorry."

Brian shrugged.

"Did not know, sir," the bartender said as he threw the drink into the sink, "did not know you didn't drink."

Brian thought about that for a while. Then he said, "I drink. I drink tonic and lime."

"Yes, sir," the bartender said.

"And when I want to go wild," Brian told him, "I drink a horse's neck."

"Yes, sir," the bartender said.

A new napkin appeared. On it, a fresh glass. In the glass, still swirling, a long red plastic stick with a red plastic seahorse wrapped around it.

Brian pushed the dollar bill still further into view.

The bartender saw it. "Oh, *that's* all right, sir," he said.

"I will *pay* for it," Brian said.

"Yes, sir," the bartender said, flicking it away, tapping the tiny cash register, putting the dollar in, taking change out, gently placing the coins on the bar in front of Brian. Brian let the coins stay.

"A compromise I say," the old man said to the bartender heartily. "I suggest the worthy deal."

But the bartender spoke only to the young man: "Like I say, always check the small print. Everything important is always there, in the small print."

The man had stopped whispering to the girl. Both were watching the bartender try to talk only to the young man.

The young man tried to help. "How do you mean?"

"I mean if it is not in the small print," the bartender said, "then it is *no* where."

"Oh," the young man said.

"And of course," the old man told the bartender, "I would only submit a sensible offer to you, with dignity."

"*No* where," the bartender told the young man. "My brother told me that, and he peddles the stuff. For a living. Fire. Life. Theft. *He* told me."

"A dignified deal," the old man said, "for all, for everyone."

"That's interesting," the young man said.

"*What is?*" the bartender asked quickly.

"That your brother sells insurance," the young man said. He smothered the remains of his cigarette. "Because my stepfather does, too."

"Yes," the bartender said, indifferently. "That is interesting."

"Dignified," the old man said, "and sure."

"He even wants *me* to go into the business," the young man said.

"Oh," the bartender said.

"Yes," the young man said.

"It is simply this," the old man said.

"But I told him No," the young man said.

"Uh-huh," the bartender said. He put out his cigarette and lighted another.

"All I need do," the old man said, "is to make the phone call and I am back home in Portland, free."

"I told him," the young man said, lighting another cigarette, "I told him I am pretty sure there is more to this world than betting a guy he won't make out."

"Um-hmm," the bartender said.

"One minor dime," the old man told him. "For the phone call. That's all. And, oh, one shot of booze, I suppose. Mere bar booze if you prefer. To gain me succor in my quest for the words."

No one said or did anything. No one was looking at the old man. They were all looking at the bartender.

The old man added: "The right words. Have to make it pretty plausible. Six men in an alley. Doped milk. All of that. For the haughty provincials, you know."

Brian glanced at the old man. He was still concentrating on the bartender, memorizing him, so Brian took a good look. He saw that he was not too old. He was anywhere from forty to sixty. It was the way he sat that made him seem old. He sat hunched up over the bar as if he carried a broken back. A thin turkey neck came out of a pressed starched and soiled shirt collar too large. He had the kind of narrow rounded shoulders Brian was always glad to see on tall welterweights because such shoulders usually meant there was going to be a good fight. He may have been, be, a tall man. Now he seemed prematurely bent, honed down too lean. That made him seem old. And his small red drinker's face made him seem old. His boy's button of a nose on his lined face made him seem old. His big red hands made him seem old. So did his old long brown suit. That brown color was the oldest brown color in the whole world. And the lapels were too large and too wide and sharp and thin. Only his chin, a small chin held high up and out—the round-shouldered hooker, hands down, inviting the lead—and his big wide eyes, though ringed with fatigue, seemed anything but outdated and overused and bruised and old. Brian looked away. He looked at the bartender.

"I tell you all of this, of course," the old man told the bartender, "and in such baroque detail, because I knew someone would sense my classical condition immediately."

The bartender briskly poured the young man's tray out, wiped it, put it back.

"And," the old man told him, "as soon as I stepped into this splendid joint, I knew that somebody was you."

He held his cigarette straight up so the ash would not fall onto the bar. His other hand was cupped under it as if prepared for another earthquake.

Without facing him, the bartender slid an ash tray over. The old man nodded once, then carefully tilted the ash down into the tray so that it did not splash.

The young man tried again. "I feel the same way about real estate."

"How?" the bartender asked wearily, sipping a small glass of water. "How do you feel about land?"

"But the crusher is," the old man confided out of the corner of his mouth, "the cruel crusher is that even if I had the dime, I would still need a short jolt to make that call."

"Real estate," the young man said, "is not real, that's all."

"Because," the old man said, "I am coming out of a constant four-day haul."

"Money is real," the bartender said.

"And I have shot," the old man said, shaking his head, "I have shot seven hundred and twenty-three dollars in that dear time."

"Sometimes," the young man said.

"So," the old man said, "I have now got to call on my Portland son-in-law. Collect, don't you see. And he is one hell of a fine old woman. My daughter was a lovely thing when she was three."

"*All* the time," the bartender told the young man.

"That is the *only* reason," the old man said, "that I presume to cadge a drink: to deal with *his* world. And also, perhaps, to divine other possibilities, other, that is, than to call my corny kith and kin I mean. *That* is the only reason I even mention the vulgar five and the parachute."

Brian saw the bartender begin to make his move. The bartender began at last to make the move to turn to face, to look directly at, the old man. Then he did. He put his hands on his hips and gave out a short snorting sigh. Then he turned and stared straight at the old man. No one else budged. They all looked at him. Sorrowfully he shook his head. Sorrowfully he spoke to the old man. "Do you know what you are?" he sorrowfully said.

With his steady smile steady and firm, eyes bright, the old man heard.

"I'll tell you what you are," the bartender said, sternly, reproachfully. "You are *really* something. That's what you are."

Respectfully the old man's smile widened a bit. "I certainly realize how deep a chance I take with a man like you," he told the bartender, "even mentioning the free five and the chancy chute."

The bartender folded his powerful arms across his chest as if his whole body ached. His brows were down, his mouth grim. He waited. Suddenly he wheeled and punched a button on the cash register. A drawer popped out. He fingered up two coins, turned, and stepped to the bar to confront the old man, who did not flinch, did not blink.

"I will tell you what I am going to do," the bartender tightly said, snipping out the words. "I am going to do this much and absolutely no more. *There!*" He threw down one coin. "There's a dime for that phone call. And *here!*" He threw down the other. "Here's another in case the first one doesn't work."

The second dime hit the rim of the bar and stopped still. The first dime was still spinning. Everyone stared at it—a tiny roulette wheel spinning low, growing lower and lower and fast and faster until it was flat and down and done.

"Very good of you," the old man said.

"Uh-huh," the bartender said. He was exhausted.

"Yes," the old man said. "But actually no surprise. I had surmised you'd comprehend my plight, considering your ken." He did not touch the coins.

"Sure," the bartender said.

"For today was the day, that lovely day," the old man said, "when I finally realized that the seven hundred was quite gone. Oh I am constantly learning the same things over and again. Besides, I gradually came to realize, as one must you know, that I had to sober up some, if only slowly and civilized, before I could begin to figure out just what had to be done."

"All right," the bartender said.

"And while I was sobering up walking around this town, I missed my flights each one. Each time I would miss my flight to Portland, Origami, and then I would go out into this cute city looking for them, for those two, the two who had helped me to stay. I missed my plane again today. Today I missed all three flights out. I was out looking for them."

"Yeah," the bartender said. "Sure."

"And I have been getting my sobriety back. But sanely of course. Slowly, sure. Which takes moola too and tonight I ran out of loot and so came here. And so home."

The bartender did not say anything.

"Each day I would remember there was a plane to catch. Paid for out of the seven hundred. And then I would get to thinking of those two and the possibility that they were out looking for me. And I would miss the plane. A curious refrain. I almost missed the plane back from my last job, from good old India. Do you know India?"

"No," the bartender said.

"Not as well," the old man said, "as you know the Islands, I suppose."

The bartender raised his eyebrows.

"Surely," the old man quickly said. "Well, where I worked in India you could not spend seven hundred cents. For two years I was in a place that makes Shangri-La seem like Twin Peaks."

The bartender began to wipe a glass.

"But I was rather bright about heading right home and handing over most of my fee. To my stately Portland daughter. Queen of bridge players at high tea. I gave her all but about one grand. I thought I'd need that to get the Ganges out of my mind. And I wanted to come here. I wanted to see this town which I love so well, which you can well understand."

"Yes," the bartender said.

"But a drinking man has got to watch out about remembering. Or perhaps it is the other way around. I do not recall. I only remember remembering about this town and drinking as I recalled. Now, during my tapering time, I need have an easy drink only now and then, like a horse or a fighter cooling out. As *you* would surely know about." He paused, grandly.

The bartender's massive shoulders and chest lifted and settled down. He sighed. "You are something," he said. "Do you know *that?*"

The old man maintained the smile, as if expecting little of a labored joke.

Again the bartender spoke: "I'll do this much. I'll give you the shot. One shot. And you drink it. And you take your time. Thinking about what to tell Portland. But then you go and *do* that. You call Portland. And you head home. And no more talk in this public place. I've got other customers. Okay?" The speech had him out of breath. He put a shot glass before the old man and poured it full of good whiskey.

The old man did not touch the drink. It sat before him a few inches away from his big hands, its faceted sides and surface reflecting many lights, stars of golden brown and yellow, curving out almost down over the thick brim, tremulous yet trim. Only once did the old man let his eyes move away from the bartender's face to gaze down at the whiskey glass. Then he looked up at the bartender again.

"I am more than pretty sure," he said, "that I would have forked over all of the money to my wife. But grown children have a way of embarrassing a grown and widowed man. Grown children, still children, can never be widowed, don't you see. And my wife and I used to do this town after a job, every time I got back. A visit not every man who goes home each night might be fully able to understand." He cautioned himself. Silenced. No one else said anything. The old man was looking at the bartender and now everyone else was looking at the old man.

"My first big job was on the Coulee," he said at last, brightly. "And she also went with me when we did the whole Tennessee. After that I pretty much moved around. And after each time away we, she and I, would have a pretty goddam good time around this town. This time I imagine I did some pretty silly things, alone. But my! they were lovely people, those two! Charming. Charming. That nice young man and his gorgeous wife. At least he said she was his wife. She did not say much. She did not have to say anything." He became silent again.

"Drink your drink," the bartender said.

The old man looked down at the quivering shot glass. Then he raised his head and smiled innocently.

The bartender stared at the glass, too. Then, quickly, he put a thick double-shot glass on the bar. Then he put it back. He picked up a small beer glass instead, a clean thin glass, and lifted the shot glass and sloshed the whiskey over into it without wasting a drop. Then he got out another still larger glass and filled it with ice. Then he threw the ice out and half filled it with water. He got out two paper coasters and put the glasses down on them in front of the old man with the water to the old man's right. He removed the small shot glass and emptied the ash tray and put it back slightly to the water's right. With a fresh bar towel he gave the bar a short, fast swipe. Then he stepped back. When he was done, and when the old man and everyone there could see that he was done, the old man casually moved his right hand to the whiskey glass and, still looking at the bartender, raised it to his mouth. He sipped some. Then he lowered the glass a few inches and looked into it. Then he sipped some more, closing his eyes. Then he opened his eyes and put the glass down.

"They reminded me, those two," he said, "of me and my wife, of course."

The bartender nodded.

"Me and my wife when we were young and invincible. He was me. Tough enough. Eager. Eager to be on his own. And that girl of his. That sweetheart of a lovely girl. I tell you that girl did for him what everybody is now so ready to tell me my wife always did for me. She. With her body bursting out. And that gorgeous head. That gorgeous hair. She trusted all to trust in her, and so in him, to care. Living proof. And so, me."

The young man's martini was done and the bartender made him another. While he did, no one spoke. The bartender served the girl and her escort more beer, and no one spoke. The bartender pointed to Brian's empty tonic glass. Brian shook his head. Everyone turned back to the old man.

"We met in that fancy little bar at the Palace," he said.

"The curvy one that is so dark, like places in crazy old Chicago. They needed the five hundred to deposit on a house in Sausalito, see. Up from Dago. He builds boats. And this house, the perfect place, would go if they did not get the firm money down that night three nights ago, and he could not cash a check because they did not know—hell, they had not even spoken to —anybody but me, the wise old traveler. After I handed her the money she went for his checkbook while he called the real estate man and I waited in that fancy mill until they shut the bloody place down. Me. The man who once outfoxed Madame Chiang Kai-shek."

The bartender nodded again. Again the old man sipped his drink.

"Now I am convinced, of course, that there is a mistake somewhere. I am convinced they are out looking for me the way I have been looking for them. Oh, I went out to Sausalito. No one ever heard of them. Not yet, naturally. And I called all around San Diego. Not a thing. And I have been missing all those airplanes. Looking. The thing is that I do not think they will ever find me. For it is not, as you know, such a small world." He lighted a cigarette. He lifted his glass. "Here's to them. To the two of them. To those two charming people." He drank his drink.

"All right, now," the bartender said.

"Certainly," the old man said. "I shall go to Portland and prepare for my next job. I know my stuff. Why, I am one of the few men around who knows what Ethiopia should do about her water-table. And all of you mountain-men: wait until we start tipping those plateaus. Yet. And yet. I would if I could rather not go creeping back up to Portland, the old bum, to face my roaring success of a son-in-law. Particularly on a Sunday. This Sunday. That is why I mention the five. Because for five dollars I can rent a parachute from the Military Air Transport boys and fly for free anywhere. They all know me. I've built more fields for them than all the Seabees put together. I was on the original Burma crew. And the Ledo. Vinegar Joe would help me out. Bright-Eyes Wingate always did. But it takes five dollars for the parachute, don't you know. Even with your kind dime to call them, to find out if a flight is going my way, they won't let me near the plane without a chute. And when we touch down, I get the five back, of course, for taxi fare in proper style to my daughter's home. She is not a bad sort once you get her laughing."

Leaning back against the cash register, the bartender gave out a little laugh. "You are *really* something," he told the old man. "Do you know what?"

"So I must work so hard to raise the five connected dollars," the old man said.

All the bartender could do was lean back and happily shake his head.

"Of course," the old man said, "even with the five for the chute, there are other problems involved. I must still get out to the field. I mean there is *that* taxi transportation to pay. And an even larger problem looms if there are no flights out tonight, this night, this particular eve, this birthday. I doubt very much that many MATS are flying out tonight."

The bartender was gently laughing now, nodding, saying, "I know, I know," as if someone were telling him his very favorite funny story, one that he enjoyed hearing even though he had already heard it many times before.

"Then again," the old man said, saying something for the first time tentatively, exploring, "there is the problem of a slight but sustaining repast."

"Yes, yes!" the bartender cried, laughing all the harder. "Food. You mean food. Right?"

"That's right," the old man said, relieved, self-confident once more. "Food. I have not eaten properly for the last two days. Oh a boiled egg here and there. And once a sardine and onion sandwich. But nothing solid, nothing to store."

"Right," the bartender said. "And your bag?"

"The bag?" the old man said.

"Your suitcase, your clothes," the bartender said. "Are they at your hotel? Or checked? Or what?"

The old man's smile widened again. "They are still at the hotel," he said. "I can pick them up on my way back through."

"Sure you can," the bartender said, laughing again, shaking his head, refilling the old man's glass of water. "And your last job was *where* did you say? Inside Iran? Idaho? Alaska?"

"Egypt," the old man said, suddenly alert. "Egypt I thought I had said."

The bartender tipped back his head and laughed quite happily. "That you did," he told the old man. "That you did." Then he leaned forward, still quietly laughing, and poured more whiskey into the old man's glass.

Brian looked at his watch. Then he pulled out another dollar and beckoned the bartender. The bartender stepped over to him, in front of him, hiding most of Brian, all but his head, from the others. Brian handed him the dollar.

With quiet intensity, the way police speak to one another in court, the bartender said, "But you have already *paid* for your drink, sir."

"I know," Brian said, in the same kind of voice, reaching for his things. "That's for you. For *your* drink."

The bartender looked at the dollar in his hand and then back at Brian. "Sir?" he said.

"*You* have a drink," Brian said, turning. "Have *two* drinks."

The bartender held the dollar as if it were an old stone, weighing it, turning it over. He looked at Brian again, who had turned. "Yes, sir," he said to Brian. Then he added, "Yes. All right, sir. All right."

Brian moved around the bar and behind the old man toward the door, moving rapidly, going beyond the old man to the door and out through the door, hearing the old man speak once again to the bartender, hearing him say, "All these additional logistics must be approached, of course, and solved, of course, without, that is, turning me into any kind of charmer myself."

"Of course," Brian heard the bartender say. "Of course. Of course. Of course."

South's Summer Idyll

A SUMMER Saturday in Dallas and the boy Howard sat out on the back steps, knees up, propping in between an old singleload twelve-gauge shotgun. While he steadied and squeezed the butt in one hand, the other, with studied unbroken slowness, wrapped a long piece of friction tape around and around the stock—for beginning at the toe of the butt and stretching up about five inches was a thin dry crack in the old wood.

His mother came out, down off the back porch carrying an enameled basin heaped with twists of wet, wrung clothes.

"You wantta be careful with that old gun," she said, making a slight frown.

A squat woman and dark-haired, almost Eastern in the intensity she tried to bear on situations, her face was perhaps too open, eyes too widely spaced, and the effect was ever what she calculated. She would not suspect, however, that within the block only a few could take her seriously.

Her boy Howard did, of course, though if others were present, he might be embarrassed or a little irritated.

"Aw now you're kiddin'," he said, wanting mainly to reassure her about the gun.

She had just given him a dollar for the weekend, and before dark he would have spent over half of it. Sitting now on the back steps, he could reckon exactly how it would go. And with her standing there talking, he was aware too that except for the show she had no idea at all how he would spend the money.

At the kitchen table his father treated it lightly. "Where you *goin'* boy? Shootin'?"

"Aw just fool aroun'," said Howard, looking away, eating slowly at a piece of bread, buttered and covered with sugar.

"Who, you and Lawrence? What're y'all goin' *after?*"

"Aw I dunno," said Howard. "Just fool aroun', I guess."

"Where're you and Lawrence *goin,'* Howie?" asked his mother, back at the sink again.

"Aw out aroun' Hampton Airport, I guess," he said.

"You wantta be careful out there at Hampton," said his mother, "with the planes comin' in and all."

Howard tried to laugh, even to catch his father's eye. "They ain't any *planes* there now," he said, sheepish at having to be impatient with her. "They closed it down, didn't you know that?"

"I don't want you goin' up in that trainer-plane either," his mother went on as unhearing, almost closed-eyed, packing faded, dripless lumps of cloth in the basin.

"Aw now you're kiddin'," said Howard. "It don't cost but three dollars for fifteen minutes. Not likely I *will,* is it?"

At the table, though, his father spoke about the gun, the danger, abstractly, as if he himself had never fired it. And yet, when he saw the box of shells on the table, he opened it and shook two or three out, holding them loosely, so as to appear casual, familiar, he who had not held a gun in thirty years.

"Look like good 'uns," he said finally. "What'd they cost?"

Howard reached Big Lawrence's house by way of the alley. Stepping through an open place in the fence two houses before and cutting across the back yards, he could hear Lawrence on at the house and he saw his shadow dark there behind a window screen.

"*Ka-pow! Ka-pow! Ka-pow!*" was what Lawrence said. It was a small room.

Big Lawrence sat out on the edge of the bed, and all down

around his feet the scattered white patches lay, fallen each as the poison cactus-bloom, every other center oil-dark, he cleaning his rifle, a 30-30 Savage.

Across one end of the bed, flat on his stomach looking at an old comic book, was Crazy Ralph Newgate, while Tommy Sellers sat on the floor, back flat to the wall. Tommy Sellers had a baseball and glove in his lap, and every so often he would flip the baseball up and it would twirl over his fingers like an electric top.

As Howard came in and sat down on the arm of a heavy-stuffed, misshapen chair, Lawrence looked up, laughing. Most of the time Lawrence's laugh was coarse and, in a way, sort of bitter.

"Well, goddam if it ain't old Howard!" he said, perhaps remembering a western movie they had seen a night before.

Somewhere, next door, a radio was playing loud, Saturday morning cowboy music from Station WRR in downtown Dallas.

Big Lawrence put the bolt back in, slapping it. "You ready?" he asked Howard, and Howard nodded. But before he could get up, Lawrence had turned around on the bed and leaned hard across Ralph Newgate's legs, sighting the rifle out over the back yard. There across the yard, out about three feet from the back fence, so crouched half-sitting that the feet were drawn way under, was a cat—a black cat—rounded small and unblinking in the high morning sun.

Big Lawrence squeezed one out on the empty chamber. "*Kapow!*" he said and brought the gun down, laughing.

On the floor, next to the wall, the baseball spun twisting across Tommy Sellers' knuckles like a trained rat.

"Goddam! Right in the eye!" said Lawrence. He raised up and with some shells from his shirt pocket loaded the rifle; then he quickly threw out the shells, working the bolt in a jerky eccentric motion. One of the shells, as they flew all over the bed, went across the comic book Ralph Newgate was holding and hit the bridge of his nose. The other three boys laughed, but Crazy Ralph muttered something, rubbing his nose, and flipped the shell back over into the rest next to Lawrence's leg, as he might have playing marbles—and Big Lawrence flinched.

"You crazy bastard!" said Lawrence. "What if it'd hit the cap!" and he picked up the shell and threw it as hard as he could against the wall behind Ralph Newgate's head, making him duck. They left the shell where it fell on the floor behind the bed. Ralph didn't speak but just kept turning the pages of the comic book, while Lawrence sat there for about a minute looking at the book that was held in front of Ralph Newgate's eyes.

Lawrence reloaded the gun and drew another bead out the window. The black cat was still sitting there, head on toward the muzzle, when Lawrence moved the safety with his thumb, and next door someone turned the radio up a little more.

In the small room the explosion was loud.

The comic book jumped in Crazy Ralph's hand as if jerked by a wire. "God*dam*mit!" he said, but he didn't look around, just shifted a little, as in settling to the book again.

The cat hardly moved. It seemed only to have been pushed back toward the fence some, still sitting there, head down, feet drawn under, staring at the screen.

But in the screen now, next to a hole made in opening the screen from the outside, was another, perfectly round, flanged out instead of in, worn suddenly by the passing of the bullet, all bright silver at the edge.

Big Lawrence and Howard walked a dirt road along one side of Hampton Airport. It was a hot, dry day.

"What's a box of shells like that cost?" Lawrence asked, and when Howard told, Lawrence said, "*Sure*, but for how many shells?"

At crossroads, the corner of a field, a place where on some Sundays certain people who made model airplanes came to try them, they found, all taped together, five or six shiny old dry-cell batteries as might be used for starting just such small engines. Howard pulled these batteries apart while they walked on, slower now beneath the terrible sun, and when Lawrence wanted to see if he could hit one in the air with the shotgun, they agreed to trade off, three rifle cartridges for one shotgun shell.

Howard pitched one of the batteries up, but Lawrence wasn't ready. "Wait'll I say '*Pull*,'" he told Howard.

He stood to one side then, holding the shotgun down as he might have seen done in a newsreel about skeet-shooting.

"Okay, now *pull!*"

Lawrence missed the first one, said that Howard was throwing too hard.

Howard tossed another, gently, lobbing it into the sun, glinting end over gleaming end, a small meteor in slow motion, suddenly jumping with the explosion, this same silver thing, as caught up in a hot-air jet, but with the explosion, coughing out its black insides.

"Got the sonofabitch," said Big Lawrence. "Dead bird goddammit!"

Howard laughed. "I reckon it is," he said softly.

Once across the field, away from the airport, they turned up the railroad track. And now they walked very slowly, straight into the sun, burning, mirrored a high blinding silver in the rails that lay for five miles unbending, flat against the shapeless waste, ascending, stretching ablaze to the sun itself—so that seen from afar, as quite small, they could have appeared as children, to walk unending between these two columns of dancing light.

With the rifle they took some long shots at the dead-glass disks on a signal tower far up the track, but nothing happened. When they were closer, though, one of the signals suddenly swung up wildly alight. A burning color. Lawrence was about to take a shot at it when they heard the train behind them.

They slid down an embankment, through the bullnettle and bluebonnets, to walk a path along the bottom. When the freight train reached them, however, they turned to watch it go by, and at one of the boxcars, Big Lawrence, holding the rifle against his hip, pumped three or four rounds into the side of it. Under the noise of the train the muted shots had no connection with the bursting way the dark wood on the boxcar door tore off angling and splintered out all pine white.

As they walked on, Howard said, "Don't reckon anybody was in *it*, do you?" Then he and Lawrence laughed.

They struck the creek hollow and followed it in file, Lawrence ahead, stepping around tall slaky rocks that pitched up abruptly from the hot shale. Heat came out of this dry stone, sharp as acid, wavering up in black lines. Then at a bend before them was the water hole, small now and stagnant, and they turned off to climb the bank in order to reach it from the side. Howard was in front now; as they came over the rise, he saw the rabbit first—standing between two oak stumps ten feet away, standing up like a kangaroo, ears winced back, looking away toward the railroad track. Then Lawrence saw it too and tried to motion Howard off with one hand, bringing his rifle up quickly with the other.

The sound came as one; but within one spurting circle of explosion, the two explosions were distinct.

On their side the half face of the rabbit twitched twice back and down even before it hit him, then he jumped straight up in a double flip five times the height he had stood and landed across one of the old burned out stumps like a roll of wet paper.

"*Goddam!*" said Lawrence, frowning. He walked slowly toward the stumps, then looked at Howard before he picked up the rabbit. "Goddammit!" he said.

One side of the rabbit, from the stomach down, looked as though it had been pushed through a meat grinder. "You must be crazy," Lawrence said. "Why didn't you let me get him, goddammit? I could have gotten him in the head." He dropped the rabbit across the stump again and stood looking at it.

Howard picked up the rabbit, studied it. "Sure tore hell out of it, didn't it?" he said.

Lawrence spat and turned away. Howard watched him for a minute walking down toward the water hole, then he put the rabbit back on the stump and followed.

They leaned the guns against the dead-grassed ground that rose at their backs and sat down. Howard got out the cigarettes and offered them, so that Lawrence took one first, and then Howard. And Howard struck the match.

"Got the car tonight?" he asked, holding out the light.

Big Lawrence didn't answer at once for drawing on the cigarette. "Sure," he said then, admitting, "but I've got a date." In this sun the flame of the match was colorless, only chemical, without heat.

"Where you goin'?" Howard asked. "To the show?"

"I dunno," said Lawrence, watching the smoke. "Maybe I will."

The water hole was small, less than ten feet across, over-hung only by a dwarfed sand-willow on the other bank, so that all around the dead burning ground was flushed with the sun, while one half of the hole itself cast back the scene in distortion.

Over and on the water, though, in and through the shadow that fell half across them, played wasps and water-spiders, dragonflies, snake-doctors, and a thousand gray gnats. A hornet, deep-ribbed, whirring golden bright as a spinning dollar, hung in a hummingbird twist just on the water surface in the deepest shadow of the tree, and Howard threw a rock at it.

Then an extraordinary thing happened. The hornet, rising frantically up through the willow branches, twisted once and came down out of the tree in a wild whining loop, and lit exactly on the back of Howard's shirt collar, and then very deliberately, as Lawrence saw, crawled inside.

"Hold still," said Lawrence, taking a handful of the shirt at the back and the hornet with it, holding it.

Howard had his throat arched out, the back of his neck all scrutched away from the shirt collar. "Did you get it?" he kept asking.

"Hold still, goddammit," said Lawrence, laughing, watching Howard's face from the side, finally closing his hand on the shirt, making the hornet crackle as hard and dry as an old matchbox when he clenched his fist.

And then Lawrence had it out, in his hand, and they were both bent over in looking. It was dead now, wadded and broken, and in the shade of his hand the gold of the hornet had become as ugly-colored as the phosphorus dial at noon. It was the stinger, sticking out like a wire hair, taut in an electric quaver, that still lived.

"Look at that goddam thing," said Lawrence of the stinger, and made as if to touch it with his finger.

"Be careful, you'll get stung," said Howard.

"*Look* at it," said Lawrence, intent.

"They all do that," Howard said.

"Sure, but not like that." Lawrence touched it with his finger, but nothing happened.

"Maybe we can get it to sting something," said Howard, and he tried to catch a doodlebug crawling on a bluebonnet that grew alone between them, but missed it. So Lawrence bent the flower itself over, to get the stinger to penetrate the stem at the bottom.

"It'll kill it," he said; "it's acid."

Lawrence held the tail of the hornet tight between his thumb and finger, squeezing to get more of the stinger out, until it came out too far and stopped moving—and Lawrence, squeezing, slowly emptied the body of its white filling. Some of it went on his finger. Lawrence smelled it, then he let Howard smell it before he wiped his finger on the grass.

They lit another cigarette. Big Lawrence threw the match in the water, and a minute after it had floated out, took up the 30-30, drew a bead, and clipped it just below the burnt head. "*Why?*" he asked Howard, handing him the rifle. "Are you going to the show tonight?"

"I might," Howard said.

"No, but have you got a date?"

"I guess I could get one," said Howard, working the bolt.

"I've gone out with Helen Ward," said Lawrence.

Howard sighted along the rifle.

"You know her *sister?*" Lawrence asked.

"Who, Louise?"

"Sure, maybe we could get 'em drunk."

Howard held his breath, steadying the rifle. Then he took a shot. "Sure I know her," he said.

They shot water targets, mostly with the rifle, Howard using the shots Lawrence owed him. Once, however, after he dug an old condensed-milk can out of the bank and sat it on the water, Lawrence took up the shotgun and held the muzzle about a foot from the can.

"H-bomb," he said, pulling the trigger.

They sat there for an hour, talking a little and smoking, shooting at crawfish and dragonflies or underwater rocks that shone through the flat yellow or, more often, dull dead brown. Then they decided to go back to the house and drink some beer.

Near the stumps Howard crossed over and picked up the rabbit, Lawrence watching him. "What're you going to do with the damn thing?" Lawrence asked.

"Aw I dunno," said Howard. "Might as well take it along."

Lawrence watched while Howard held it by the ears and kicked at a piece of newspaper, twisted dry and dirty, yellow in the grass. He got the paper, shook it out straight, and he wrapped it around the rabbit.

They started across the field, Lawrence not talking for a while. Then he stopped to light a cigarette. "I know what," he said, cradling the 30-30 to one arm; "we can cook it."

Howard didn't answer right off, but once, as they walked back toward the stumps, he looked at the sun. "I wonder what time it is anyhow," he said.

Using Howard's knife, Big Lawrence, once it was decided, sat on one of the stumps to skin the rabbit while Howard went pushing around through the Johnson grass, folding aside with his feet, peering and picking, bundling back, to build the fire.

At the stumps, Lawrence cursed the knife, tried the other blade, and sawed at the rabbit's neck, twisting it in his hand.

"Wouldn't cut hot niggerpiss," he said, but somehow he managed to get the head off and to turn the skin back on itself at the neck, so that he pulled it down like a glove reversed on an unborn hand, it glistened so.

He had to stop with the skin halfway down to cut off the front feet, and in doing this, hacking once straight on from the point of the blade, the blade suddenly folded back against his finger. He opened the knife slowly, saying nothing, but he sucked at the finger and squeezed it between two others until, through all this heavy red of rabbit, sticking, covering his whole hand now, he could almost see, but never quite, where in one spot on his smallest finger he himself, up through the blood of the rabbit, was bleeding too.

He went down to the pool to clean his hands, but he finished skinning the rabbit first.

When he got back, Howard was down, ready to light the fire.

"Are we goin' to the show or not?" Lawrence said.

"I don't care," said Howard, staring up at him. "Do *you* want to?"

"Well, we better get back if we're goin'."

Howard got the old newspaper from where he had put it to burn and wrapped it around the rabbit again, and he put this inside his shirt. He folded the skin square and put it in his pocket.

Lawrence had the rabbit's head. He tried to get the eyes to stay open, but only the white showed when he sat it on the stump. He took a brick from the windbreak Howard had built for the fire and put this on the stump too, behind the head, and they started across the field. When they were a little way out, they took shots at the head, and finally Lawrence used the last of the shells he had coming to go up close and shoot the head, brick, and even part of the stump away with the old twelve-gauge.

Before they reached Rosemont Street, they could hear Tommy Sellers cursing and Crazy Ralph Newgate farther away yelling, "*All the way! All the way!*" and as they turned in, Tommy Sellers was there, coming toward them, walking up the middle of the street swinging his glove by one finger.

Howard pulled the wad of newspaper out of his shirt and held it up to show, and Tommy Sellers stopped and kicked around at some dead grass piled in the gutter. "*Okay, all the way!*" Ralph Newgate was yelling halfway down the block, and Tommy Sellers found the ball with his foot. Then, bending over, in a low twisting windup from the gutter, never once looking where, he threw it—the ball that lifted like a shot to hang sailing for an instant in a wide-climbing arc.

Big Lawrence brought the rifle off his shoulder. "*Ka-pow!*" and the barrel point wavered, sighting up the lazy wake of the ball. "Dead sonofabitch bird," he said.

Tommy Sellers was standing close, hands on his hips, not seeing down there an eighth of a mile where Ralph Newgate, with his eyes high, nervously tapping the glove palm, was trying to pick the bouncing throw off the headlight of a parked car.

"God it stinks," said Lawrence, making a face when Howard

opened the newspaper. The paper now was like a half-dried cloth, stiff, or sticking in places and coming to pieces. Almost at once a fly was crawling over the chewed-up part of the rabbit.

"You know what it's like?" said Lawrence—"*goddam rotten afterbirth!*" and he spat, seeming to retch a little.

"What is it?" asked Tommy Sellers, looking close at the rabbit, then up, away, not caring in dancing out to take the wild looping throw from Ralph Newgate.

They walked on. Howard wrapped the newspaper around the rabbit again and put it in his shirt.

"It's already beginning to rot," said Big Lawrence.

"Aw you're crazy," Howard said.

"*Crazy!*" repeated Lawrence. "You're the one who's crazy. What'll you do, eat it?" He laughed, angrily, spitting again.

They were walking in the street in front of Lawrence's house now. Tommy Sellers and Ralph Newgate were at the curb, throwing their gloves up through the branches of a cedar tree where the ball was caught.

There were some people standing around the steps at Lawrence's front porch. One was a youngish woman wearing an apron over her dress, and a little girl was holding on to the dress with both hands, pressing her face into the apron, swinging herself slowly back and forth, so that the woman stood as braced, her feet slightly apart. She stroked the child's head with one hand, and in the other she was holding the cat.

They watched Howard and Lawrence in the street in front of the house. Once the woman moved her head and spoke to the fat man standing on the porch who frowned without looking at her.

Howard didn't turn in with Lawrence. "See you at the show," he said.

As he walked on, the fall of their voices died past him. "How'd it happen, son?" he heard Lawrence's dad ask.

He turned off on a vacant lot that cut through toward his house. Halfway across, he pulled out the paper and opened it. He studied it, brought it up to his face, and smelled it.

"*That rake'll reach!*" Crazy Ralph was yelling way behind him. "*That rake'll reach!*"

GEORGE P. ELLIOTT

Among the Dangs

I GRADUATED FROM Sansom University in 1937 with honors
in history, having intended to study law, but I had no money
and nowhere to get any; by good fortune the anthropology department, which had just been given a grant for research, decided that I could do a job for them. In idle curiosity I had
taken a course in anthro, to see what I would have been like
had history not catapulted my people a couple of centuries ago
up into civilization, but I had not been inclined to enlarge on
the sketchy knowledge I got from that course; even yet, when
I think about it, I feel like a fraud teaching anthropology. What
chiefly recommended me to the department, aside from a friend,
was a combination of three attributes: I was a good mimic, a
long-distance runner, and black.

The Dangs live in a forested valley in the eastern foothills of
the Andes. The only white man to report on them (and, it was
loosely gossiped, the only one to return from them alive), Sir
Bewley Morehead, owed his escape in 1910 to the consternation
caused by Halley's comet. Otherwise, he reported, they would
certainly have sacrificed him as they were preparing to do; as it
was, they killed the priest who was to have killed him and then
burned the temple down. However, Dr. Sorish, our most dis-

tinguished Sansom man, in the early thirties developed an interest in the Dangs which led to my research grant; he had
introduced a tribe of Amazonian head-shrinkers to the idea of
planting grain instead of just harvesting it, as a result of which
they had fattened, taken to drinking brew by the tubful, and
elevated Sorish to the rank of new god. The last time he had
descended among them—it is Sansom policy to follow through
on any primitives we "do"—he had found his worshipers holding
a couple of young Dang men captive and preparing them for
ceremonies which would end only with the processing of their
heads; his godhood gave him sufficient power to defer these
ceremonies while he made half-a-dozen transcriptions of the
men's conversations and learned their language well enough to
arouse the curiosity of his colleagues. The Dangs were handy
with blowpipes; no one knew what pleased them; Halley's
comet wasn't due till 1986. But among the recordings Sorish
brought back was a legend strangely chanted by one of these
young men, whose very head perhaps you can buy today from a
natural science company for $150 to $200, and the same youth
had given Sorish a sufficient demonstration of the Dang
prophetic trance, previously described by Morehead, to whet
his appetite.

I was black, true, but as Sorish pointed out, I looked as
though I had been rolled in granite dust and the Dangs as
though they had been rolled in brick dust; my hair was short
and kinky, theirs long and straight; my lips were thick, theirs
thin. It's like dressing a Greek up in reindeer skins, I said, and
telling him to go pass himself off as a Lapp in Lapland. Maybe,
they countered, but wouldn't he be more likely to get by than
a naked Swahili with bones in his nose? I was a long-distance
runner, true, but as I pointed out with a good deal of feeling,
I didn't know the principles of jungle escape and had no desire
to learn them in, as they put it, the field. They would teach me
to throw the javelin and wield a machete, they would teach me
the elements of judo, and as for poisoned darts and sacrifices,
they would insure my life—that is, my return within three years
—for five thousand dollars. I was a good mimic, true; I would
be able to reproduce the Dang speech and especially the trance
of the Dang prophets for the observation of science—"make a

genuine contribution to learning." In the Sansom concept the researcher's experience is an inextricable part of anthropological study, and a good mimic provides the object for others' study as well as for his own. For doing this job I would be given round-trip transportation, an M.S. if I wrote a thesis on the material I gathered, the temporary insurance on my life, and one hundred dollars a month for the year I was expected to be gone. After I'd got them to throw in a fellowship of some sort for the following year, I agreed. It would pay for filling the forty cavities in my brothers' and sisters' teeth.

Dr. Sorish and I had to wait at the nearest outstation for a thunderstorm; when it finally blew up, I took off all my clothes, put on a breechcloth and leather apron, put a box of equipment on my head, and trotted after him; his people were holed in from the thunder and we were in their settlement before they saw us. They were taller than I; they no doubt found my white teeth as disagreeable as I found their stained, filed teeth, but when Sorish spoke to me in English (telling me to pretend indifference to them while they sniffed me over) and in the accents of American acquaintances rather than in the harsh tones of divinity, their eyes filled with awe of me. Their taboo against touching Sorish extended itself to me; when a baby ran up to me and I lifted him up to play with him, his mother crawled, beating her head on the ground till I freed him.

The next day was devoted chiefly to selecting the man to fulfill Sorish's formidable command to guide me to the edge of the Dang country. As for running—if those characters could be got to the next Olympics, Ecuador would take every long-distance medal on the board. I knew I had reached the brow of my valley only because I discovered that my guide, whom I had been lagging behind by fifty feet, at a turn in the path had disappeared into the brush.

Exhaustion allayed my terror; as I lay in the meager shade recuperating, I remembered to execute the advice I had given myself before coming: to act always as though I were not afraid. What would a brave man do next? Pay no attention to his aching feet, reconnoiter, and cautiously proceed. I climbed a jutting of rock and peered about. It was a wide, scrubby valley; on the banks of the river running down the valley I thought I saw a dozen mounds too regular for stones. I touched the handle of the hunting knife sheathed at my side and trotted down the trackless hill.

The village was deserted, but the huts, though miserable, were clean and in good repair. This meant, according to the movies I had seen, that hostile eyes were watching my every gesture. I had to keep moving in order to avoid trembling. The river was clear and not deep. The corpse of a man floated by. I felt like going downstream, but my hypothesized courage drove me up.

In half a mile I came upon a toothless old woman squatting by the track. She did not stop munching when I appeared, nor did she scream, or even stand up. I greeted her in Dang according to the formula I had learned, whereupon she cackled and smiled and nodded as gleefully as though I had just passed a test. She reminded me of my grandmother, rolled in brick dust, minus a corncob pipe between her gums. Presently I heard voices ahead of me. I saw five women carrying branches and walking very slowly. I lurked behind them until they came to a small village, and watched from a bush while they set to work. They stripped the leaves off, carefully did something to them with their fingers, and then dropped them in small-throated pots. Children scrabbled around, and once a couple of them ran up and suckled at one of the women. There remained about an hour till sunset. I prowled, undetected. The women stood, like fashion models, with pelvis abnormally rocked forward; they were wiry, without fat even on their breasts; not even their thighs and hips afforded clean sweeping lines undisturbed by bunched muscles. I saw no men.

Before I began to get into a lather about the right tack to take, I stepped into the clearing and uttered their word of salutation. If a strange man should walk in your wife's front door and say "How do you do" in an accent she did not recognize, simultaneously poking his middle finger at her, her consternation would be something like that of those Dang women, for unthinkingly I had nodded my head when speaking and turned my palm up as one does in the United States; to them this was a gesture of intimacy, signifying desire. They disappeared into huts, clutching children.

I went to the central clearing and sat with my back to a log, knowing they would scrutinize me. I wondered where the men were. I could think of no excuse for having my knife in my hand except to clean my toenails. So astonishing an act was unknown to the Dangs; the women and children gradually approached in silence, watching; I cleaned my fingernails. I said the word for food; no one reacted, but presently a little girl ran up to me holding a fruit in both hands. I took it, snibbed her nose between my fingers, and with a pat on the bottom sent her back to her mother. Upon this there were hostile glances, audible intakes of breath, and a huddling about the baby who did not understand any more than I did why she was being consoled. While I ate the fruit, I determined to leave the next move up to them. I sheathed my knife and squatted on my hunkers, waiting. To disguise my nervousness I fixed my eyes on the ground between my feet, and grasped my ankles from behind in such a way—right ankle with right hand, left with left—as to expose the inner sides of my forearms. Now this was, as I later learned, pretty close to the initial posture taken for the prophetic trance; also I had a blue flower tattooed on my inner right arm and a blue serpent on my left (from the summer I'd gone to sea), the like of which had never been seen in this place.

At sundown I heard the men approach; they were anything but stealthy about it; I had the greatest difficulty in suppressing the shivers. In simple fear of showing my fear I did not look up when the men gathered around; I could understand just enough of what the women were telling the men to realize that they were afraid of me. Even though I was pelted with pebbles and twigs till I was angry, I still did not respond, because I could not think what to do. Then something clammy was plopped onto my back from above and I leaped high, howling. Their spears were poised before I landed.

"Strangers!" I cried, my speech composed. "Far kinsmen! I come from the mountains!" I had intended to say *from the river lands*, but the excitement tangled my tongue. Their faces remained expressionless but no spears drove at me, and then to be doing something I shoved the guts under the log with my feet.

And saved my life by doing so. That I seemed to have taken,

though awkwardly, the prophetic squat; that I bore visible marvels on my arms; that I was fearless and inwardly absorbed; that I came from the mountains (their enemies lived toward the river lands); that I wore their apron and spoke their language, albeit poorly; all these disposed them to wonder at this mysterious outlander. Even so they might very well have captured me, marvelous though I was, possibly useful to them, dangerous to antagonize, had I not been unblemished, which meant that I was supernaturally guarded. Finally, my scrutinizing the fish guts, daring to smile as I did so, could mean only that I was prophetic; my leap when they had been dropped onto my back was prodigious, "far higher than a man's head," and my howl had been vatic; and my deliberately kicking the guts aside, though an inscrutable act, demonstrated at least that I could touch the entrails of an eel and live.

So I was accepted to the Dangs. The trouble was that they had no ceremony for naturalizing me. For them every act had a significance, and here they were faced with a reverse problem for which nothing had prepared them. They could not possibly just assimilate me without marking the event with an act (that is, a ceremony) signifying my entrance. For them nothing *just happened*, certainly nothing that men did. Meanwhile, I was kept in a sort of quarantine while they deliberated. I did not, to be sure, understand why I was being isolated in a hut by myself, never spoken to except officially, watched but not restrained. I swam, slept, scratched, watched, swatted, ate; I was not really alarmed, because they had not restrained me forcibly and they gave me food. I began making friends with some of the small children, especially while swimming, and there were two girls of fifteen or so who found me terribly funny. I wished I had some magic, but I knew only card tricks. The sixth day, swimming, I thought I was being enticed around a point in the river by the two girls, but when I began to chase them, they threw good-sized stones at me, missing me only because they were such poor shots. A corpse floated by; when they saw it, they immediately placed the sole of their right foot on the side of their left knee and stood thus on one leg till the corpse floated out of sight; I followed the girls' example, teetering. I gathered from what they said that some illness was devastating their people; I hoped it was one of the diseases I had been inoculated against. The girls' mothers found them talking with me and cuffed them away.

I did not see them for two days, but the night of my eighth day there the bolder of them hissed me awake at the door of my hut in a way that meant "no danger." I recognized her when she giggled. I was not sure what their customs were in these matters, but while I was deliberating what my course of wisdom should be, she crawled into the hut and lay on the mat beside me. She liked me, she was utterly devoid of reticence, I was twenty-one and far from home; even a scabby little knotty-legged fashion model is hard to resist under such circumstances. I learned before falling asleep that there was a three-way debate among the men over what to do with me: initiate me according to the prophet-initiation rites, invent a new ceremony, or sacrifice me as propitiation to the disease among them as was usually done with captives. Each had its advantages and drawbacks, even the news that some of the Dangs wanted to sacrifice me did not excite me as it would have done a week before; now, I half-sympathized with their trouble. I was awakened at dawn by the outraged howl of a man at my door; he was the girl's father. The village men gathered and the girl cowered behind me. They talked for hours outside my hut, men arrived from other villages up and down the valley, and finally they agreed upon a solution to all the problems: they proposed that I should be made one of the tribe by marriage on the same night that I should be initiated into the rites of prophecy.

The new-rite men were satisfied by this arrangement because of the novelty of having a man married and initiated on the same day, but the sacrifice party was visibly unmollified. Noticing this and reflecting that the proposed arrangement would permit me to do all my trance research under optimum conditions and to accumulate a great deal of sexual data as well, I agreed to it. I would of course only be going through the forms of marriage, not meaning them; as for the girl, I took this vow to myself (meaning without ceremony): "So long as I am a Dang, I shall be formally a correct husband to her." More's the pity.

Fortunately, a youth from down the valley already had been chosen as a novice (at least a third of the Dang men enter the novitiate at one time or another, though few make the grade), so that I had not only a companion during the four-month preparation for the vatic rites but also a control upon whom I might check my experience of the stages of the novitiate. My mimetic powers stood me in good stead; I was presumed to have a special prophetic gift, and my readiness at assuming the proper stances and properly performing the ritual acts confirmed the Dangs' impressions of my gift; but also, since I was required to proceed no faster than the ritual pace in my learning, I had plenty of leisure in which to observe in the smallest detail what I did and how I, and to some extent my fellow novice, felt. If I had not had this self-observing to relieve the tedium. I think I should have been unable to get through that mindless holding of the same position hour after hour, that mindless repeating of the same act day after day. The Dangs *appear* to be bored much of the time, and my early experience with them was certainly the ennui, though never again ennui so acute as during this novitiate. Yet I doubt that it would be accurate to say they actually are bored, and I am sure that the other novice was not, as a fisherman waiting hours for a strike cannot be said to be bored. The Dangs do not sate themselves on food; the experience which they consider most worth seeking, vision, is one which cannot glut either the prophet or his auditors; they cannot imagine an alternative to living as they live or, more instantly, to preparing a novice as I was being prepared. The people endure; the prophets, as I have learned, wait for the time to come again, and though they are bitten and stung by ten thousand fears, about this they have no anxiety—the time will surely come again. Boredom implies either satiety, and they were poor and not interested in enriching themselves, or the frustration of impulse, and they were without alternatives and diversions. The intense boredom, which is really a controlled anxiety, they are protected from by never doubting the worth of their vision or their power to achieve it.

I was assisted through these difficult months, during which I was supposed to do nothing but train, by Redadu, my be-trothed. As a novice I was strictly to abstain from sexual intercourse, but as betrothed we were supposed to make sure before marriage that we satisfied one another, for adultery by either husband or wife was punishable by maiming. Naturally, the theologians were much exercised by this impasse, but while they were arguing, Redadu and I took the obvious course—we met more or less surreptitiously. Since my vatic training could not take place between sunrise and sundown, I assumed that we could meet in the afternoon when I woke up, but when I began making plans to this effect, I discovered that she did not know what I was talking about. It makes as much sense in Dang to say, "Let's blow poisoned darts at the loss of the moon," as to say, "Let's make love in broad daylight." Redadu dissolved in giggles at the absurdity. What to do? She found us a cave. Everyone must have known what I was up to, but we were respectable (the Dang term for it was harsher, *deed-liar*), so we were never disturbed. Redadu's friends would not believe her stories of my luxurious love ways, especially my biting with lips instead of teeth. At one time or another she sent four of them to the cave for me to demonstrate my prowess upon; I was glad that none of them pleased me as much as she did, for I was beginning to be fond of her. My son has told me that lip-biting has become if not a customary at any rate a possible caress.

As the night of the double rite approached, a night of full moon, a new conflict became evident: the marriage must be consummated exactly at sundown, but the initiation must begin at moonrise, less than two hours later. For some reason that was not clear to me, preparing for the initiation would incapacitate me for the consummation. I refrained from pointing out that it was only technically that this marriage needed consummating and even from asking why I would not be able to do it. The solution, which displeased everyone, was to defer the rites for three nights, when the moon, though no longer perfectly round, would rise sufficiently late so that I would, by hurrying, be able to perform both of my functions. Redadu's father, who had been of the sacrifice party, waived ahead of time his claim against me; legally he was entitled to annul the marriage if I should leave the marriage hut during the bridal night. And although I in turn could legally annul it if she left the hut, I waived my claim as well so that she might attend my initiation.

The wedding consisted chiefly of our being bound back to back by the elbows and being sung to and danced about all day. At sunset we were bound face to face by the elbows (most awkward) and sent into our hut. Outside the two mothers waited—a high prophet's wife took the place of my mother (my Methodist mother!)—until our orgastic cries indicated that the marriage had been consummated, and then came in to sever our bonds and bring us the bridal foods of cold stewed eel and parched seeds. We fed each other bite for bite and gave the scraps to our mothers, who by the formula with which they thanked us pronounced themselves satisfied with us. Then a falsetto voice called to me to hurry to the altar. A man in the mask of a moon slave was standing outside my hut on his left leg with the right foot against his left knee, and he continued to shake his rattle so long as I was within earshot.

The men were masked. Their voices were all disguised. I wondered whether I was supposed to speak in an altered voice; I knew every stance and gesture I was to make, but nothing of what I was to say; yet surely a prophet must employ words. I had seen some of the masks before—being repaired, being carried from one place to another—but now, faced with them alive in the failing twilight, I was impressed by them in no scientific or aesthetic way—they terrified and exalted me. I wondered if I would be given a mask. I began trying to identify such men as I could by their scars and missing fingers and crooked arms, and noticed to my distress that they too were all standing one-legged in my presence. I had thought that was the stance to be assumed in the presence of the dead! We were at the entrance to The Cleft, a dead-end ravine in one of the cliffs along the valley; my fellow novice and I were each given a gourdful of some vile-tasting drink and were then taken up to the end of The Cleft, instructed to assume the first position, and left alone. We squatted as I had been squatting by the log on my first day, except that my head was cocked in a certain way and my hands clasped my ankles from the front. The excitements of the day seemed to have addled my wits; I could concentrate on nothing and lost my impulse to observe coolly what was going on; I kept humming "St. James Infirmary" to myself, and though at first I had been thinking the words, after a while I realized that I had nothing but the tune left in my head. At moonrise we were brought another gourd of the liquor to drink and were then taken to the mouth of The Cleft again. I did, easily, whatever I was told. The last thing I remember seeing before taking the second position was the semicircle of masked men facing us and chanting, and behind them the women and children—all standing on the left leg. I lay on my back with my left ankle on my right and my hands crossed over my navel, rolled my eyeballs up and held the lids open without blinking, and breathed in the necessary rhythm, each breath taking four heartbeats, with an interval of ten heartbeats between each exhalation and the next inspiration. Then the drug took over. At dawn, when a called command awakened me, I found myself on an islet in the river dancing with my companion a leaping dance I had not known or even seen before and brandishing over my head a magnificent red and blue, new-made mask of my own. The shores of the river were lined with the people chanting as we leaped, and all of them were either sitting or else standing on both feet. If we had been dead the night before, we were alive now.

After I had slept and returned to myself, Redadu told me that my vision was splendid, but of course she was no more permitted to tell me what I had said than I was able to remember it. The Dangs' sense of rhythm is as subtle as their ear for melody is monotonous, and for weeks I kept hearing rhythmic snatches of "St. James Infirmary" scratched on calabash drums and tapped on blocks.

Sorish honored me by rewriting my master's thesis and adding my name as co-author of the resultant essay, which he published in *JAFA* (*The Journal of American Field Anthropology*): "Techniques of Vatic Hallucinosis among the Dangs." And the twenty-minute movie I made of a streamlined performance of the rites is still widely used as an audio-visual aid.

By 1939, when I had been cured of the skin disease I had brought back with me and had finished the work for my M.S., I still had no money. I had been working as the assistant curator of the University's Pre-Columbian Museum and had

developed a powerful aversion to devoting my life to cata-
loguing, displaying, restoring, warehousing. But my chances of
getting a research job, slight enough with a Ph.D., were nil
with only an M.S. The girl I was going with said (I had not
told her about Redadu) that if we married, she would work
as a nurse to support me while I went through law school; I
was tempted by the opportunity to fulfill my original ambition,
and probably I would have done it had she not pressed too
hard; she wanted me to leave anthropology, she wanted me to
become a lawyer, she wanted to support me, but what she did
not want was to make my intentions, whatever they might be,
her own. So when a new grant gave me the chance to return to
the Dangs, I gladly seized it; not only would I be asserting
myself against Velma, but also I would be paid for doing the
research for my Ph.D. thesis; besides, I was curious to see the
Congo-Maryland-Dang bastard I had left in Redadu's belly.

My assignment was to make a general cultural survey but
especially to discover the *content* of the vatic experience—not
just the technique, not even the hallucinations and stories, but
the qualities of the experience itself. The former would get me
a routine degree, but the latter would, if I did it, make me a
name and get me a job. After much consultation I decided
against taking with me any form of magic, including medicine;
the antibiotics had not been invented yet, and even if there
had been a simple way to eradicate the fever endemic among
the Dangs, my advisers persuaded me that it would be an error
to introduce it since the Dangs were able to procure barely
enough food for themselves as it was and since they might wor-
ship me for doing it, thereby making it impossible for me to do
my research with the proper empathy. I arrived the second time
provided only with my knife (which had not seemed to impress
these stone-agers), salve to soothe my sores, and the knowledge
of how to preserve fish against a lean season, innovation enough
but not one likely to divinize me.

I was only slightly worried about how I would be received
on my return, because of the circumstances under which I had
disappeared. I had become a fairly decent hunter—the women
gathered grain and fruit—and I had learned to respect the
Dangs' tracking abilities enough to have been nervous about

getting away safely. While hunting with a companion in the hills south of our valley, I had run into a couple of hunters from an enemy tribe which seldom foraged so far north as this. They probably were as surprised as I and probably would have been glad to leave me unmolested; however, outnumbered and not knowing how many more were with them, I whooped for my companion; one of the hunters in turn, not knowing how many were with me, threw his spear at me. I side-stepped it and reached for my darts, and though I was not very accurate with a blowpipe, I hit him in the thigh; within a minute he was writhing on the ground, for in my haste I had blown a venomous dart at him, and my comrade took his comrade prisoner by surprise. As soon as the man I had hit was dead, I withdrew my dart and cut off his ear for trophy, and we returned with our captive. He told our war chief in sign language that the young man I had killed was the son and heir of their king and that my having mutilated him meant their tribe surely would seek to avenge his death. The next morning a Dang search party was sent out to recover the body so that it might be destroyed and trouble averted, but it had disappeared; war threatened. The day after that I chose to vanish; they would not think of looking for me in the direction of Sorish's tribe, north, but would assume that I had been captured by the southern tribe in retribution for their prince's death. My concern now, two years later, was how to account for not having been maimed or executed; the least I could do was to cut a finger off, but when it came to the point, I could not even bring myself to have a surgeon do it, much less do it myself; I had adequate lies prepared for their other questions, but about this I was a bit nervous.

I got there at sundown. Spying, I did not see Redadu about the village. On the chance, I slipped into our hut when no one was looking; she was there, playing with our child. He was as cute a little preliterate as you ever saw suck a thumb, and it made me chuckle to think he would never be literate either. Redadu's screams when she saw me fetched the women, but when they heard a man's voice, they could not intrude. In her joy she lacerated me with her fingernails (the furrows across my shoulder festered for a long time); I could do no less than

bite her arm till she bled; the primal scene we treated our son to
presumably scarred him for life—though I must say the scars
haven't shown up yet. I can't deny that I was glad to see her
too, for, though I felt for her none of the tender, complex emotions I had been feeling for Velma, emotions which I more or
less identified as being love, yet I was so secure with her sexually,
knew so well what to do and what to expect from her in every
important matter that it was an enormous, if cool, comfort to
me to be with her. *Comfort* is a dangerous approximation to
what I mean; being with her provided, as it were, the condition for doing; in Sansom I did not consider her my wife and
here I did not recognize in myself the American emotions of
love or marriage, yet it seemed to me right to be with her and
our son was no bastard. *Cool*—I cannot guarantee that mine
was the usual Dang emotion, for it is hard for the cool to gauge
the warmth of others (in my reports I have denied any personal
experience of love among the Dangs for this reason). When we
emerged from the hut, there was amazement and relief among
the women: amazement that I had returned and relief that it
had not been one of their husbands pleasuring the widow. But
the men were more ambiguously pleased to see me. Redadu's
scratches were not enough and they doubted my story that the
enemy king had made me his personal slave who must be bodily
perfect. They wanted to hear me prophesy.

Redadu told me afterward, hiding her face in my arms for
fear of being judged insolent, that I surpassed myself that night,
that only the three high prophets had ever been so inspired.
And it was true that even the men most hostile to me did not
oppose my re-entry into the tribe after they had heard me
prophesy; they could have swallowed the story I fed them about
my two-year absence only because they believed in me, the
prophet. Dangs make no separation between fact and fantasy,
apparent reality and visionary reality, truth and beauty. I once
saw a young would-be prophet shudder away from a stick on
the ground, saying it was a snake, and none of the others except
the impressionable were afraid of the stick; it was said of him
that he was a beginner. Another time I saw a prophet scatter the
whole congregation, myself included, when he screamed at the
sight of a beast which he called a cougar; when sober dawn

found the speared creature to be a cur, it was said of the prophet that he was strong, and he was honored with an epithet, Cougar-Dog. My prophesying the first night of my return must have been of this caliber, though to my disappointment I was given no epithet, not even the nickname I'd sometimes heard before, Bush-Hair.

I knew there was a third kind of prophesying, the highest, performed only on the most important occasions in the Cave-Temple where I had never been. No such occasion had presented itself during my stay before, and when I asked one of the other prophets about the ceremony, he put me off with the term Wind-haired Child of the Sun; from another I learned that the name of this sort of prophesying was Stone Is Stone. Obviously I was going to have to stay until I could make sense of these mysteries.

There was a war party that wanted my support; my slavery was presumed to have given me knowledge which would make a raid highly successful; because of this as well as because I had instigated the conflict by killing the king's son, I would be made chief of the raiding party. I was uneasy about the fever, which had got rather worse among them during the previous two years, without risking my neck against savages who were said always to eat a portion of their slain enemy's liver raw and whose habitat I knew nothing of. I persuaded the Dangs, therefore, that they should not consider attacking before the rains came, because their enemies were now the stronger, having on their side their protector, the sun. They listened to me and waited. Fortunately it was a long dry season, during which I had time to find a salt deposit and to teach a few women the rudiments of drying and salting fish; and during the first week of the rains every night there were showers of falling stars to be seen in the sky; to defend against them absorbed all energies for weeks, including the warriors'. Even so, even though I was a prophet, a journeyman prophet as it were, I was never in on these rites in the Cave-Temple. I dared not ask many questions. Sir Bewley Morehead had described a temple surrounded by seventy-six poles, each topped by a human head; he could hardly have failed to mention that it was in a cave, yet he made no such mention, and I knew of no temple like the one he had described. At a time of rains and peace in the sky the war party would importune me. I did not know what to do but wait.

The rains became violent, swamping the villages in the lower valley and destroying a number of huts, yet the rainy season ended abruptly two months before its usual time. Preparations for war had already begun, and day by day, as the sun's strength increased and the earth dried, the war party became more impatient. The preparations in themselves lulled my objections to the raid, even to my leading the raid, and stimulated my desire to make war. But the whole project was canceled a couple of days before we were to attack because of the sudden fever of one of the high prophets; the day after he came down five others of the tribe fell sick, among them Redadu. There was nothing I could do but sit by her, fanning her and sponging her till she died. Her next older sister took our son to rear. I would allow no one to prepare her body but myself, though her mother was supposed to help; I washed it with the proper infusions of herbs, and at dawn, in the presence of her clan, I laid her body on the river. Thank heaven it floated or I should have had to spend another night preparing it further. I felt like killing someone now; I recklessly called for war now, even though the high prophet had not yet died; I was restrained, not without admiration. I went up into the eastern hills by myself and returned after a week bearing the hide of a cougar; I had left the head and claws on my trophy in a way the Dangs had never seen; when I put the skin on in play by daylight and bounded and snarled, only the bravest did not run in terror. They called me Cougar-Man. Redadu's younger sister came to sleep with me; I did not want her, but she so stubbornly refused to be expelled that I kept her for the night; for the next night, for the next; it was not improper.

The high prophet did not die but lay comatose most of the time. The Dangs have ten master prophets, of whom the specially gifted, whether one or all ten, usually two or three, are high prophets. Fifteen days after Redadu had died, well into the abnormal dry spell, nearly all the large fish seemed to disappear from the river. A sacrifice was necessary. It was only because the old man was so sick that a high prophet was used for this occasion, otherwise a captive or a woman would have served the purpose. A new master prophet must replace him, to keep the complement up to ten. I was chosen.

The exultation I felt when I learned that the master prophets had co-opted me among them was by no means cool and anthropological, for now that I had got what I had come to get, I no longer wanted it for Sansom reasons. *If the conditions of my being elevated,* I said to myself, *are the suffering of the people, Redadu's death, and the sacrifice of an old man, then I must make myself worthy of the great price. Worthy*—a value word, not a scientific one. Of course, my emotions were not the simple pride and fear of a Dang. I can't say what sort they were, but they were fierce.

At sundown all the Dangs of all the clans were assembled about the entrance to The Cleft. All the prophets, masked, emerged from The Cleft and began the dance in a great wheel. Within this wheel, rotating against it, was the smaller wheel of the nine able-bodied master prophets. At the center, facing the point at which the full moon would rise, I hopped on one leg, then the other. I had been given none of the vatic liquor, that brew which the women, when I had first come among the Dangs, had been preparing in the small-throated pots, and I hoped I should be able to remain conscious throughout the rites. However, at moonrise a moon slave brought me a gourdful to drink without ceasing to dance. I managed to allow a good deal of it to spill unnoticed down with the sweat streaming off me, so that later I was able to remember what had happened, right up to the prophesying itself. The dance continued for at least two more hours, then the drums suddenly stopped and the prophets began to file up The Cleft, with me last, dancing after the high prophets. We danced into an opening of the cliff from which a disguising stone had been rolled away. The people were not allowed to follow us. We entered a great cavern illuminated by ten smoking torches and circled a palisade of stakes; the only sound was the shuffle of our feet and the snorts of our breathing. There were seventy-six stakes, as Morehead had seen, but only on twenty-eight of them were heads impaled, the last few with flesh on them still, not yet skulls cleaned of all but hair. In the center was a huge stone under the middle of which a now dry stream had tunneled a narrow passage; on one side of the stone, above the passage, were two breastlike protuberances, one of which had a recognizable nipple in the suitable place.

Presently the dancing file reversed so that I was the leader. I had not been taught what to do; I wove the file through the round of stakes, and spiraled inward till we were three deep about The Stone; I straddled the channel, raised my hands till they were touching the breasts, and gave a great cry. I was, for reasons I do not understand, shuddering all over; though I was conscious and though I had not been instructed, I was not worried that I might do the wrong thing next. When I touched The Stone, a dread shook me without affecting my exaltation. Two moon slaves seized my arms, took off my mask, and wrapped and bound me—arms at my side and legs pressed together in a deer hide—and then laid me on my back in the channel under The Stone with my head only half out, so that I was staring up the sheer side of rock. The dancers continued, though the master prophets had disappeared. My excitement, the new unused position, being mummied tightly, the weakness of the drug, my will to observe, all kept me conscious for a long time. Gradually, however, my eyes began to roll up into my head, I strained less powerfully against the thongs that bound me, and I felt my breathing approach the vatic rhythm. At this point I seemed to break out in a new sweat, on my forehead, my throat, in my hair; I could hear a splash, groggily I licked my chin—an odd taste—I wondered if I was bleeding. Of course, it was the blood of the sick old high prophet, who had just been sacrificed on The Stone above me; well, his blood would give me strength. Wondering remotely whether his fever could be transmitted by drinking his blood, I entered the trance. At dawn I emerged into consciousness while I was still prophesying; I was on a ledge in the valley above all the people, in my mask again. I listened to myself finish the story I was telling. "He was afraid. A third time a man said to him: 'You are a friend of the most high prophet.' He answered: 'Not me. I do not know that man they are sacrificing.' Then he went into a dark corner; he put his hands over his face all day." When I came to the Resurrection, a sigh blew across the people. It was the best story they had ever heard. Of course. But I was not really a

Christian. For several weeks I fretted over my confusion, this new, unsuspected confusion.

I was miserable without Redadu; I let her sister substitute only until I had been elevated, and then I cast her off, promising her however that she and only she might wear an anklet made of my teeth when I should die. Now that I was a master prophet, I could not be a warrior; I had had enough of hunting and fishing and tedious ceremonies. Hunger from the shortage of fish drove the hunters high into the foothills; there was not enough; they ate my preserved fish, suspiciously, but they ate them. When I left, it was not famine that I was escaping but my confusion; I was fleeing to the classrooms and the cool museums where I should be neither a leftover Christian nor a mimic of a Dang.

My academic peace lasted for just two years, during which time I wrote five articles on my researches, publishing them this time under my name only, did some of the work for my doctorate, and married Velma. Then came World War II, in which my right hand was severed above the wrist; I was provided with an artificial hand and given enough money so that I could afford to finish my degree in style. We had two daughters and I was given a job at Sansom. There was no longer a question of my returning to the Dangs. I would become a settled anthropologist, teach, and quarrel with my colleagues in the learned journals. But by the time the Korean War came along and robbed us of a lot of our students, my situation at the university had changed considerably. Few of my theoretical and disputatious articles were printed in the journals, and I hated writing them; I was not given tenure and there were some hints to the effect that I was considered a one-shot man, a flash-in-the-pan; Velma nagged for more money and higher rank. My only recourse was further research, and when I thought of starting all over again with some other tribe—in northern Australia, along the Zambesi, on an African island—my heart sank. The gossip was not far from the mark—I was not a one-hundred-per-cent scientist and never would be. I had just enough reputation and influential recommendations to be awarded a Guggenheim Fellowship; supplemented by a travel grant from the university, this made it possible for me to leave my family comfortably provided for and to return to the Dangs.

A former student now in Standard Oil in Venezuela arranged to have me parachuted among them from an SO plane. There was the real danger that they would kill me before they recognized me, but if I arrived in a less spectacular fashion, I was pretty sure they would sacrifice me for their safety's sake. This time, being middle-aged, I left my hunting knife and brought instead at my belt a pouch filed with penicillin and salves. I had a hard time identifying the valley from the air; it took me so long that it was sunset before I jumped. I knew how the Dangs were enraged by airplanes, especially by the winking lights of night fliers, and I knew they would come for me if they saw me billowing down. Fortunately, I landed in the river, for though I was nearly drowned before I disentangled my parachute harness, I was also out of range of the blowpipes. I finally identified myself to the warriors brandishing their spears along the shore; they had not quite dared to swim out after so prodigious a being; even after they knew who I said I was and allowed me to swim to shore, they saw me less as myself than as a supernatural being. I was recognized by newcomers who had not seen me so closely swinging from the parachute (the cloud); on the spot my epithet became, and remained, Sky-Cougar. Even so, no one dared touch me till the high prophet—there was only one now—had arrived and talked with me; my artificial hand seemed to him an extension of the snake tattooed onto my skin, he would not touch it; I suddenly struck him with it and pinched his arm. "Pinchers," I said, using the word for a crayfish claw, and he laughed. He said there was no way telling whether I was what I seemed to be until he had heard me prophesy; if I prophesied as I had done before I had disappeared, I must be what I seemed to be; meanwhile, for the three weeks till full moon I was to be kept in the hut for captives.

At first I was furious at being imprisoned, and when mothers brought children from miles about to peek through the stakes at the man with the snake hand, I snarled or sulked like a caged wolf. But I became conscious that one youth, squatting in a quiet place, had been watching me for hours. I demanded of him who he was. He said, "I am your son," but he did not treat me as his father. To be sure, he could not have remembered what I looked like; my very identity was doubted; even if I were myself, I was legendary, a stranger who had become a Dang and had been held by an enemy as captive slave for two years and had then become a master prophet with the most wonderful vision anyone knew. Yet he came to me every day and answered all the questions I put to him. It was, I believe, my artificial hand that finally kept him aloof from me; no amount of acquaintance could accustom him to that. By the end of the first week it was clear to me that if I wanted to survive—not to be accepted as I once had been, just to survive—I would have to prophesy the Passion again. And how could I determine what I would say when under the vatic drug? I imagined a dozen schemes for substituting colored water for the drug, but I would need an accomplice for that, and I knew that not even my own son would serve me in so forbidden an act.

I called for the high prophet. I announced to him in tones all the more arrogant because of my trepidations that I would prophesy without the vatic liquor. His response to my announcement astonished me: he fell upon his knees, bowed his head, and rubbed dust into his hair. He was the most powerful man among the Dangs, except in time of war when the war chief took over, and furthermore he was an old man of personal dignity, yet here he was abasing himself before me and, worse, rubbing dust into his hair as was proper in the presence of the very sick to help them in their dying. He told me why: prophesying successfully from a voluntary trance was the test which I must pass to become a high prophet; normally a master prophet was forced to this, for the penalty for failing it was death. I dismissed him with a wave of my claw.

I had five days to wait until full moon. The thought of the risk I was running was more than I could handle consciously; to avoid the jitters I performed over and over all the techniques of preparing for the trance, though I carefully avoided entering it. I was not sure I would be able to enter it alone, but whether I could or not, I knew I wanted to conserve my forces for the great test. At first during those five days I would remind myself once in a while of my scientific purpose in going into the trance consciously; at other times I would assure myself that it was for the good of the Dangs that I was doing it, since it was not wise or safe for them to have only one high prophet. Both of these reasons were true enough, but not very important. As scientist I should tell them some new myth, say the story of Abraham and Isaac or of Oedipus, so that I could compare its effect on them with that of the Passion; as master prophet I should ennoble my people if I could. However, thinking these matters over as I held my vatic squat hour after hour, visited and poked at by prying eyes, I could find no myth to satisfy me; either, as in the case of Abraham, it involved a concept of God which the Dangs could not reach, or else, as with Oedipus, it necessitated more drastic changes than I trusted myself to keep straight while prophesying—that Oedipus should mutilate himself was unthinkable to the Dangs and that the gods should be represented as able to forgive him for it was impious. Furthermore, I did not think, basically, that any story I could tell them would in fact ennoble them. I was out to save my own skin.

The story of Christ I knew by heart; it had worked for me once, perhaps more than once; it would work again. I rehearsed it over and over, from the Immaculate Conception to the Ascension. But such was the force of that story on me that by the fifth day my cynicism had disappeared along with my scientism, and I believed, not that the myth itself was true, but that relating it to my people was the best thing it was possible for me to do for them. I remember telling myself that this story would help raise them toward monotheism, a necessary stage in the evolution toward freedom. I felt a certain satisfaction in the thought that some of the skulls on the stakes in the Cave-Temple were very likely those of missionaries who had failed to convert these heathen.

At sundown of the fifth day I was taken by moon slaves to a cave near The Cleft, where I was left in peace. I fell into a troubled sleep from which I awoke in a sweat. "Where am I? What am I about to do?" It seemed to me dreadfully wrong that I should be telling these, my people, a myth in whose power, but not in whose truth, I believed. Why should I want to free them from superstition into monotheism and then into my total freedom, when I myself was half-returning, voluntarily, down the layers again? The energy for these sweating questions came, no doubt, from my anxiety about how I was going to perform that night, but I did not recognize this fact at the time. Then I thought it was my conscience speaking, and that I had no right to open to the Dangs a freedom I myself was rejecting. It was too late to alter my course; honesty required me, and I resolved courageously, not to prophesy at all.

When I was fetched out, the people were in assembly at The Cleft and the wheel of master prophets was revolving against the greater wheel of dancers. I was given my cougar skin. Hung from a stake, in the center where I was to hop, was a huge, terrific mask I had never seen before. As the moon rose, her slaves hung this mask on me; the thong cut into the back of my neck cruelly, and at the bottom the mask came to a point that pressed my belly; it was so wide my arms could only move laterally. It had no eye holes; I broke into a sweat wondering how I should be able to follow the prophets into the Cave-Temple. It turned out to be no problem; the two moon slaves, one on each side, guided me by prodding spears in my ribs. Once in the cave they guided me to the back side of The Stone and drove me to climb it, my feet groping for steps I could not see; once, when I lost my balance, the spears' pressure kept me from falling backward. By the time I reached the top of The Stone, I was bleeding and dizzy. With one arm I kept the mask from gouging my belly while with the other I helped my aching neck support the mask. I did not know what to do next. Tears of pain and anger poured from my eyes. I began hopping. I should have been moving my arms in counterpoint to the rhythm of my hop, but I could not bear the thought of letting the mask cut into me more. I kept hopping in the same place for fear of falling off; I had not been noticing the sounds of the other prophets, but suddenly I was aware they were making no sounds at all. In my alarm I lurched to the side and cut my foot on a sharp break in the rock. Pain converted my panic to rage.

I lifted the mask and held it flat above my head. I threw my head back and howled as I had never howled in my life, through a constricted, gradually opening throat, until at the end I was roaring; when I gasped in my breath I made a barking noise. I leaped and leaped, relieved of pain, confident. I punched my knee desecratingly through the brittle hide of the mask and threw it behind me off The Stone. I tore off my cougar skin, and holding it with my claw by the tip of its tail, I whirled it around my head. The prophets, massed below me, fell onto their knees. I felt their fear. Howling, I soared the skin out over them; one of those on whom it landed screamed hideously. A commotion started; I could not see very well what was happening. I barked and they turned toward me again. I leaped three times and then, howling, jumped wide-armed off The Stone. The twelve-foot drop hurt severely my already cut foot. I rolled exhausted into the channel in the cave floor.

Moon slaves with trembling hands mummied me in the deerskin and shoved me under The Stone with only my head sticking out. They brought two spears with darts tied to the points; rolling my head to watch them do this, I saw that the prophets were kneeling over and rubbing dirt into their hair. Then the slaves laid the spears alongside the base of The Stone with the poisoned pricks pointed at my temples; exactly how close they were, I could not be sure, but close enough so that I dared not move my head. In all my preparations I had, as I had been trained to do, rocked and weaved at least my head; now, rigidity, live rigidity. A movement would scratch me and a scratch would kill me.

I pressed my hook into my thigh, curled my toes, and pressed my tongue against my teeth till my throat ached. I did not dare relieve myself even with a howl, for I might toss my head fatally. I strained against my thongs to the verge of apoplexy. For a while I was unable to see, for sheer rage. Fatigue collapsed me. Yet I dared not relax my vigilance over my movements. My consciousness sealed me off. Those stone protuberances up between which I had to stare in the flickering light were merely chance processes on a boulder, similes to breasts. The one thing I might not become unconscious of was the pair of darts waiting for me to err. For a long time I thought of piercing my head against them, for relief, for spite. Hours passed. I was carefully watched.

I do not know what wild scheme I had had in mind when I had earlier resolved not to prophesy, what confrontation or escape; it had had the pure magnificence of a fantasy resolution. But the reality, which I had not seriously tried to evade, was that I must prophesy or die. I kept lapsing from English into a delirium of Dang. By the greatest effort of will I looked about me rationally. I wondered whether the return of Halley's comet, at which time all the stakes should be mounted by skulls, would make the Dangs destroy the Cave-Temple and erect a new one. I observed the straight, indented seam of sandstone running slantwise up the boulder over me and wondered how many eons this rotting piece of granite had been tumbled about by water. I reflected that I was unworthy both as a Christian and as a Dang to prophesy the life of Jesus. But I convinced myself that it was a trivial matter, since to the Christians it was the telling more than the teller that counted and to the Dangs this myth would serve as a civilizing force they needed. Surely, I thought, my hypocrisy could be forgiven me, especially since I resolved to punish myself for it by leaving the Dangs forever as soon as I could. Having reached this rational solution, I smiled and gestured to the high prophet with my eyes; he did not move a muscle. When I realized that nothing to do with hyprocrisy would unbind me, desperation swarmed in my guts and mounted toward my brain; with this question it took me over: *How can I make myself believe it is true?* I needed to catch hold of myself again. I dug my hook so hard into my leg—it was the only action I was able to take—that I gasped with pain; the pain I wanted. I did not speculate on the consequences of gouging my leg, tearing a furrow in my thigh muscle, hurting by the same act the stump of my arm to which the hook was attached; just as I knew that the prophets, the torches, the poisoned darts were there in the cave, so also I knew that far, far back in my mind I had good enough reasons to be hurting myself, reasons which I could find out if I wanted to, but which it was not worth my trouble to discover; I even allowed the knowledge that I myself was causing the pain to drift back in my mind. The pain itself, only the pain, became my consciousness, purging all else. Then, as the pain subsided, leaving me free and equipoised, awareness of the stone arched over me flooded my mind. Because it had been invested by the people with a great mystery, it was an incarnation; the power of their faith made it the moon, who was female; at the same time it was only a boulder. I understood Stone Is Stone, and that became my consciousness.

My muscles ceased straining against the bonds, nor did they slump; they ceased aching, they were at ease, they were ready. I said nothing, I did not change the upward direction of my glance, I did not smile, yet at this moment the high prophet removed the spears and had the moon slaves unbind me. I did not feel stiff, nor did my wounds bother me, and when I put on my cougar skin and leaped, pulled the head over my face and roared, all the prophets fell onto their faces before me. I began chanting and I knew I was doing it all the better for knowing what I was about; I led them back out to the waiting people, and until dawn I chanted the story of the birth, prophesying betrayal, sacrifice, and victory of the most high prophet. I am a good mimic, I was thoroughly trained, the story is the best; what I gave them was, for them, as good as a vision. I did not know the difference myself.

But the next evening I knew the difference. While I performed my ablutions and the routine ceremonies to the full moon, I thought with increasing horror of my state of mind during my conscious trance. What my state of mind actually had been I cannot with confidence now represent, for what I know of it is colored by my reaction against it the next day. I had remained conscious, in that I could recall what had happened, yet that observer and commentator in myself of whose existence I had scarcely been aware, but whom I had always taken for my consciousness, had vanished. I no longer had been thinking, but had lost control so that my consciousness had become what I was doing; almost worse, when I had told the story of Christ, I had done it not because I had wanted to or believed in it but because, in some obscure sense, I had had to. Thinking about it afterward, I did not understand or want to understand what I was drifting toward, but I knew it was something that I feared. And I got out of there as soon as I was physically able.

Here in Sansom what I have learned has provided me with material for an honorable contribution to knowledge, has given me a tenure to a professorship—thereby pleasing my wife—

whereas if I had stayed there among the Dangs much longer, I would have reverted until I had become one of them, might not have minded when the time came to die under the sacrificial knife, would have taken in all ways the risk of prophecy—as my Dang son intends to do—until I had lost myself utterly.

Peacetime

They marched, Raggedy-Andy time, straight up the sand-packed road. The five of them, ordered by the big inch taller or shorter they were than one another, dusty-headed and laughing. Junius, who'd found the village weeks ago on a snipe hunt, led the way. Sometimes he hopped around and marched backwards, pumping his skinned elbows and chugging like the yellow locomotive that screamed out of Charleston to the Army camp. That way he could talk to the others.

"Remember," he said, "I'm the mayor."

"Your stomach's sticking out," said Henry Lee.

"So what?"

"It's a lazy backbone."

"I'm the mayor. I can do what I want."

Then there was Robert Lee, Henry Lee's brother, who was having his first boil and had to sit off the corners of chairs, and Minor, who was much too short to be such a fat kid, and Lizard. Besides Henry Lee, who thought it was time somebody else got to be mayor.

"When're we goin' to have an election?" he asked.

"Don't need one," said Junius.

"I nominate Minor," said Henry Lee.

"I nominate Robert Lee," said Minor.

"I nominate Junius again," said Robert Lee.

Junius laughed. "And I nominate Lizard." He laughed again and hopped around to march frontwards. "Nobody's goin' to nominate you, Henry Lee. I found it. I'm the mayor."

Henry Lee tried to hit his brother a charley horse in the arm, but Robert Lee ducked him. "You watch out for my boil, or else."

"That ain't where your boil is."

"That's how I got it. From spanking."

"You did not."

"Mother says Father shouldn't—"

"You did not!"

"I nominate Junius *again*. I nominate him a hundred times. I nominate Junius, one, I nominate Junius, two, I nominate Junius, three, I nominate Junius, four, I nominate Junius, five, I nominate . . ." He ran out of breath.

There was nothing for Henry Lee to do except try Lizard, who was trailing them all, slightly in their dust.

"Who do you nominate?"

Lizard looked up at him, his eyes nearly lidless, blue-beaming, a little frightened. There was a large black pine cone ahead of him in the tank track that the others had missed. He wanted to get to it, maybe start a game going.

"I don't know."

Henry Lee blocked his way.

"Two, four, six, eight, who do you a-nominate?"

"I don't know!"

"My name's Henry Lee," said Henry Lee, and still blocked his way.

"I nominate Henry Lee," said Lizard.

Henry Lee whirled around and laughed at his brother.

"He don' know. He ain't been here before," said Robert Lee. "I nominate Junius, ninety-nine, I nominate Junius, a hundred."

But Henry Lee didn't care. "You didn't count all the way. You skipped." Then he saw the pine cone in the tank track and backed around to line himself up with it. Lizard bumped into him. "Out of my way!" Henry Lee shouted at him.

"I saw it first," Lizard said, but Henry Lee shoved him, and ran forward. He didn't kick it right. It skittered along the hard sand on its blunt thorns and quickly twisted out of the road. Henry Lee ran it down and stomped on it brutally.

"Better not, better not," said Junius.

"Butter nut, butter nut!" Henry Lee said back.

"Government property."

"A lousy ol' pine cone? It just fell off of some rotten ol' stupid pine tree." He stomped on it again, but the life had gone out of it. It ground in crackles into the sand.

"We're *on* gober'ment property," Minor yelled at him. "Everything on gober'ment property belongs to the gober'-ment, and if it fell off a tree, it's a gober'ment tree, and a gober'ment pine cone. You better not!"

"It's Army," said Henry Lee, "not gober'ment."

"The Army's gober'ment! Don' you know that?" Minor said. "You better watch out, *boy!* I'm telling you. If you destroy gober'ment property, one of them Army tanks'll come running down the road and you're flat!"

This scared Henry Lee, but it scared Lizard more. He hadn't been out here before. It was vast. Nothing but scrub oak and scrub pine and tall pine with long green, hairy needles, and all the way up and down the cracked, sandy road the deep, double, square-toed track of the tank. He couldn't tell which way it was coming. Panicky, scuffing sand into his shoes, he climbed out of the road and began hopping clumsily along the bunkers of saw grass overhanging the water-gutted road. It's a game, he pre-tended, a new game. But he fell farther and farther behind.

"What're you doin', Lizard?" called Junius.

"I'm coming."

"Walk in the road!"

"Can't. I'll hurt the tank." The sod began cracking behind him, and he grabbed at the saw grass to hold himself.

"He's scared!" Henry Lee laughed.

"He's got yellow on his belly," said Minor. "All lizards got yellow on their belly."

"Yellow belly!"

The saw grass sliced his tiny hands, and he pitched forward, tumbling with the bunker into the road. He kicked back and back with his feet, but he sprawled anyhow. And the track ran right under his stomach, big toe after big toe.

"Look at him cry!" said Henry Lee, running up.

"Lizards can cry!" shouted Robert Lee. "Lookit, little lizards can cry!"

Lizard got up, full of sand. One cheek felt raw, and he brushed the sand out of the skin, wincing. "Lucky it was me, Robert Lee," he said. "You would've hurt your boil."

Robert Lee reached around behind himself protectively. "I can take a spanking. Anytime."

Junius chugged up fast, turned around, and started chugging away again. "Come on, Lizard, let's go." He whistled for a crossing to let the others catch up. "There isn't no tank. It's a half-track, and it was here *weeks* ago. I saw it. On maneuvers. Robert Lee saw it too, only he didn't know what it was."

"I nominate Henry Lee!" shouted Robert Lee.

"Shut up, stupid," said Henry Lee.

They began running toward the village. Lizard kept up.

"Now, remember," said Junius, over his wind. "We're on government property, but it's our village, and when we get to it, we're safe. Nobody'll know us, and nobody'll see us, and . . ." He stopped short, jamming up Henry Lee behind him. "Hide, hide, hide!" he shouted.

They scattered off the road into the pines, and crouched around Junius, looking up where he pointed over the highest green spike of needles at the sky. They heard the chopping, and then saw it twirling in toward them, catching the sun like a fish in its glass bubble.

"M.P.'s!" cried Minor. "M.P. air patrol."

"No, it's just an ol' egg beater," said Robert Lee.

"Just an ol' whirlybird," said Henry Lee.

It bent around in a whirling sunflash of blades and floated nearer. They could see the pilot inside the bubble, and beside him a stiff old man with gold braid on his cap down over his eyes, and his hands crossed over a brief case. They stood in the air, and it churned all around them.

"That's the General!" said Junius.

The helicopter seemed to come right down on top of them, sinking into the pine trees on a breast of wind. Suddenly Lizard jumped up and began waving.

"Hi, General! Hi, General! Hi there, General!"

Junius and Henry Lee grabbed him. They wrestled him to the ground and out of his shirttail. Henry Lee hit him a charley horse.

"I'm not scared of him!" Lizard said tearfully. "He's just an ol' general."

"Shut up, Lizard," snapped Junius.

Henry Lee charley-horsed him again.

Overhead, the old man looked down from under braid at where they were for a long time, but he was passing, drifting sideways. Then the egg beater rose up and leaned away from them with a roar, chopping down the wind above it, flailing up toward the clouds like an angry bug. It disappeared.

They all stood up except Lizard. They pulled him up and shoved him out of the woods into the road. Then they set him between Henry Lee and Robert Lee and started running. Henry Lee yelled at his brother, "Race you to the sign," and everybody raced. Before they reached the sign, Lizard's feet hurt, and he was coughing. Henry Lee won, but Robert Lee knocked him down coming in, so it was even. Junius was next, with Minor after, and then Lizard. He stumbled in, head down, his droopy blond hair lightly toweling his forehead. He lolled his head back until his neck cracked, and from there he could read the sign.

Up it went:

| U S ARMY |
| Range No. 401 |
| Guerrilla Tactics |

"Now we gotta be careful," said Junius.

They scuttled out of the road again and edged their way through the scrub pine and saw grass toward a slight rise. Lizard saw it ahead, shimmering with heat, waving in his sight. Then, above it, he saw something else shimmering.

"What's the red flag?" he whispered.

"Is the flag up?" said Minor, worried.

They all stopped and crouched even lower.

"I can see it," said Henry Lee. He flattened out.

"Better go back," said Robert Lee. "Gober'ment property."

"Butter goo!" said Henry Lee. "I don't hear any firing."

"Wait," said Junius. "Crawl up and look. Come on, Lizard."

He couldn't not. Together they inched up the ridge, raw-kneed on the sand and pine needles.

"Is this where we're goin' to play?" Lizard asked.

"We don't play," said Junius. "It's different. It's ours, and nobody else knows about it. We do it all by ourselves. It's dangerous."

"That's why we're hiding?"

"We're not hiding. We're scouting."

They got to the ridge, and the shimmering traveled on beyond to another hillock where the red flag hung down from a tall pole, limply, like a fireman's shirt from a hook. Lizard watched Junius and raised himself on his elbows to look down when the other did.

"They're not here yet," Junius said. "They're coming, but we'll beat 'em there." He stood up and pointed down into the sandy gully. "That's my village."

He saw it.

"Come on. You can stand up."

He didn't want to. He wanted to stay down in the saw grass, peeping through at the five little houses below him. Black boards, slopped over with tar, and old. Old, old boards, cracked through with sunlight, and nailed wrong, or broken, or split apart. Through the torn tarpaper roofs the beams bellied, and the stairways were fallen, and no door stood. The window frames crooked and sagged. One of the little houses had a cross of slats on its ridgepole and a mound of sand blown rolling through the front wall. The others leaned together in a splintered pile over a raked street of dirty sand.

"It's haunted," he guessed.

Junius shook his head. "It's better than that. You'll see." He signaled the others with an Indian sign, and they ran up the rise. Lizard stood up. They lined up together on the ridge, waiting for another sign from Junius.

"Nobody knows about it but us," said Junius. "And any-body who tells—" He looked around at all four of them, but only Lizard had to shake his head.

"You know what about it?" asked Robert Lee.

Lizard nodded.

"You *do?* Already?"

He nodded again.

"O.K., what about it?"

"It's dangerous."

"Yeah, why?"

"It's not a toy place."

"Yes!" said Minor.

"It's real."

"Yes!" cried Henry Lee.

"You can do real things in it. It's better than real."

They cheered Lizard, howling around him and whooping him into their charmed little circle of real things.

"We run around without any clothes on if we want to!" said Henry Lee.

"We can go in the church and cuss!" said Minor.

"It's old and dirty, and if you wanta kick it down, you can kick and kick and kick, and I'm the mayor!" shouted Junius, starting suddenly down the hill, already losing himself in a wild cry that Robert Lee and Minor and Henry Lee took up. It split itself against their ears, and they raised it higher, until they rolled down into the gully and drove with its echo into the deserted, wood-cluttered street.

Then they stopped and hushed. Crouching low, they followed Junius along the gaping black boards of the houses. Lizard could feel why. Other people seemed to be there, not quite left yet.

"Where to?" said Henry Lee, low.

"Where first?" whispered Minor.

"The movies," ruled Junius.

He skulked the corner, and the others followed round, loping and crouching. Lizard was last again. He stumbled over too much to see. There were signs everywhere along the dark slab-bing. Across the street the toppling wall had a painted door with a sickle moon and a hammer through it. It said:

THE PEOPLE'S PRIVY

Higher up on the wall it said:

VOLGA'S BEST VODKA

and by his thin shoulder, as he slipped along, picking up splinters through his T shirt, it said:

FIVE & TEN
RUBLE STORE

But the tiny holes. The bright tiny holes that sparkled at him through the black boards, like needles run through. Hundreds and hundreds of them, blinking from the sun raised behind.

"Line up!" Junius said. "Line up, and don't push!" He began to take tickets under another sign, straight on a slant building, that had more tiny holes in it.

RED PASTURES
Filmed in Glorious Siberiascope!
Starring the Rumanian Beauty
Comrade OLGA

He couldn't read it. The words were too big. He was beginning to feel dizzy, tiny holes twinkling in his head.

"Come on, pay up." Junius nudged him.

Lizard rubbed his eyes.

"Costs a nickel."

"Haven't got a nickel."

"You *haven't?*" Lizard was supposed to be a rich kid.

"No." He took his hands away from his eyes, and they stung with needles of sunlight. "Where are we?"

"You really want to know?"

"Uh-huh."

Junius leaned to his ear and whispered in long sounds, "Si-ber-i-a!"

"Where?"

"Siberia! Don' you know?"

"Where's that?"

"Right here!"

Lizard stared around at the baked, blank street, the broken houses, the strange signs, and the sun-hardened sand hills humming with saw grass above him. He shook his head. Then he pointed to the red flag hanging tallest of all on the ridge and asked, "Is that what it's for?"

"No," said Junius. "That's for firing. Why we gotta hurry." He forgot about the nickel. "Come on, you get in free the first time."

They went inside the falling house, where it was hot and the gnats bothered.

"Who's goin' to be the movie?" said Henry Lee.

"Pull down the shades," said Minor. "Pitchers!" He ran around the house, pulling down all the shades that weren't there over the gashed windows. One rolled up on him, he pretended.

"Lizard has to be the movie!" said Robert Lee.

"It's Lizard's turn," said Minor. "First time."

"Next time," said Junius. "This time Robert Lee."

"*Why?*" yelled Robert Lee. "I was last time!"

"That's dirty!" yelled Henry Lee. "You're mayor too much!"

Junius smiled. "Don't you wanta see his boil?"

It struck them all. Robert Lee reached around behind himself again.

"It'll hurt!"

"Chicken liver."

"He don't have to," said Henry Lee, weakly.

"Chicken liver with giblets!" yelled Minor.

"Shut up!" But he resigned himself. "How long's it gotta be?"

"Just a newsreel," Junius bargained.

"I'm goin' keep my shoes on," Robert Lee said, holding out. "And my underwear till the last part."

"Sure," said Junius, and sat down in the sand for the lights to dim. "Sure."

They all sat down, and Robert Lee went to the far corner. Angrily he undressed, keeping his back to them. His elbows got jammed in his T shirt, which was badly shrunk and pulled his hair. His pants fell like a shot, because they were his brother's. He hung both on a raw nail hammered in naked from the other side of the wall, and turned around. His ribs combed under the pink skin, and his belly button curled. He scratched nothing at all on his chest.

"Movies!" shouted Minor, and began to whir like a projector, grinding his fist in a great circle around his ear.

Robert Lee pressed his back against the wall and pushed off. He landed in the center of the room, and a speckle of sunflake from the tiny holes sprayed over him, blotching his skin. He began to dance to no music with no rhythm, toeing and heeling in the sand floor, until the dance turned into a war. He was cannon and grenade, fire and shrapnel, impact and recoil. With a huge childish violence he exploded internally and fell dead. But they made him get up.

"That's not enough," said Junius. "More."

He worked himself up into a war again. This time he came by as a jet, swooping with his arms spread delta-wing, until the dive, when he pulled them in suddenly and gripped both handles on his machine gun. He riddled Junius and pulled out. Then he swung back and strafed his brother and Minor and Lizard. They rocked back on their haunches and died laughing. Then Robert Lee idled down, banked quietly into a landing. He jounced and stopped. He swung his tail slowly toward them, and at the dramatic moment bent down double, ripping his underpants to his dirty ankles. He let them look for ten seconds. Then he clawed up his skivvies and ran for his clothes. They cheered and clapped.

"Terrific!" yelled Minor. "Goin' to bust any minute."

"It should have a bandage," said Lizard.

"He should be in bed," said Robert Lee.

"Didn't hurt, did it?" asked Junius.

"Hurts all the time," said Robert Lee, buckling his brother's pants to his thin waist. He was starting to be proud of his boil. "I got to be careful from now on."

"Great movie!" said Minor. "Terrific war pitcher!"

"I took Lizard's turn," warned Robert Lee. "He's got to take mine."

Henry Lee stood up. "Where now?"

"Church," said Junius. "Got to hurry."

They gathered at the angled doorway quickly, and one by one sneaked out after the mayor. They went through the houses now, instead of skirting them, crawling in windows and sliding out doors a leg at a time. It was fast work among rusty nails, broken glass, and loose, breaking boards. Lizard breathed hard, careful not to touch the tarpaper, which burned. He couldn't see now without things rolling and pitching a little. In the second house a slat rose and barked his shin. When he bent over to rub it, Henry Lee pushed him against the wall. The house shivered and shook hornets loose in the flimsy roofing. The hornets went out the window with him whining. Then, the last house, cluttered with old planks and chewed slabs, clattered under him, spilling sand, and out the door, across a scape of rusty wire and stubble, stood the church. It said:

THE PEOPLE'S CHURCH

The sight of it almost toppled him. He rubbed his stinging eyes again, but the church stayed the same, racked through with brutal sunlight, gigged everywhere with those tiny holes. The little wooden cross at the peak tilted its arm steeply, just catching its balance on the ridgepole. Below, everything gaped. The tarred boards warped away from their clawing nails. The front wall, trumped in sand, was pushed over, and the weak frame buckled to it. Nothing was hidden. It was all swept together and jacked high and beaten apart. It frightened him.

It hushed them all.

"What happened to it?" Lizard asked.

"It looks worse'n last time," said Minor. "They been practicing on it."

"What do they do to it?" Lizard asked.

"You'll see it happen," said Robert Lee, "maybe." He started edging toward the church. "Hurry up!"

They formed a circle, and then Junius broke the circle out

into an Indian file, which crossed the sand at a weave. This time they kept step. Lizard bumped Minor's heels ahead of him. He heard them whispering something harsh and low, but before he could make it out, he was inside the church, like a cage of wooden bars. Then he could hear clearly. They were chanting. It went "Bap-" on one foot, and then "*tist!*" on the other. "Bap-*tist!* Bap-*tist!* Bap-*tist!*" They hissed the word, taking it slowly around the walls. It marked their cadence and died in a burst of laughter. They hugged each other gleefully and started around again, chanting, "Jew-*ISH!* Jew-*ISH!* Jew-*ISH!*" They laughed that one down, too, and danced around Junius, rubbing knuckles in his hair. Then Minor remembered. "We ain't finished. What about Lizard?"

Henry Lee turned on him quickly. "What church you go to?"

"Piscopalian," said Lizard carefully.

"That's too *long!*"

"We'll speed it up."

"Congo line!" said Minor.

They rushed together, grabbing each other's shoulders, and started off. It was out of beat at first, but they picked it up.

" 'Pisco-PAY-lian! 'Pisco-PAY-lian! 'Pisco-PAY-lian!"

They laughed harder than ever, howling at Lizard, hugging him.

"Now you're in it," said Junius. "They can't touch us."

Minor warned Lizard, "Just *don't* go out of the circle, that's all."

He looked around him at the beaten track in the sand, drawing him in. It's like being trapped, he suddenly realized, only you're safe. He laughed out loud. "What do we do now?"

"Anything!" yelled Minor. He punched Lizard in the shoulder. "Go ahead, whatever you want."

They were all watching him hopefully, but he was still frightened. "I'll . . . I'll be next."

Henry Lee jeered him.

They all sank their eyes. The silence weighed briefly under the twinkling holes. Junius said again, "Got to hurry. They'll be here."

Minor jumped up. "Me," he said.

"What?"

"I'm goin' to preach."

Henry Lee grabbed sand with both hands, yelled, and threw into the air. They got it down all their necks. "Minor's goin' to preach," he said. "You better listen, God!"

"Like on the radio," said Minor. "Preach the end of the world." He raised his fist and his craning voice. "The LOR' GAWD A'MIGHTY SEND FIRE TO BURN THE EARTH AND I'S SINNIN' PEOPLE!" He cleared his throat. "Like that, and you got to yell, 'Amen, brother, amen!' when I have to breathe."

"Amen, brother, amen," they said, catching on already.

Minor set about him for the right footing. In the corner, under the bending-out eave, was a crate on end. He kicked it over and stepped up. The lettering on the slats was upside down.

```
       ЯƎᛒI⅃∀Ɔ 0Ɛ˙
      ƧƎ⅁ᗡIЯTЯ∀Ɔ I-M
```

"BROTHEREN!" Minor started off at full pitch.

"Don't shout," Junius warned. "They're around."

"You're supposed to shout," said Minor. "We're under the big tent."

"Anyway, don't shout!"

Minor flicked his loose rubber heel twice on the edge of the crate, thinking rebellion, but he lowered his voice. "Brotheren!" He looked at Junius, who nodded. "Lor' GAWD A'mighty put His Son on th' sinnin' earth to save us."

Henry Lee grabbed another double handful of sand and rolled it into nothing between his palms. "Amen, brother, amen!"

"But it didn' do Him no good. It was *all* no good. So He call in His angels and ask 'em for a staff study."

"A what?" said Robert Lee.

"A staff study!" Minor's father was a colonel. "Get the target lined up. You'll see." He cleared his throat back to the sermon. "Anyhow, they staffed it and decided to—" he looked them all defiantly in the eye—"to push ahead on a crash basis!"

Henry Lee jeered him.

"They drew it all up and cleared it and finalized it. End of the world is coming!" He was working himself up, standing on his toes and bending slats of the crate. "The angels are goin' to launch a big attack! They're coming in waves and blast us! Angels are worse than missiles. They'll get us 'fore we know it, and no plane'll ever even get off the ground!"

He was breathing hard.

"Amen, brother, amen!" they yelled.

"And God," he went on, "Gawd A'mighty is goin' to watch over from His whirlybird. He's goin' to look down through that glass bubble and point out with His fiery finger all th' sinners on earth and yell, 'Damned!'" He thrust out his arm, sweeping. "He's goin' to point out 'em all, every one, and yell, 'Damned . . . Damned . . . Damned'"—he arched his finger at Lizard—"'DAMNED!'"

Lizard felt prickles rising through his shoulders. Quickly he reached up to rub his neck, but instead, the touch freed a shudder that sank through his whole body. It felt like holes. He hugged himself hard.

"Yessir, they're comin' over the North Pole at high altitude and whomp us!" Minor preached. "Angel after angel, stacked up! Prepare to meet up with yo' Maker 'cause He's comin' in His whirlybird to judge us all!" He jumped off the cartridge box. "How's that?"

"Amen, brother, amen!"

"Amen."

"Amen, broth—"

But Junius suddenly waved his hand for silence. "Quiet."

"Amen, brother," said Henry Lee, giggling.

"Shut up!" Junius snapped. "Listen . . ."

They listened. Nobody moved. The sun steeped them in its unbending light through the torn walls, and the sand cut their knees. Lizard strained his ears until they hummed.

"What?" Minor whispered.

"Listen."

They all caught it at once. A low grunting and whining behind the ridge, and they knew what made it.

"Jeeps!" said Minor.

"Church is over," said Robert Lee.

"It's time," said Henry Lee, already crawling over. "We got to bug!"

"Bug quick!" said Robert Lee.

"O.K. After me," ordered Junius. "Keep low."

None of them got up. They stayed on their knees, scrubbing across the sand, crowding each other to the door. They looked out and up the slope they'd come down. It was a long dash, where you fell back if you didn't scramble.

"Everybody ready?" said Henry Lee, out of turn.

Junius growled at him to shut up. The sound of motors was louder, shaking inside the church. "I'll ask." Then he turned around and saw Lizard far back in the corner by the cartridge box.

"Lizard," he cried low, "move up."

Lizard, still kneeling, shook his head.

"What's a matter?" said Robert Lee.

"Nothing," Lizard said.

"You got to come! It's terrible what happens!"

"No."

"You can't stay! You want to?"

"Yes."

"Why?"

He didn't know exactly why he wanted to, but he answered, "You're scared!" It thrilled him to say it. "You're all chicken."

Henry Lee snarled. He cupped a handful of sand and threw it viciously at Lizard. "Come ON!" he yelled. "Y' dummy!"

They could hear the jeeps heavier now, grinding in a lower gear, bucking the ridge. Lizard turned around and peeped out a crack. "Can't see 'em yet." Secretly he wiped Henry Lee's sand out of his eyes.

"Come ON!"

"I can do whatever I want!" Lizard yelled back. "It's my turn."

"You'll get—" Henry Lee started to say, but a flurry of sand caught him stinging in the face. Lizard had another ready to throw.

"Come and get me!" he defied them. "Back inside the circle!"

Junius raised up slowly, brushing the sand off his stomach.

Then he blew his lower lip. He said, "Are you coming, or what?" It was final.

"No."

He watched them run off at a break. When they were out of sight from his corner, he crawled to the church door and on his belly watched their last scramble uphill. They stood up all the way, raising a dusty smoke, clawing for handholds in the dry grass and tumbling sand. Minor was the last one to scuttle out of sight. The dust settled where their toes had dug, and behind him, the jeeps gained the ridge, roaring their motors, spitting exhaust, and once backfiring.

Suddenly frightened, he rolled over on his back, stiffened out his arms, and shut his eyes tight against the sounds. Then he relaxed, and for comfort, slowly winging, made an eagle in the sand. He jumped up and looked down at the eagle to see if it made him feel any bigger. A speckle of stark sunlight from the tiny holes touched the sand where it lay.

He knelt down and reached his hands into the speckles, trying to catch them on his fingers. He could hear men now, yelling, swearing, crashing metal. He cupped his right hand and slowly raised it toward his face, so that a single sun speckle shrank down almost round on his sandy palm. He held it steady and then shifted its tiny warmth and light into his left hand, pretending to pour it. He poured it back.

The first fire came from the ridge.

He dropped it.

HUGHES RUDD

The Shores of Schizophrenia

I STARTED SPOUTING off the other night about how I'd always wanted to have a conducted tour through a mortuary, with somebody along to explain what it was all about, exactly how they do it and so forth, when I remembered that I did take a tour like that once, although it didn't turn out too well. I'd forgotten all about it—it just shows you how useless everything is, how absurd it is to try and tell kids anything. You give them an experience like that, something you'd think they could never forget, and within a week they don't know what you're talking about.

I had to shut up when I thought of it; I was sitting in the garden behind the Peanut at one of the tin tables, swilling beer and working up to a good speech, really getting ready to insult somebody, but it plugged me right up. The other people at the table decided I hated them, they couldn't understand it, it wasn't like me at all. I just sat there; I couldn't tell them about it because they wouldn't have understood it, it would have meant a lot of babbling and shouting, before it was all over

118]

we'd have been down on the gravel, rolling around and beating each other with beer bottles while the fat rats skipped back and forth, trying to stay out of range. That's the way it is out at the Peanut, sometimes; the place attracts that sort. You can curse and shout and belch all you want, as long as you don't pull anything funny, anything unusual. If you do—blooey! out you go.

That mortuary trip was just one of several we had at that time. We were in the fourth grade, somewhere around there, at Dean Highland School in Waco, Texas, a building stuck out on the muddy edge of town like an unsuccessful factory, with two mulberry trees in the front yard.

The teacher was absolutely the meanest bitch I have ever known in my life, nothing pleased her, she snarled and slapped and snorted until everybody in the class was terrified, we worked like dogs. But we didn't seem to learn anything, we just went through the motions, almost hysterical, so of course things got worse and worse. Nothing did any good, you could have cut your throat to please her and she still would have hated your guts. An average schoolteacher, in fact.

And then she started those damn trips of hers. As I remember it, at first we thought it was a terrific idea, anything to get out of that gloomy, hideous building, with its smell of cedar sawdust and stale, infantile pee, we couldn't wait for the first outing. Everybody had to show up in their best clothes that day, washed and combed and buttoned up to the eyeballs, like a Sunday School class. The kids from the other rooms nearly split themselves laughing at us, they thought we were out of our minds and you know nothing gives you such a belly laugh as a real loony walking around in your everyday world. They got a real kick out of it. But for once we didn't give a damn, we were the ones who were getting out, and we piled aboard the bus like we were headed for the Crystal Theater or a calf cutting.

Well, teacher soon fixed that. It was slap, slap, slap, up and down the aisle, pulling ears and twisting cowlicks until we were almost in a panic, ready to kick the windows out. For some reason it never occurred to us to gang her. By the time we pulled up in front of German's Funeral Home everybody's clean clothes had all gone to hell and we were covered with dirt, there

was chewing gum in hair and eyebrows, and two or three of
the more timid souls had wet their pants, including little
Robert, of course; he never failed us. We looked like a wild-
eyed rabble lined up on the grass in front of the funeral home,
like we'd broken out of prison and crawled through a hundred
miles of dust to get there, to be on time for the guided tour
through the mortuary.

The first thing, of course, was to explain what the hell it
was all about. In school we had been reading about the Egyptians and their mummies, the King Tut tomb business happened about that time and it set everybody off, I never knew
why. The teacher started brooding about what a stupid bunch
we were, I suppose, not understanding embalming and so on,
she was sick and tired of trying to explain what it was all about
so she decided the hell with it, we'd go to the source. And, too,
she probably was just as happy to get out of that damned building as we were, I don't know. Anyway, she lined us up on the
grass and tried to make it clear what was about to happen,
which was a mistake. Up till then I don't think anybody had
any idea what was going on, but as soon as she put it across
that we were going in there and look at a lot of dead people,
the ranks faltered, then broke, and in a split second most of the
girls and some of the boys were squawling like turpentined cats.
She had a nimble time for a few minutes, running all over the
lawn after kids who wanted to go home, hopping around the
house, plunging through the canna beds, dodging around among
the iron deer and sundials that Mr. German had all over the
place. The people passing by must have thought one of our
little classmates had kicked off and we had turned up in a group
at the funeral, unable to contain our grief. It was lively, but
it wasn't getting things done, and pretty soon Mr. German's son
came out in his black suit and helped her round up the strays.
Little Robert got away, though; he wandered around downtown all that day, wetting his pants every fifteen minutes, until
somebody recognized him and took him home. So he missed it.

It was cool inside, but you really couldn't see much. Mr.
German's place had been just a house to begin with, the mortuary stuff was all in the basement and the upstairs was pretty
much like our own houses, only darker and a good deal tidier,

and somehow that made it seem even worse. We trailed around in the gloom in a chorus of little moans, everywhere you looked you could see eyeballs shining. We held on to each other for dear life, and there were squeaks and grunts and sighs and other nervous noises while we were led around through the rooms, completely aimlessly. It was really senseless. Finally, the teacher started arguing with Mr. German about letting us go down in the basement where the meat of the matter was, but he refused to do it, he was against the whole idea, in fact, and they had a real go-around while we stood there looking on, waiting for our fate like a bunch of pigs. After a while the teacher gave up and led us back to the bus, and we reloaded and went back to school. All we had seen that was unusual was the portable organ and an empty casket, unlined. The rest of it was just rooms and folding chairs, we couldn't understand what the hell it was all about. A field trip!

The next thing was the compress. Naturally, we were involved with cotton all the time, no matter what you were studying they always managed to drag cotton into it somehow, and with the Egyptians it was a cinch. As usual, we had to bring bolls of it to school, and we made little speeches about it, the way it had been in every class since we had started school, but you couldn't keep coasting along on your old speeches. Oh, no. Some jerk would snitch if you did that. You had to come up with new facts every year, and you had to have a novel way of presenting your cotton boll to the collection, too. We pasted the damn things on cards, we wired them into little trees, we made leis out of them, we dyed them with watercolors, we did every damn thing you can think of with cotton before it was over. Well, of course there was no pleasing this bitch, she didn't think much of our efforts. She flung the silly things back in our faces, she ranted and howled and redoubled her pinching and slapping. We were a spineless bunch, we just took it. She wasn't even reported to the school board by an outraged mother, as far as I know. Of course, she had a lot on her mind, a lot of worries, as it turned out, she probably expected the ax to fall at any minute, but apparently that just made her bear down harder on this cotton business. We'd never had such a siege of it, it made us shudder to think what must be ahead of us in the

grades to come. If it was this bad here, what would they expect
in junior high school? Would you have to go out and pick the
stuff, gin the goddam cotton yourself? For Christ's sake! We
worried our little heads about it, I can tell you. Little Robert
was soaked, every day.

Well, after we'd done everything possible with our bedraggled
cotton bolls and had brought in tons of newspaper clippings
about it, all smeared around and pasted on cards and in scrap-
books, we had to show up in our best clothes again to go to the
compress. The compress! There's not a damned thing to see
in one of those places, and every kid in town knew it. They pile
the cotton in a hopper and a big weight comes down and packs
it into a bale. That's all, and you can't even see that, there's always so much dust and lint in the air, and the machinery isn't
out where you can stick your finger in it, anyway. A hell of an
uproar, but you can't see what they're doing, and if you don't
look out, one of those tough bastards will knock you on your
ear, clear off the loading dock. We all knew that, but we packed
ourselves into that stinking bus, a little troop of smelly martyrs,
and off we went. We had no guts at all.

The compress manager thought everybody had gone nuts.
They'd told him we were coming, all right, but Jesus! A busload,
piling out all over the joint! What a day for the compress
manager! And the terrible thing for him, of course, was that he
couldn't figure out what the hell we were doing there. He'd
been around compresses all his life, he didn't see anything unusual about it at all. What else did we expect him to do with
the cotton, for Godsake, tie it up with string? Of course they
baled it, of course the plunger came down and packed it tight,
of course, of course, and we agreed with him. What the hell, we
knew all that as well as he did, we weren't idiots, you know. We
just stood around and looked at the poor devil, getting filthier
by the minute, dirt and lint settling all over us, in our ears, in
our nostrils; we could hardly breathe. It was like the rope factory in a prison, and the noise! You couldn't hear yourself
scream, so of course we did, we opened our little mouths and
bellowed like maddened bulls, looking at the compress manager.
To that poor sod it looked like our mouths were hanging open
in astonishment at his machine, he couldn't hear a thing. We

were all hoarse when we got out of there, and nobody had heard us make a sound. That was getting even, all right! That was one up the teacher's nose! We enjoyed that, but it wasn't over yet. She lined us up, the usual business, out in the road this time in dust deeper than our sweaty little ankles, and everybody had to describe what he had just seen. Not just, "They bale cotton." Hell, no! The first one tried that and got a real wallop. You had to go into ecstasies over the crumby place, really tear your heart out about that compress. To be successful at it, you needed a degree in hydraulic engineering and a steam boiler operator whispering in your ear. We stood there in the dust and took it, we were absolutely no damned good to Dean Highland School whatsoever. We thought any minute she was going to give us the order to go hop in the compress bin, under the plunger, it was the only honorable way out and we knew it. We were ready, it was tough, but that's the way it was, so what the hell. Let's get it over with. But no, back in the bus, slap, smack, pinch, somebody puking on the floor, a splendid little outing, the teacher behaving like a drunken storm trooper. Well, we've seen the compress, now what? Mass suicide? Why not, what else? There's nothing left, is there? Come on, we'll all do it together, out on the playground. We can hang ourselves from the swing supports, in relays of ten.

Well, that took care of cotton. Let's see, what's next, now? Oh, yes, coffee, of course. Is there anybody here who doesn't know what coffee is? Of course there isn't, we have it all over the house, we practically live on the stuff. Well, that doesn't make a goddam bit of difference, you little slobs! What a filthy bunch! What parents you must have! Wipe your noses and get into that bus, or I'll wring every one of your grimy necks! We're going to the coffee works.

If anybody else had told us there was a place in town where they ground coffee, we wouldn't have believed it. They'd drummed it into us that the stuff came from South America, we knew what the score was. We'd seen a thousand pictures of it growing down there, or over there, or wherever the hell South America was, we'd even seen pictures of it lying on the ground, with people walking around on it barefooted. What the hell! You didn't have to tell us about coffee, we'd all had nightmares

about it at some time or other, at one point we had to go
around to the grocery stores begging for a coffee bean to take
to class, just to show some teacher we knew what she was talking about. Coffee! Why bother! We weren't even allowed to
drink it, yet here it was, coffee, coffee and still more coffee, you
heard nothing else. What a world!

They were waiting for us at the coffee works, I suppose they
were more accustomed to the screwballs in town than the
compress manager was, they were a high-class bunch. You'd
have thought we were little movie stars, for the first five minutes. There we were, all cleaned up again, they thought it was
downright sweet. Sweet! Jesus, why didn't they put us to work
digging sewers? We were getting a little sick of all this idiocy
by now, we were beginning to figure maybe all this wasn't in
the contract, that they were putting one over on us, in fact. We
hadn't been idle, we'd been asking around.

Well, there it was, the coffee! Now what? There were tons of
it, in all stages, and that was all right, we had nothing against
it, but so what? Sure, it was coffee, we admitted that, didn't
we? What did they want us to do, throw ourselves in it? What
good would that do anybody? What was all the fuss about, anyway?

Well, here's the kind they drink in New Orleans, somebody
said. See? It's ground up finer than the rest, like powder. New
Orleans? What the hell are they talking about? Sure, we supposed they drank coffee in New Orleans, why not, when you
think of it? And we dawdled around, an impossible scene. It's
really hell in a coffee mill, you know, especially if you don't
drink it. Instead of dust in the air you have little motes of
coffee, I suppose from the batch those New Orleanians had to
have, trying to be different. We figured that out, and we began
to hate New Orleans' guts. We breathed the stuff, that
powdered coffee filled up our lungs and passed into our blood-
streams until we were as hopped up as if we'd gotten bugged on
cocaine. We didn't know what the hell we were doing, it was
a colossal coffee jag. Our nerves were shot, we almost got bags
under our little eyes, and not one of us slept a wink that night.
It upset the whole west end of town. For a week we puked

every time we saw a cup of the nasty stuff. We were feverish with caffeine.

Well, that was another one under our belts. Live and let live, that was us, we could stand anything, Powder River, let 'er buck! We hadn't lost anybody yet, we were a damned tough crowd. They were going to have trouble polishing us off, all right. We were ready to go back to the mortuary and start all over again, we'd drag the damn stiffs out in the front yard if we had to, if that was what they wanted. A hardy little class!

We could've kept it up forever, we were just hitting our stride when the whole thing blew up. I got on the streetcar one afternoon and who was sitting in front of me but the teacher, with some woman I'd never seen before. I was on my way down to the Crystal and I didn't want to miss any more of the show than I had already, I just sat there scared stiff, afraid she'd see me and start grilling me about streetcars or electricity or some damn thing. But I got by, she just bawled on the other woman's neck all the way downtown, it was quite a scene, everybody was disgusted, and after that I never saw her again.

The next day we had a new teacher and she had to break the bad news. The old bitch had pinched our little savings, the dough she'd extorted from us a dime at a time so our room would look good on the chart out in the hall, she'd blown the whole seven bucks! Jesus, no! We set up quite an uproar, but there it was, nothing anybody could do about it, we'd just have to lump it. They'd found out about it and fired her, but that didn't get our money back. We wanted her arrested, we wanted the cops to beat hell out of her, but they let her go, of course. That's always the way it is. If *we'd* hooked the seven bucks— brother! They'd have taken us down in the coal bin and buried us alive. But we finally figured, what the hell, you know, at least those idiotic tours where finished with, and just in time. She'd been raving about dragging us out to the cement factory, just before the roof fell in. God knows what would have happened out there, it was a rugged place.

JAMES BLAKE

Day of the Alligator

Riding back to the stockade after the long and leaden day on the road, Dooley sat stripped to the waist on a plank that crossed the body of the truck, looking at the pines, sand and palmettos.

Friday. The weekend Olympics again. Night games. God, if only— I hope he can't get any ephedrine tonight.

He looked back at Barton sitting massively on the tailgate, brown back and yellow hair gleaming in the late sunlight. He was swinging his feet and singing "When It's Twilight on the Trail"—*doy-doy doy doy doy doy doy, doy-doy doy doy doy*— the raucous voice rebounding from the wall of the woods.

Why did I feel so absurdly pleased when I found out he knew that tune? Like watching him graduate. You've come a long way from your civilian days, father of none.

Barton caught Dooley looking at him, and the look he returned mixed amusement with irritation.

"Whose baby are you?" he said sternly.

"Daddy's baby," said Dooley.

"What kind of a daddy?"

"High-rollin' daddy."

"And who's your high-rollin' daddy?"

"You are, Daddy."

"Just don't forget it."

The other cons roared at the stale and familiar exchange. Dooley turned to stare again at the passing trees.

An evil night when I fell into that routine. Even a straight delivery doesn't save anything.

The truck was passing through heavily wooded country now, pine forest on either side. This was the spot where so many prisoners had jumped off into the woods. He looked back at the two shotgun guards in the trailer behind the truck. When they remembered, they would sit up straight at this spot, grasp their guns, and look straight ahead with such a charged air of dissembling alertness that Dooley always felt oddly gratified.

The truck slowed at the approach to a wooden bridge across a creek. Looking down, Dooley saw a huge alligator, looking up.

Everybody yelled at once. "Stop the truck, Cap'n!" " 'Gator back here, Cap'n!" Somebody banged on the top of the truck's cab.

The truck drew to a stop at the side of the road. Cap'n Clark slowly unfolded his long old bones from the front seat of the truck. He pulled off the cork tropical helmet he wore and stood glaring wildly from the guards to the prisoners.

"Big 'gator back here, Cap'n," Barton explained. "Could we please go back and see him, Cap'n? He's a great *big* bastard, sir."

The two guards had dismounted from the trailer and stood leaning on their shotguns. The driver of the truck, a burly young cracker with the eyes of a doe, got out and started back toward the bridge, pulling his pistol from the holster.

"Better put that gun up, Kern," the old man stopped him. "You know better than to shoot a 'gator."

The driver, coloring, put up his gun.

"All right, c'mon everybody wants to see the 'gator." Cap'n Clark started toward the bridge.

The men jumped in noisy confusion off the truck to follow, trying to rattle one of the guards, who was new on the job and had been getting it all day.

The alligator lay in a sunlit mud-patch on the bank. Someone made a sudden noise, and with a great heave and flash of its belly it slid into the water and vanished beneath the bridge.

Some of the crew hung over the railing, peering, anxious to pro-long the diversion.

Cap'n Clark turned toward the truck. "All right, all right, let's ramble, we're runnin' late now."

"Ramble!" they hollered, and scrambled noisily back up on the truck.

All the way in to the stockade Barton kept outlining to Bayou Boy, the big ramrod of the crew, a scheme for capturing the alligator alive, involving a rope and "downwind" and a leap from the bridge onto the alligator's back.

Dooley heard eager excited snatches of it as he faced into the wind.

He's transported by it. And I feel touched and warmed by his eagerness. Fearful for the boyish awkwardness. Aaah God.

In the prison dormitory Dooley waited his turn at the long row of taps in the washroom. He washed slowly and the room was deserted when he was combing his hair.

Canfield came in, a plump young man with a crew cut from San Francisco. An airline pilot, in for forgery, to Dooley his coming to the prison farm had been an advent. Riding out in the morning to the job, back at night, each had discovered in the other a listener and a companion.

Canfield knew all the names and labels, Fauré, Firbank, Fonteyn, Fats, and told long serpentine stories of rainy week-ends in New Haven, of what the boy from Amherst had said, all in a half-petulant tone that suggested everything had been a tedious mistake.

He stood beside Dooley at the mirror, combing his hair, carefully pressing forward the beginning of a small curl over his forehead. He said wearily:

"How are you and Apollo Belvedere getting along?"

"Not too bad." Dooley leaned into the mirror. Dishing with Canfield was a thing he would never understand, and never forego. "He found an alligator he wants to rassle."

"He found a what?"

"An alligator." Dooley gave a small pained shrug. "And he's going to leap off a bridge onto its back. Bring it back alive."

"Oh no. Mowgli the Alligator Boy."

A small shame crept into him, but he went on, "Bayou Boy

is coming from *downwind*, with a rope—I think— Well, it's not too clear, of course— But we all goan have *alligator* shoes by-'n'-by."

"All God's *chillun* got alligator shoes!" They collapsed into silent laughter. The room was suddenly quiet, only the soft, pleasantly stricken sounds of muffled mirth. Dooley straightened and saw himself in the mirror.

"C'mon, cut it out now, man; yawl act like yawl against alligators." He reached for the comb and looked up to comb his hair.

In the glass he saw Barton, buttoning his pants, coming around from a row of toilets that was screened from the mirror. He came over and stood behind them, examining his nails.

Canfield hurriedly finished combing his hair. "Time for chow," he muttered, and fled.

Dooley watched his own stricken face in the glass and combed his hair with careful attention.

Barton stood inspecting himself, yellow hair, brown face, brown shoulders, in the mirror.

"Alligator shoes for all," he murmured. "I've always wanted to deck you good anyway, Carhart."

The washed-blue eyes that Dooley sought in the mirror were implacable with hatred.

"Bart, I didn't want—"

"It was *amusing,* wasn't it?" He gave it the languid inflection of Canfield.

"Bart, look—"

Chow call sounded. Barton turned away from the mirror. "You better not go in for chow tonight. If I have to look at you, I'll puke. Get over on the bunk and stay there."

"Jesus Christ, Bart, I'm hungry as a bitch! Look, man, don't—"

Barton turned, motioned with his head. "Over on the bunk. And when I come back, I'm going to try to kill you."

He lay face down across the double bunk in the deserted dormitory, listening to the busy clacking of spoons on plastic plates in the mess hall. Heavy with a dreary certainty, he reached over and turned on the radio. Sarah Vaughan came on, singing

"If You Could See Me Now." The sinuous silver of the music
trailed in the air . . .

He thought of how quietly expectant the piano used to look
when he sat down at it. Rush Street in Chicago on a misty
night, the neon signs of all the night clubs haloed, the taxi
horns muted in the gentle fog.

How many worlds away?

MacLean came in from chow, first out, fastest eater. He bent
over Dooley, long eager nose.

"You better hide, kid. He's really pissed."

"Don't get excited, Mac. And don't do me any favors. Just
go away."

"Just trying to help you, kid."

"Yeah, I know."

And waited.

Dooley Carhart was a piano player from Chicago who'd been
bouncing around Florida for a year, lightly tea-d up most of
the time, drunk on gin and the climate. He played the piano
in bars until he ran out of jobs, began to steal, and wound up
on the chain gang with two years to build.

The only law of the prison dormitory, he discovered immediately, was that of violence. Except for shakedowns and riots, no
guards ever entered it. Authority was represented by a trusty,
of whom it was said that he would get out with better than
a thousand dollars.

On the first night Dooley made up his bunk, an upper on the
top tier, and flopped into it. The noise in the dormitory was
deafening. Radios brayed, all different, voices shouted, sang,
cursed.

The rack shook, and a brown face under wheat-yellow hair
looked over the top. "Mind if I come up?"

Dooley said no.

He swung himself over the top and perched on the side of
the bunk, a half-naked brown giant in faded-gray prison pants.

"Barton's my name. You're the new cock came in today."

"That's right. I'm Carhart."

"What'd you bring?"

"Two years."

"This your first bit?"

"My first."

"You'll find it ain't so bad when you get used to it. You can build easy time or do it the hard way. I could make this standing on my head in the shit-jacket. All you got to do here is beat your brains out on the road, and they don't care what else you do."

"I ain't exactly looking forward to that road department."

"It'll be rough at first, but you'll get used to it. After a while you'll learn how to goof so they can't see it— Hey, I was on my way to get a Coke. You wanna Coke or something? Ya got cigarettes?"

Dooley said yes, and yes he had cigarettes.

When Barton returned with the Cokes, he said, "I've been thinking, there's a lower bunk vacant down in my rack. I don't know why the hell he put you up here. Ya gotta climb up and down every time you have to piss. That's nowhere. Let's move your gear over there, you wanna?"

Dooley wanted to be alone and read, but he thought of the hassle he was due to face out on the road in the morning. It would help to know somebody, and this guy acted like a wheel. If it was some kind of a pitch, he would just pull out.

"Good deal," he said, and they rolled everything up in the mattress and carried it down to the back end of the long room, through the inquiring stares of other prisoners.

"You sure this is all right? The houseman—"

"He don't mean anything. If he says anything, I'll straighten him out."

The bunk was on the bottom tier of a rack in the back corner of the dormitory, another bunk beside it. Hanging across the back of the rack was a blanket covered with pin-up pictures, and on a shelf across the head of the bunks were an overseas radio, some pipes, tobacco, shaving gear.

"This is fine, man," Dooley said, unrolling the mattress and distributing his belongings.

"Beats sleeping up on a shelf. They call this the Mourner's Corner back here."

Dooley noticed for the first time that Barton was wearing shackles.

"What did you get those for?"

"Oh these? Runnin'." He stretched out on the bunk. The stout chain was about two feet long, fastened to thick steel rings around his ankles. "I ran about a month ago, but I got drunk and fouled up. They'll take 'em off maybe in a month or so. Hey, I think I'll make some coffee."

He reached under the bunk and pulled out a glass half-gallon jar. "I'll get some water from the bathroom."

He brought the jar back half-full and put it on the shelf, then opened the back of the radio and drew out an electric cord with a plug on one end. "Shakedown all the time, but they never find this baby." The other end of the cord was an exposed wire wrapped around the handle of a spoon.

"This is what they call a bug. Put the spoon in the water, plug in, pretty soon hot water."

They drank the coffee out of glasses, and talked. Dooley learned that Barton had been in the Marines and got a DD for black-marketing in Manila during the war—that he was a light-heavy professional boxer when not in jail—that he had made time in Leavenworth and Raiford, the state pen—and that he wanted someday to return to Manila to stay.

Barton assured him that there was nothing to the road that couldn't be handled, and that anyway he'd be around to help him out.

Dooley went to sleep with an easier mind.

In the morning he was assigned to the bull gang, Barton's crew, under the boss-guard, Cap'n Tig.

Tig was a towering fat man with a whiskey-raddled face and bright, malign, squeezed-looking eyes.

He fastened on Dooley early in the day. Dooley was down in a ditch, wrestling with the unfamiliar shovel. Tig came sauntering along the line of digging men, holding an open lunch bucket in his hand and eating a pork chop. The crew worked silently as he stood watching Dooley.

"What'd you bring, fella?"

"Two years, Cap'n."

"Hmmf. Where you from?"

"Chicago, sir."

"Yankee, eh? What'd you do outside?"

"Played the piano, sir."

"Played the piano. You mean for a living?"

"Yessir."

"Hmmf. Well, play me a tune on that ignorant stick you got there—" The crew laughed dutifully. "We'll show you how to—"

"Pardon me, Cap'n." Barton carried on his shoulder a long-handled wide-bladed bush knife. "I thought I'd go down and cut that bamboo thicket. It's going to hold us up when we get down there otherwise."

"Good idea. Take somebody along with you to drag them out of your way." He looked around.

"How about the new cock, Cap'n? He'll have to learn how to use a bush hook sometime."

"Hmmf. O.K., take him with you."

"If he tries to run, I'll cut his legs off, Cap'n."

"Go on, ramble, ramble."

They walked up the road toward the bamboos, Barton's shackles jingling in the morning quiet.

"Wonderful," Dooley said. "How do you get away with it?"

"I'm the ramrod of this crew, lad. And I don't get away with much. If we were on a heavy job, like putting in a culvert, I'd be working my ass off, me and Bayou Boy. On a chicken-shit job like this he lets me horse around, as long as I keep working. We'll go down here and goof a little."

"Man! That fat son of a bitch sure builds up a lot of pressure. I was waiting for my ears to pop."

"You might as well figure you're going to spend some time in the hole. After a while he'll get a new one to play with and forget about you. He's gotta have fresh meat."

They were at the bamboos. Barton brandished the long wicked bush knife over his head, shouting: "Flash Barton in the Philippines! Take that and that and that!" attacking the bamboos with a wild joyous fury, toppling them like matches. "Die like a dog, Mr. Moto! Take that, and that!"

The guard leaned on his shotgun and grinned at Barton whirling and slashing and yelling in the bamboos, knife flashing in the sun.

Dooley had a good time. It felt good to laugh again, pulling

the cut saplings across the road in the warm misty sunlight of
an early morning in Florida.

Noon chow was eaten under any convenient trees, where the
con who did the cooking dug a fire-pit in the sand and heated
a crock of lima beans with pieces of hog-back floating in it,
like pieces of a football. They ate from tin plates, sitting on the
ground.

Dooley finished eating and lay back in the thick flattened
grass, smoking a cigarette. Bart was sleeping under a tree across
the clearing, as were most of the crew. One of the cons walked
over and sat down beside Dooley. A thin, scrawny, sinewy
redhead with popping brown eyes. His face and body were
burned brown, and he looked to Dooley like a rawhide thong.
Or one of those long brown bugs with their eyes on stems.

"How ya makin' it?"

"Pretty good so far."

"You'll get used to it. Daddy Bart's sure takin' care of you."

"Barton? He's a fine guy."

"Didn't take you two long to get together. You know him in
some other rock?"

Another con sat down, the massive body blocking Dooley
off from the clearing. He curled a huge hand around Dooley's
ankle, thrust forward the thick neck and cropped bullet-head.
Bayou Boy.

"Hiya, baby. We gonna take a shower after lights out tonight?"

Dooley shook his head.

"What's the matter, afraid of Bart?"

"I like to sleep at night."

"You ain't gettin' much sleep around Bart."

"If you mean he snores—"

"You know what I mean, punk." He got up. "I'll see you in
the shower room an hour after lights out tonight. Don't
lemme have to come and get you."

Boneyard got up too. "You better be there, punk. Just ask
Barton what happened to Sweet Pea."

"Sweet Pea?"

"Yeah, Sweet Pea."

Dooley was too busy staying ahead of Cap'n Tig for the rest

of the day to think of anything else, but that night after chow as they lay listening to the radio, he said, "Who was Sweet Pea?"

"What do you know about Sweet Pea?"

"Nothing. I was told to ask you."

"Boneyard and Bayou Boy been giving you trouble?"

"Not trouble, really. They made me a little uneasy, but—"

"Uneasy, is it? Well, Sweet Pea was a young kid that was here a while back. Pink skin, long eyelashes, not very bright. He used to bunk right here, but he moved out and got those two on his tail. He said no, so they and some other guy took him back in the shower room and beat the shit out of him. He had to agree eventually, anyway— He could have saved himself a lot of grief—just not bright."

"What happened to him?"

"How should I know? They took him to the County Hospital from here."

"Wasn't there any investigation?"

"Oh, some chicken-shit questions. Nobody found out anything. He was just a punk and not a very good worker anyway. They probably turned him loose. He never came back."

He sat up in the bunk, lit a cigarette.

"As long as it came up—I wanted to take my time, but Boneyard kinda—I think we oughta get with it and build some easy time. Whaddya say?"

Dooley was silent.

"I'm not a very patient man."

"Bart, I'd like to make use of all this dead time to get some reading done and learn something. It's the only way to pull out of this ahead. That's all I want to do, Bart."

"Look, lad, you saw today how I can help you, out on the road. I can also make it so goddam hot for you out there that you'll have to run, or try to run, and if you move out of here, you'll have Boneyard and Bayou Boy on your trail—a stork and a bear. A great big-ass bear! Would you like that? Just relax— I'll tell you what, you can rub my back with mineral oil, that'll relax you. Here."

In the months of sadism and calculated brutality that followed, Dooley clung to the blind determination that he would somehow come out alive and ahead. There were periods when Barton was contrite and subdued and would express guarded curiosity about the books that Dooley read. And Dooley, eager to divert him, to fan the small spark, would read aloud to him the lyric poems of Millay (which Barton grudgingly admitted he liked: "Really loused up, wasn't she?"), the polished nonsense of Perelman, anything to lure him along the road of mental pursuits, to rouse the throttled humanity that must be somewhere in him.

From this, Barton would emerge silent, restless, morose—and arrange a series of crushing humiliations for Dooley, designed to show his contempt, reaffirm his dominance: inviting a crony on the crew to spend the night ("Eskimos do it all the time"), forcing him to paint his face with cosmetics and parading him around the dormitory. Dooley endured it with stony self-possession, sometimes even evincing apathetic enjoyment in a forlorn effort to deprive Barton of satisfaction.

In all this a small thing helped to comfort and sustain him. Sitting on the edge of Barton's bunk, by the high barred window open to the soft tropic night, he could see, across the dark and silent land, a red winking signal light on a radio tower. Watching it night after night, he came to imagine himself a swimmer at sea, the distant winking light, a light on the shore of safety. Barton would growl with impatience, and having to turn away from the winking light was like giving himself up to drowning. But there stayed in his mind the resolve that he would come to that shore safely.

Along about that time Canfield arrived at the stockade. The plump languid airline pilot and forger was salvation to Dooley. Just to talk to someone, even a mannered exquisite, about books and plays and music restored a little his shattered confidence and reassured him that his identity had not been totally lost.

Bart hated Canfield and told him to stay away from the bunk —but Dooley had need of those yammering camps with the malicious one, the opportunity to pour malice on the head of the absent Bart, to hear the sardonic Canfield make wearily deprecatory remarks about him. It was a small source of strength to Dooley, seeking strength from any source at all.

And even then, during these furtive and frantic conversations, he could not escape a small twinge of shame and disloyalty.

Shortly after his arrival Canfield sought the protection of Bo Braswell, a barrel-chested hooligan from Center Street in Macon.

"I know he's a little outré," he apologized to Dooley, "but the material for molding is there. I'll take him to the Coast and polish him up, make a vogue of him."

Dooley waited on the bunk, dreading Barton's return, casting about in his mind for the attitude, the words, that would confuse Bart, divert him, diminish his anger.

Canfield stopped and bent over Dooley. "Are you just going to lie there and make like Camille?"

"I know what I'm doing. It's what he expects to see."

"Oh Jesus you make me sick. Of course it's what he expects. If you're going to hold still for another dreary degrading beating, I just—"

"Well, what should I do, what the goddam hell should I do?"

"Throw him a curve, for Christ's sake! If you can't snow that big dumb blond ox, you oughta quit the business. That guy has got you so utterly— Honestly, I give up!"

He went wearily up the long aisle between the bunks.

When Bart came back from chow, Dooley was writing a letter.

He leaned against the rack indolently. "I hope you're making out your will."

"Just a letter. I'm writing to Fort Worth about those ankle-boots you wanted."

"I call that mighty sweet. But you can't buy me, Madam. And you can't slide out of what's coming to you, you two-faced—"

"Bart, I'll ask you again—let me go. Let's be sensible. I'll get a bunk by myself, and we'll forget all this argling and bargling."

"*Bart, let me go!*" he mimicked, falsetto. "Jesus. You don't even tell yourself the truth any more. Two weeks after you came to me, I couldn't have run you off with a baseball bat. You don't really want to go anywhere."

He came around the end of the bunk. "—But if you stay here, you're gonna improve."

He sat down on the bunk, watching Dooley, ominous brightness in his eyes. A long brown hand came to rest on Dooley's leg just above the knee. He gave a tentative squeeze, just tuning-up, and Dooley gave a small involuntary jump.

"Today I found out you've got a mean little streak in you. I used to wonder what you and that California poppy talked about all the time—"

"Bart, if you'll listen—"

"I don't need any chicken-shit explanations—"

"Bart, you remember the night you made me paint my face and led me all over the barracks?"

"Yeah, you were chicken-shit then, too."

"I went through a lot of humiliation that night. Man, it went deep. And the night your friend Dago called here, panting like a spaniel? C'mon in, Dago, have a cigar."

"What humiliation? You're a punk, you're supposed to act like a punk. You ain't got any rights."

"I give up. I'll never find it. It's there, but I'll never find it."

"Whaddya talking about now?"

"About you. I've thought about this a lot, Bart. Somewhere inside you there's a guy with a natural instinct for what's good, in music, poetry, books, different things. And he's unhappy and crowded in there, because there's two other guys living there too, a bank-robber and a fourflusher. If you could get the third man to move, there'd be more room and less argument, and it might not be a bad place to live."

"I knew if I let you talk, you'd make me mad. On your feet, you wise son of a bitch."

"I'm not finished. I'd just as soon be hit for something as nothing."

"On your feet, before I—" Barton turned at the hand on his shoulder.

Canfield: "Bart, I want to tell you that it was all my—"

"I thought I told you to stay away from here, shit-bird."

"Dear boy, I just want to say that we're sorry for—"

"Blow, before I slap you loose from that phony accent!"

"Just a minute, I'm not poor Dooley, you know. Don't you jump bad with me, you alligator-bait you—"

Barton leaped from the bunk and hit him a slashing backhand across the face that staggered him backwards. He hit the bars of the window with a jarring crash.

Uproar broke loose, all Canfield.

"He hit me, he hit me, the sonovabitch hit me! Help! Bo! Help! He broke my jaw! Bo! Help, Bo!"

Cons came running from all over the dormitory. The houseman went to the window and called down. "Hey, Cap'n! Up here, Cap'n!"

Bo elbowed his way swiftly through the crowd, grim and purposeful.

Canfield was still screaming.

"You broke my jaw, you dirty bastard!" He kicked viciously at Barton, who caught the leg and held it. Canfield danced around him on one leg, screaming bloody murder.

Bo broke through the crowd and launched himself at Barton, who threw Canfield on the bunk. The blow landed on Barton's neck, and he leaped at Bo, hitting him in the jaw and driving him back into the crowd. Bo came hurtling back and grabbed Barton around the waist, carrying him to the floor.

"All right, all right, break it up, break it up! What's goin' on here?"

Three guards with blackjacks came through the crowd. They pulled the struggling pair on the floor apart.

"A little time in the hole will cool you boys off. Come on, come on." The guards led them away. The cons, disappointed, went about their business.

Dooley, alone, lay back on the bunk blank-eyed, exhausted.

"Is this where I apply for a widow's pension?"

He looked up. Canfield stood there, holding a blanket and pillow.

"Can I sleep with you tonight? My father's out getting drunk and he beats me when he comes home. I brought my pajamas and some bananas. I know you're starved."

"Idiot. You'll bring down the wrath of the rabble on us."

"I don't think so. Wasn't Bo magnificent? How did you like

my little production?" He got into Barton's bunk and lay down.

"Baby, baby, you took an awful chance."

"I left nothing to chance, sweetie. I got Bo half-ribbed-up over Bart before I came down here, and I gave the houseman three bucks to call the law whenever the fight started. Those people are so predictable, I love that in them."

"Poor Bo. Poor Bart."

"Oh my god. Listen, with Bo in the hole for a while, I'm saving money. And don't think he did anything for *me!* He's been honing for Bart for a long time. I merely staged it."

"But when they come out—"

"They'll be buddies. Suffering brings people closer together."

"Canfield, you are positively—"

"Do I not know it. Didn't you like that first bit I did, 'He hit me, he hit me!' Like a Birmingham housewife blowing the whistle on a colored masher."

"*Most* effective."

"And later, that line, 'He broke my jaw!' A fine touch."

"Never better, Ethel. And they said you were through."

"The choreography could have been better, but I had to ad lib."

"I thought it was fresh and inventive. Of course you had to mention 'alligator' to Bart."

"Certainly. You can't ignite anything with wet matches. It's all chemical."

They fell silent at the approach of Bayou Boy, the big ram-rod of the crew. He stood at the foot of the bunk, glowering.

"I suppose you know that on account of you two butter-flahs the crew'll be short the two best men tomorrow. I'll make it mah business to see you take their place. You'll roll to-morrow!" He turned and walked away.

Canfield sat up, peeling a banana.

"Thank goodness. I thought it was going to be something sticky."

"But tomorrow—what'll we do?"

"I'm tired tonight. We'll think about it tomorrow." He lay down.

There was a long silence in the bunk. Dooley stirred rest-lessly.

"Poor Bart. I'll bet he's miserable down there."

"Get him a nice alligator bag. Good night, pet."

"Good night."

. . . And somewhere far off, he seemed to hear a taxi horn, half muted in the gentle fog.

SAUL BELLOW

Address by Gooley MacDowell to the Hasbeens Club of Chicago

Fellows: There have been rumors running concerning me, some funny and some two-sided, and some old ones, getting boring. I am not always against bores; I used to argue that they should be sacred, like strangers and lunatics in the simpler societies, because they keep the mysteries at the right depth; but I realize that this position overlooks great dangers. However, there's the rumor again that I'm going to marry, which is nothing but a joke on my appearance and personal neglect of years. There's a rumor that *People's Gas* wants to make me personnel director—I'm used to that one, too. And then there's this new thing, that the Nobel committee wants to start a prize for general secular intelligence or leading laymanship, and that I'm the top candidate from the Middle West. This is some

142]

satire that people think I'm beginning to lose my edge, and with perhaps a hum of sadness to it that I'm a little calcified and the blood supply to my head is not so swift as once—when, say, I first failed in business, first got married, first became a Unitarian. But it is not a well-planned joke. It overlooks my loss to the Hasbeens, should I get that famous money; and, also, that having the reverse Midas touch, all the gold I ever came in contact with having turned into something less universally desired, I wouldn't bring the Nobels anything but peril, wearing their medal.

But this joke about my falling off aims right, though physical deterioration is not what I believe to be back of it. Only, what I have been saying in bits and drabbles has waked that suspicion, so that now I will try to report my changed views or new doubts.

It's true, fellows, that I used to be very intelligent, and now don't know but what I should give it up. I've seen too many hard times, and these days I've been starting to reconsider to what end I hoped to be so smart.

Kindness sent me forward and I got praise from the first. What is there better for learning? My mother put up my exercise books in ribbons. My long-dress teachers, in the mud and shack days of this town, gave me encouragement, and I sprung my elbow waving to answer questions; and later on, with intelligence tests and so forth, I was up amongst the brightest apes, and have no doubt but that I would have conquered a box of Milky Ways from Professor I. Q. had the times been more advanced. But I did my best. I set much store by correspondence schools, where there were cerebellar doctors in the picture; the more confident in them if they had log cabins drawn in behind them, and ploughs and lonesome prairie, and now were qualified to rise up to a point of information in the thick of intellectual Boston about Lycurgus or Pitt the Younger, or which birds fly longest in migration. It was so, in the hard-collar and wisely bearded photos of these men in the back pages of magazines where they advertised, that you could see the close weave of brain back of their eyes, like the reward of gazing into radio tubes—pardon, germanium crystal diodes of thought-machines—to examine the secret of their potency. And furthermore, when I was a young bachelor, I was put wise to Herbert

Spencer, the great practical man, with snap-purse lips and head
economized of all hair and wrinkles, cleared as if for the
smoother work of brain. I was in favor of all he proposed, even,
for a moment, of his plan for the painless execution of crimi-
nals. Who remembers that piece of kindness? A centrifuge
wheel: bind your murderer to it, start him spinning slowly and
then accelerate until he dies by anemia of the brain. True capi-
tal punishment, humaner than rope, and also more noble or
Copernican that society should punish into the head and by a
law of motion that also rules in the stars. Yes, yes, in all the de-
partments of life it was intelligence connected to human ad-
vancement. You might not have thought well of big money, but
nevertheless there was the capacity of the Wall Street man and
his major brain, displacing so much black water of finance with
ticking calculations, making head into Europe and China. And
as the wizard with flashing synapses rose on the world, the engi-
neers went forward—Mr. Goethals, Mr. Eiffel, the makers of
industrial bread, Mr. Sullivan raised the Monadnock Building
here, Mr. Roosevelt, the first, sat in a white suit at the controls
of a steam shovel in the Panama Canal, voices came out of the
telephone, the country and earth filled with light forced up
from Menlo Park, the front of life coruscated, the Dying Gaul
was promoted to be Rodin's Thinker, a higher immolation, with
his fist to his forehead—as all this happened, what was it to be
wondered at that clever young fellows were wetting a finger to
turn pages and set themselves ahead? As, today, the International Business Machine Company in its showroom on
Michigan Boulevard prints THINK! on its walls with identical
inspiration.

Now I see some of my friends putting out a foxy jaw of
skepticism about me, and I know they have in reserve the
memory of my little pamphlets on T. H. Huxley and my
Haldeman-Julius Kansas bluebook *Evolution and Mind* with
foreword by Clarence Darrow; or else my long association with
the Yellow Kid whose financial genius was of such interest to
the State Prosecutor and courts of Illinois, a man of great intellectual refinement. And also the fact that for years I have
had the same seat, more formal than the stock exchange, under
the portrait of M. le duc D'Aumale wearing his noble knickers,

this clean and rational French gentleman, in the science reading room of the Crerar, or our homespun Bodleian. They will want to know why I have it in for thought, suddenly. To them I say—Archie, Boggs, you boys—there's an interesting explanation coming, that I'm not preparing to say I'm p.o. with reason and brain.

How is any man going to account for having closed up in his head, above his teeth and palate and below his hair, what there is? This folding! This isthmus! This finding! That baroque pearl of an inmost thing! You think I'm not in awe of it? Why, here's this earth, chained down of mountains where I sway, in its silk buffets of atmosphere; here's the rooster breaking into peaks of day, while the clucks are his base, the pecking and the fostering of the eggs: the relation of the brain and other organs is what I mean. And isn't it maybe the curiosity over these internal discoveries that leads us to have captive animals—eagles in the park, canaries at home? We keep pets within and without. Imprisoned power. The heart in its cage of bone. I had goldfish myself, in the days of my victrola shop, and loved the bulge-eyed blackies so swift after flies.

This, about pets and mascots, is not so far from the subject, inasmuch as we are in the habit of regarding and considering ourselves no matter which direction we look. Is that something to surprise us? It's in the book of rules among the first and commonest of human things, and it doesn't have to be as disagreeable as it's become. But no debate, either, that it has become so, and tiresome, a complication from what was a process, and thereby makes mathematics and physics a comfort. For there it seems surest that you're not talking about yourself. In fact they probably wouldn't have developed so far, these sciences, in a less selfish age. Because this kind of consciousness can be like sharing a bed with a pal who is running a high fever, and at last you would rather shake down on the hard floor of fact, where no humanity is, in the fair cool space of vectors and the topless tent of laws, open to the universe. That's for removal from the burning *me*. And why should it be so? Fellows, there's a question!

What, Mr. President, and you others, do you think I'm turning into a Jack Cade, enraged with people who don't sign

themselves with crosses, or a Know Nothing, and out to tear
down the flag of *cogito*; or that pretty soon I'm going to break
out with old arguments—Bishop Berkeley rocks, Paley watches?
Even the latest about Percy Lowell's planet that should have
been there by mathematics but didn't show up for its appoint-
ment ever? Not I. At last even Dr. Skinner's little pigeons
who play ping-pong or pick out *Annie Laurie* on the piano can
be justified in my sight, though my willingness is slow here and
would be even if they played the *Moonlight Sonata*, for I think
of Noah's messengers coming up from Ararat with little leaves.
But, *grosso modo*, I give my okay because of the sublimity of
the greater enterprise. Only it's in another direction I'm looking
today, of thought in the singular and personal, and what you
manage by it.

Around our heads we have a dome of thought as thick as
atmosphere to breathe. And what's about? One thought leads
to another as breath leads to breath. I find it barren just to
breathe or only to have thoughts. By pulling into universal
consciousness, can explain everything from Democritus to
Bikini? But a person can no longer keep up, and plenty are
dying of good ideas. We have them in the millions, in com-
pilations from the *Zend-Avesta* to now, all on file with the best
advice for any and all human occasions. What a load you can
buy for a buck, in anthologies, out of Augustine, Pascal, Aris-
totle, Nicholas of Cusa, superbrain Goethe, and it's a confusion for us. Look at us, deafened, hampered, obstructed, im-
peded, impaired, and bowel-glutted with wise counsel and good
precept; and the more plentiful our ideas, the worse our headaches. So we ask, will some good creature pull out the plug and
ease our disgusted hearts a little? We are not free to use it,
that is why the advice is a loaded burden. What's the laugh on
Polonius, if not just in that? And, besides, is my heart going to
authorize me in this day to play chivalry and Roland, or Roman
senator or good bishop? And if a good idea isn't also a law of
the body, then what is it to us? There was the Mahatma in his
baken-earth back yard one day, in Africa, striving with his wife
that she didn't carry the chamber pots of strangers with a will-
ing enough pleasure. Now if you're looking for the pattern of
the foundation of new great things, this man and wife bicker

is what to start with; and when my soul feels its privations, and the cut-end branches of inclinations that were not allowed, I also say a knowledge to be true must be confirmed or arrive with a happiness, and we're a little thin on that side, too.

Now I awoke this fine summer morning with a fly bustling in the hairs of my foot, and went to spit in the sink of my hall bedroom in the house belonging to my brother's widow, and heard the steam of the tailor pressing below, and had a gander at the say-nothing tragedian clouds upstairs of me. Then the question rose in me, "Gooley, what is the score, you poor-man's Socrates? What is the pay-off of your devoted studies?" And I saw that I could not stand any more self-improvement originating in thought. And just a note here is necessary, that as you get better by the correction of intellect, you may lose your nature and have less and less to say, because what your nature prompts, your betterness turns down, so you become silent and are otherwise in danger of becoming better than you can afford. As, also, there is an acquaintance with thought whose widening cannot be stopped because the question of what it is that you yourself believe only forces you faster after what has been said, and soon that saying is all, and the record everything.

While as to being dry on the chaos waves by the management and steering of wit, haven't we taken care of that in our charter, declaring nobody can trust knowing the angles to obtain salvation? Intelligent? What for, you subject-man and personal ant, when you're so much at the mercy and soldered up inside determinations? Intelligence is the Brillo of the brave! And slaveys when they scour with it shine up a disappointed face; and then what a moment on the bottom of the pot. And can you, ambitious to think the deepest penetration into manhood, tell me what effectively rules in your life and how much you are, at sixty, still your mother's and your father's child, not unfastened from that close happiness, swaying from it still with a lifted upper body like the tit-footed caterpillar? And how much great and vast sense there is to be waked up in your last years from that almost lifelong state? (Not to lose love nor yet be prevented from clear thought, is what I intend to say.) Or also what things happened, seeming neither intrinsic nor even called-for: what have these done to you, what have they made of you? And I must ask, when I see these many, ignorant of their others, and fearful, and faithless of happiness: how wise and clever must you become to be well, and what kind of specialist to stand even average among so many hard griefs and difficult bafflements, when even to be decent needs heroism? What education is misery, that now is the main teacher, or the word of intelligence to human cookery and soap-manufacture? Why, then, I feel compelled to admit it seems only natural for people to confine themselves in the far corner from the largest power of their minds, which may come and whiff after them like the elephant after its peanut, and lose them in its huge digestion.

Nevertheless, I'm still in doubt and not ready yet to draw all my hopes out of the old deposited account. Except I see there are feelings of being that go beyond and beyond all I ever knew of thought, and a massive existence of man that comes to question even in me, who was so easily hammer-locked in the first trial-grips of my life. And have the sense, as well, that there is always a furthest creature that wears various lives or forms as a garment, and the life of thought as one of the greatest of these.

JAMES LEO HERLIHY

The Sleep of
Baby Filbertson

Rudy was awake now but his body had not changed
from its position of sleep. Under the sheet he lay coiled like a
serpent, his knees and elbows and his face all nestled in a fat
and private circle. His mother stood at his bedside.

"Baby Filbertson, I'm tired and I'm mad. It's two o'clock in
the afternoon. Dammit, I said P.M. Tell *me* you never dipped
into my phenobarbitals last night!"

He answered without moving: "Mother, I swear hand on the
Bible, if I touched one pheeny in this house last night, God
strike me dead an' you along with me!"

"Leave me the hell out of it, brother," she said.

"Anyway I'm sick," Rudy said, "somethin' wrong with
m'head."

"You think your head's in bad shape *now* . . ." She held
up the back of her hand and threatened his face with it.
"Groggy from stolen phenobarbs is your trouble."

"I already swore on the Bible may I be struck dead," he
said, still without moving. "I wasn't struck, was I?"

[149

"Show me somebody sleeps fourteen hours 'thout a pill, and
brother, I'll show you a cockeyed snake-in-the-grass wouldn't
know the truth 'f he got hit on his head with it." She closed
her fat hand over the corner of the sheet and ripped it from
the bed. "Git up!"

Rudy rolled over on his back and covered his private section
with the pillow. Then he looked up at his mother who stood
with arms akimbo, smoke pouring from her nostrils, and an inch
of cigarette hanging from her lips, grinning like a nasty car-
toon bulldog. Rudy sat up: "You're a sonofabitch," he said.

Her hand landed with great force and speed on the side of
his face. Rudy screamed as his head struck the mattress.

"Make me sick," she said, waddling out of the room, her
bedroom slippers going whoosh-slap whoosh-slap under her like
the fins of some walking dream-fish. "Nineteen years old, I
think he's still in di'pers." The door slammed shut.

Rudy lay looking at his body, the breasts as full as a young
girl's; below them, a larger more distant hill of stomach and
near the foot of the bed, two groups of toes like uncooked
sausages pointed vaguely toward the ceiling. Rudy was good
and damned fed up. Trying to get one puny little sleeping
capsule from her was like sticking up the First National Bank.
He had a good notion just to pack up a few things, including
enough money to get as far as Hollywood, and just leave her
there in the middle of New York to shift for herself. And
brother, when it came to that, she knew how to shift. She got
her sleeping pills, didn't she? You bet your bottom dollar she
got hers. And enough money to last for life, too: had his father
certified mentally non-something-or-other and locked up at
Belle Grove (not that the skunk didn't deserve it), then went
to court and had the separation made legal, tied up half of the
old cuss's money in a trust fund so she could give up day
nursing and sit on her fat tail for life without twitching a
muscle she didn't want to twitch. Except the one under her
left eye. That'n probably be twitching from now on. Doctor
called it nerves.

Maybe he'd go away alone, to anywhere, even if it was back
to New Orleans, then get himself a job, though Lord knew
where: perhaps a loan office could use him for evaluating pearls,
or the movies in funny fat person parts, or maybe he'd brush

up on his piano and take voice, if they ever stayed in one place long enough, and get himself a job singing and playing in a saloon. Eventually, of course, Rudy knew he'd end up in Hollywood.

He could hear the whoosh-slap of her slippers approaching on the other side of the door. He got out of bed and stepped into his trousers. She opened the door and stood watching him.

"If you ain't a sight," she said. "Gain another pound, you be a *real* hog, that's for damn sure!"

" 'Bout like you, Mother?" he said. "That's what I'm aimin' for."

"Yeah, 'bout like me, son. Titties an' all."

The ironing board was set up in the main room of the apartment. There were three altogether: two bedrooms and this main room which was used for everything but sleeping and bathing. In an alcove near the bathroom door stood a cream-colored refrigerator on which a previous tenant had glued a picture of a yellow swan eating a pink water lily. Rudy opened the door. Inside were four bottles of Coca-Cola, half a melon, a bottle of chocolate milk, and a pound of bacon. He took one of the Coca-Colas and the melon, sat on the couch, turned on the radio, and began to eat.

Daisy Filbertson held the iron upside down under her face. "If you wasn't so soft in the head, you'd get you a nylon shirt, don't need pressin'." She spat on the iron; it sizzled. "Listen t'me, Baby Filbertson, turn off that damn radio, your mother's talkin'. I know you don't give one lovely hoot if I iron from now till hell won't have it, but I do, brother. *Turn that damn thing off!*"

Rudy was listening to a radio commercial paid for by a correspondence school that taught Spanish in six weeks. Maybe he'd slip away to Trinidad and become a calypso singer.

". . . don't leave it sit there," Daisy was saying as the commercial gave place to a song called "Give Me a Kiss to Build a Dream On." "Put that rind in the pail and take it all on down t' the street. Been bad pork in there since last night, startin' t' smell."

The entire island seemed to have been submerged in an ocean of hot light and walking through it required a swimmer's effort. Women invented parasols made of newspapers to blind them from the sun, and men blotted their foreheads with handkerchiefs and squirmed inside their suits. Yet it seemed to Rudy more bearable on the street than it had been inside where Daisy's ironing sent the temperature even higher.

He wandered down Broadway and after only a few blocks he was tired. He went into the subway station at 72nd Street, stuck a dime in the slot, pushed through the turnstile, and descended the stairway into an airless chamber illuminated by naked light bulbs. Several people stood about, with the unhappy but patient air of travelers to Hell who realize the journey is inevitable, waiting for the Seventh Avenue Local.

When the train arrived, Rudy boarded the last car. He stood at the rear and looked out the window, and then he watched the station platform grow smaller and smaller as he and the train were drawn deeper and deeper with greater and greater speed into the tunnel. It was like that quick and sensuous falling into sleep on a night when he'd stolen one of the magic pheenies. Occasional shafts of sudden light dropped from gratings in the street above and made flaws in the blackness.

Now ordinarily he'd go to bed and the dreams took him right smack back to Louisiana where there was nothing but trouble: night before last he'd barely closed his eyes but what he found himself going through that car accident all over again. Started out by driving down Jackson Street, turned the corner into Chinaberry Avenue, got to looking at that same coon leaning on the lamppost, and just like it was happening all over again only this time faster, forgot to straighten up in time and there he was parked on the sidewalk with the car buried up to its windshield in Hodgeson's furniture store, and the same fat policeman lying flat on his back on one of the display beds in the window, his right leg bleeding like a live pig stuck through the middle with a barbecue sword.

Every time he dreamed it, Rudy'd wake up laughing—also just as it'd really happened: sat there laughing like a fool hyena and made the policeman all the madder—but in his dreaming the laughing hurt him some, like it was his own leg bleeding. And then all day long he'd see, as if through a window in his mind, way off somewhere, that colored boy leaning on the lamppost like he was holding up the world.

Rudy did not want to think about the people of his dreams, but they often visited his mind uninvited. The principal figure was the young Negro. Rudy would always see, as if tattooed in pink on the man's brown neck, a long sickle-shaped scar which stretched from his left ear to his Adam's apple and then descended down the length of his throat. His eyes were kind and warm, but in the kindness itself Rudy sensed some terrible store of violent energy that attracted him at the same moment that it repelled him. Rudy could not imagine the nature of the harm this kind-eyed Negro's dark and unfathomable cunning would one day inflict upon him. Nor could he remember any longer whether the Negro on the street corner looked like the person he knew from dreaming, or if his identifying marks, the eyes and the pink scar, had been placed there by that other dark and unknown stranger, the artisan who designed the dreams.

The train came to a stop at 50th Street. Rudy climbed out of the subway pit, his energy by now at a low ebb. He hated New York for its heat and for its concrete that sustained the heat even through the night all summer long, and his mother for her strange restlessness that had brought them here several weeks ago.

It was her often stated intention, now that she had achieved a degree of economic freedom from her husband whom she hated, to see the world. But Rudy could not understand why it was that each time they arrived in some new city—San Francisco, Santa Fe, Chicago, and now New York—she would install herself like a hibernating bear in some unpleasant cave and refuse to move outside the door. It made their traveling absurd and their lives pointless. On the journey itself she would fill herself with phenobarbital, and seldom looked out the train window except perhaps to discern whether it was night or day. After they had been in a city for several weeks or months, he might come home at almost any moment to find that, without warning or even a hint of any kind, she had packed their bags and had engaged space for them on a train or a bus to some new destination.

"Seen enough o' this damn town," she'd said on the afternoon they'd left San Francisco. "Get your face washed, Baby,
we got a train to catch at four-thirty."

"Seen *enough* of it!" Rudy had said. "Seen nothin' of it's
the fact of the matter!"

"Lousy cotton-pickin' fog!" she grumbled. "Come on, get
your shirt on!" Rudy remembered that in Santa Fe there'd
been too much cotton-pickin' sunshine and in Chicago, the
factory smoke; it was yet to be learned which aspect of New
York she would find too damn cotton-pickin'.

During their first days here she had said at least six different
times: "Goin' out Monday morning t'see that dame with the
torch in New York Harbor, providin' the weather's decent."
But when the weather had been decent, a backache had
stopped her, or she'd had to stick around the place as she was
expecting some imaginary telegram.

It was as if Daisy had reached a point in her living at which
she suspected that life held no further promise, and rather
than risk finding this true, she went through it grumbling,
complaining, and partially hypnotized by sleeping capsules, her
unconscious mind artfully avoiding direct contact with whatever remained to be experienced.

Now, from the top of the subway steps, Rudy could see the
marquee of the Roxy Theatre. It was featuring a Ginger
Rogers picture and on its stage was an ice show. He bought a
ticket and went inside: the temperature was thirty degrees
cooler; a girl with yellow hair sold him a package of Life Savers;
ushers stood like palace guards at a dozen inner doors; on either
side of the stage, high in the theater's lofts, were golden stairways that led to no one knew what secret chambers, and covering it all, like the ceiling of heaven itself, were delicate designs
carved in wood and lighted by dim hidden sources; on the
screen Miss Rogers was seated at a cocktail bar quarreling with
an elderly gentleman.

But Rudy's mind was never quite so taken up with what
happened on the screen as with what might be happening instead if he were playing a particular role himself and could
follow random impulses and take the story in directions more
to his own choosing. Now and then the entrance of a beautiful

person required some quick revision of the plot, or the music under the story would speak out some fevered crescendo that brought his dreaming to a new beginning. And in this way the hottest hours of Rudy's afternoon passed.

Finally, the ice show came to an end. The magnificent curtains descended like the skirts of a mammoth goddess from between the golden stairways. A swift march began to play as the people left their seats and pushed their way up the aisles, fighting those now coming in. In the back of Rudy's neck was that cotton-candy ache that comes of looking too long at too many bonbon colors of changing lights and glitter-spangled costumes. His eyes ached and he was hungry.

He wandered, somewhat dizzy, into the daylight. By the time he reached the sidewalk, his hunger had grown almost to pain. He walked west on 50th Street in search of hot dogs, but before he reached a restaurant, some sweet aroma gripped his nose like a claw and drew him into a shop where a dozen varieties of popcorn and nuts had been dipped in a golden liquid candy.

He bought a bag of caramel corn and returned to the street; the first mouthful was delicious, but at the moment it reached his stomach he began to feel ill. Rudy could never understand this chemistry of pleasure, the way it seemed that all sweetness was in reality a poison. But the hunger drove him to take another mouthful, and then a third.

All at once a police whistle shrieked, an automobile sounded in his ear, a woman's voice said: "Watch out, mister!" and Rudy felt a sudden heavy push in his stomach. Then he was lying on his back in the street, surrounded by a steadily growing crowd.

"Here's the driver of the car," said a woman's voice.

"You hurt, kid?" a man asked.

Rudy's right hand was bruised where he had tried to break his fall, and in his left, as if it had been the widow's baby snatched in the nick of time from the burning house, he clutched the white sack of caramel corn. He was not seriously hurt and he knew it. More than anything else he felt humiliated and foolish. "Why don't everybody go away and leave me alone?"

The man who had driven the car helped Rudy to his feet. "You hurt?"

"No, I ain't hurt; just get back in your damn car and drive away."

A woman's voice behind Rudy said: "It was your fault, sonny, you walked right into him."

"You want me to take you home, kid?" the driver asked.

Rudy felt caged in by the crowd. He moved sullenly to the sidewalk. "I'm not hurt for Chrissake, lea' me alone."

He tried to walk as if nothing were wrong, but his bruised knee caused him to limp. He was less than half a block away when he could see from the corner of his eye someone following him. This irritated him and he began to walk faster.

One night he had dreamed he was walking down Chinaberry Avenue with a parasol over his head—stark naked! He felt like that now. The young man behind him ran to catch up with Rudy. He was a Negro, tall, copper-skinned, athletic, probably somewhere in his twenties. "You want me to get you a taxi?" he said. "There's something wrong with your foot."

His first impulse was to send the stranger away, but when Rudy frowned and looked into the man's face, the smile he found there was so kind and warm that he was instantly disarmed by it. In the Negro's manner was some deeply appealing intimacy, the unequivocal sympathy of an animal. It was as if a pair of invisible arms, brown and strong as an animal's, had reached out and surrounded him to protect him from the eyes of the street, and to soothe his hurts for which he suddenly felt no shame.

The young Negro called a taxi. He opened the door and Rudy climbed in. "I think you better go right on up to a doctor," the Negro said. Rudy watched as the young man closed the cab door.

"Won't you get in and ride uptown with me?" Rudy said. The stranger smiled and shook his head. "Naw, I'll just catch a bus."

As the Negro turned to walk away, Rudy was suddenly gripped with panic. "Hey, wait a minute!" he said. When the young man returned to the taxi and lowered his head through the window, Rudy could find nothing to say. But the thought of being separated from the stranger terrified him. "I don't even know your name," he said finally. The other man thrust his hand through the open window: "I'm Clyde," he said, "Clyde Williams."

Rudy took Clyde's hand in both of his and held it tightly. "My name's Rudy. I want you to ride with me, hear? Come on, Clyde, please!"

Clyde continued to smile, but a frown settled into his face between his eyebrows: "You got money enough to pay the cab?"

Rudy said he had.

"Well, you're all right then, Rudy; you just tell the fella where you want to go, and he'll take you there. Everything's going to be all right. I'll see you some more, Rudy."

Clyde withdrew his hand from Rudy's. The frown left his face, he smiled broadly, waved his hand, and walked away. The taxi started to move. Rudy moved forward onto one of the small folding seats and stuck his face out the window. As the cab reached the corner, Rudy saw Clyde again. He was waiting for a bus, and as he waited, he leaned on a lamppost.

The traffic light was green, and the driver placed the gears into second position and withdrew his foot. As the car moved more rapidly forward, Rudy was able to get a last good look at his friend. He was certain that he could discern, on Clyde's neck, glistening from his ear to his throat and disappearing down into his shirt, a scar which was like a sickle tattooed in pink.

Rudy got out of the cab in front of his apartment house. He paid the driver and walked slowly up the steps to the third floor. He was no longer aware of the pain in his leg.

Daisy was lying on the couch with her eyes closed, her glasses on, a small cigarette butt protruding from her lips. When Rudy closed the door, her eyes popped open.

"Where you been, brother?"

Rudy flopped into a chair and said nothing. The muscle under Daisy's left eye began to twitch as she came more fully

awake. "Baby Filbertson, I said where you been?" Rudy slowly
drew his pantleg up past his knee, baring a red bruise the size
of a quarter.

"Well!" Daisy said, "Twinkletoes fell on his ass!" She went
into the bathroom and returned with a first aid kit. "It's iodine
and it's gonna hurt, so keep your mouth shut." Then she painted
the wound liberally, and when she had finished, the edges were
a deep orange. "Didn't flinch, did he? I believe m'soul he's
turnin' into a man! Now what happened?"

Rudy was slumped deep into the chair; it contained him like
giant arms. "Like t'got killed is all," he said. "Damn Grey-
hound bus come tear-assin' around 50th Street corner o'Broadway. I'd got squashed good haddin been for some coon shoved
me outa the way, nick o'time. Anyway, fell on m'knees."

"You let a nigger shove you on the sidewalk?"

"Yeah. I let'im. Saved m'neck. You talk like a damn fool!"

Daisy went to the stove which was above the refrigerator
and boiled some spaghetti. She opened a can of tomato soup
and poured that over the top of it. Then she fried several strips
of bacon. Daisy and Rudy ate their dinners in irritated silence.
Then Daisy returned to the couch. She switched the radio on
and began to thumb through a paperbacked detective novel.

Rudy went to his room. The air was still moist and warm
even though the sun was gone. He removed his clothes and lay
on the bed. In his mind he reproached himself for the way he
had mishandled the events of the day. Should've got out of that
damn taxicab right there'n'then, he thought; should've walked
right over to that one called hisself Clyde Williams and said
to him: Boy, who the hell're you, followin' me all the way up
here from Louisiana? Could swear I seen you in N'Orleans,
Shreveport, Santa Fe, and Lord knows how many dreams you
poked your black nose into. Should've had it right out with
him there'n'then, make an end to it one way or the other.

Rudy went through this dialogue in his mind several times
until he had memorized it, and through several variations of
the same words in which he tried to improve on the original,
and soon he was in a light sleep, a haunted ordinary non-
pheeny sleep in which all the dreams were wild, terrible, filled
with blazing Technicolor violence: He was the captive of a

band of dark-skinned gypsies who had taken him into a southern wood where they had built a large fire and tied him to a tree alongside of it. Then like black magicians or voodoo madmen they danced and mumbled and shrieked grinning curses to an unbearable thump-thump-*thump* drumbeat which seemed to go on for a hundred days and nights. They had removed all of Rudy's clothes, and as he stood tied to the tree by the stifling heat of the fire, the perspiration fell like blood from his body and caused itches impossible to scratch.

Suddenly there was complete silence. The gypsies sat by the fireside with brilliant savage-toothed grins fixed on their faces, as if painted there. A fat gypsy squaw appeared before Rudy and stood so close to him that he could smell her sour air on his face. Her eyes held his in a kind of hypnotic trance for a long moment and then, with a movement so quick he could not follow it with his eyes, she had withdrawn, from under her great shawl, a shining silver-bladed breadknife; with her free hand she took hold of his sex and with the knife she severed it from his body and threw it into the fire. Rudy was instantly released from the tree. He was handed a small pink parasol and ordered to dance.

Then there was a loud tapping sound that seemed to be made by the contact of a man's knuckles on a pane of glass.

This noise awakened him and the dream ended. Rudy sat up and looked about the room. But no one was there. After the raucousness of the dream the entire world seemed to be in a state of iced silence. The table lamp issued a shrill white light that made the bedsheets look like icebergs gleaming under moonlight. The articles on the bureau seemed fragile, useless, as if they had been dried up while he slept and covered by invisible dust like objects in a museum which, once removed from their glass cases or unglued from their mountings, might crumble like sculptures in sand.

There was no accounting for this strangeness that had settled on the world. He wanted desperately to get away from it, perhaps into a pheeny sleep in some country so far away that when he woke he would never remember where he'd been, some deep dark warm sleep from which he would wake in some other place, a new and quiet land not on this earth.

Once more he heard the noise that had caused his dream to
end. He was certain that someone was knocking on his bedroom window. He remained in bed, transfixed, chilled with
fear, eyes on the window, listening. Now he could hear a voice
calling to him: "Rudy, let me in, Rudy. I won't hurt you,
Rudy, I'm your friend."

Rudy was no longer afraid. When Clyde's face appeared at
the window, he recognized it instantly, and the long sickle-
shaped scar as well. "Clyde, what you want?" he said. "What's
the idea followin' me all over hell'n'back, and now come scarin'
me like this, the middle of the night? You crazy?" But he no
longer felt impelled to reproach Clyde. It was as if they had
been friends for a long time and once again, as on the street
in the afternoon, Rudy trusted the warm animal eyes, and he
could feel the brown strength of invisible arms reaching out,
surrounding him to protect him. He heard Clyde's voice again:
"Rudy, let me in. Please let me in."

"Wait a second, you black idiot," Rudy said, gently mocking
his friend. "Wait'll I get m'drawers on." He scrambled into his
trousers. Inside of him there was excitement, happiness.

By placing his foot on the steam radiator, Rudy was able to
hoist himself up to the window sill where he sat and looked
out. The ground was three stories below. There was no fire
escape anywhere and the small concrete garden was empty.
Rudy called from the window: "Clyde, Clyde! Where in hell
did you go, you sonofabitch? Come back here."

Across the courtyard a woman stood in a window. But no
one else could be seen. A tall elm that grew out of the concrete
garden stood perfectly still. The woman in the window watched
Rudy. "Hey, mister," she said in a loud stage whisper: "Pipe
down, will you. We got sickness here."

Climbing back into his room, Rudy's foot slipped from the
radiator. He fell to the floor and landed once again on his
hands and knees. The irritation of his early bruises angered
him. He sat on the floor cursing and grumbling, at first to himself, then gradually louder and louder. Everything seemed to
have been conspiring for his annoyance: the heat, which
brought perspiration from his pores to roll down and cover
that which had dried on his body while he slept; Clyde, who

probably at this very moment sat crosslegged on the roof, laughing at him; and his mother, who dragged him with her from city to city and never would stay in one place long enough for him to get a start on his voice lessons—she didn't care if he ever got to Hollywood; the truth was that no one cared a good cotton-picking goddam for him, there it was, the fact of the matter right on the line—and he began to weep.

He leaned his head on the bed. The sheet felt mercifully cool against his cheek. He stopped crying for a moment to look longingly at that endless desert of icebergs made by the rumpled sheet. They were like the lifeless mountains and valleys one might find on a planet such as the moon was thought to be.

He drew himself to his feet and left his room in search of the sleeping capsules. He looked on the floor of the closets, behind the stacks of magazines on the mantelpiece, in all of the strange unlikely places his mother might think of, even back behind the cushions on the davenport and in a box of shredded wheat on the kitchen shelf. He knew she had them stashed away all over the apartment. Last night he'd found a bottle of them in an old shoe away under a pile of laundry on the bathroom floor and another, believe it or not, buried in a box of sanitary napkins on top of the toilet.

Several minutes later Rudy found himself digging with his bare hands into the depths of the garbage pail.

Finally, with the courage of utter desperation, silent as a burglar, Rudy turned the doorknob and eased open the door of his mother's bedroom.

She was snoring. The room was partly illuminated by moonlight. He could see Daisy's face. The light shone on her moist eyelids and they glistened like false eyes. A bottle of capsules stood on the small table next to the head of her bed. Rudy crept slowly toward them, slowly, taking care to set his weight down a little at a time in order to test the strength of the boards: the weak ones were sure to creak.

He reached the side of her bed. Daisy's snoring continued. He stood stock-still, taking one long moment just to look at her. Her nightgown was torn and one of her breasts was revealed. It seemed limp and liquid, as if its shape depended entirely upon gravity; the large brown nipple gaped blindly at the ceiling. It

was just possible she'd be playing possum, waiting to catch him
in the act. No, it was a real sleep. Her breathing was slow and
noisy, her eye did not twitch at all as it would if she were awake.

Rudy had just put his arm forward, toward the table, when
Daisy's hand sprung forward and gripped his wrist like a claw.
Her eyes snapped open at the same instant. Rudy jumped
back and cried out, and his heart was beating fast. At the same
moment, he could not help admiring her speed.

"Caught ya damn sneak thief," she said, glowering at him,
her hand still fixed bearlike on his wrist.

"Let go, dammit, you're hurtin' me."

"I've heard tell o' people that kill sneak thieves in the night,
kill 'em dead as hell!" she said.

"You'd laugh out o' the other end, 'f I was to have a heart
attack cause o' you."

"Attack ahead, Filbertson; g'on, turn blue! Could'n' care
less."

"I should've snuk in here 'th a breadknife 'n' stuck it in yer
gizzard. Better keep on sleepin' like a sly damned old fox, or
one o' these days I'm apt to."

Her eyes glared through the dark at him like false eyes
with some nightmare knowledge frozen dead inside of them:
"Brother, where you're headin' there won't be any breadknife
left lyin' around."

Rudy's heart continued to beat too rapidly, and the palms
of his hands and the arches of his feet were moist and hot. His
breath came in short nervous gasps, and in his mind were the
ghosts of a hundred or more dark-skinned gypsies. His mother's
eyes were steady and cold as they penetrated his mind. Then a
small grin disfigured her mouth, and her eye began to twitch.

"Mother," Rudy said in a sad voice that was almost a
whimper, "can I have a pheeny?"

"*One*," she said.

He took a capsule from the bottle and replaced the lid.

"Thanks. M'damned head hurts."

He turned quickly and left the room. When he reached the
bathroom, he could hear her calling to him: "Baby Filbertson!
Baby Filbertson!" He drew a glass of cool water from the tap.
She was still calling to him as he swallowed the capsule. "Baby

Filbertson, come kiss your mother good night." But he pretended not to hear. He hurried to his bedroom and turned out the light. "Baby Filbertson," she called. Her voice was heavy and angry, and it filled the house like an air raid siren in a doomed city. "Come kiss your mother, goddammit! Hear now?"

She could go to hell, he thought. Clyde was probably still seated on the roof, his head and shoulders silhouetted against the sky. He could go to hell too.

Rudy believed he could feel the capsule exploding inside of him, soothing him with its thousands of warm hands that massaged gently every vessel of his bloodstream. One pheeny was not very strong, he knew that, but there were many tricks for getting to sleep fast: for instance, arithmetic, get to thinking about figures and pretty soon you drop off.

Ninety years from now, he began, I'll be a hundred and nine. Five years ago I was fourteen and weighed two hundred and eleven pounds. Nine years ago I was ten and weighed a hundred. Fifteen years ago I don't know what I weighed but I was four, and five years before that I wasn't even thought of yet and didn't weigh an ounce.

Imagining himself weightless, even unborn, he was soon fast asleep, wrapped into himself, knees and elbows and head grouped together. A sheet covered him entirely, so that his bed was like a slab on which lay the corpse of some giant foetus.

CHANDLER BROSSARD

The Closing of This Door Must Be Oh, So Gentle

Harrison's wife Edith looked like a dwarf. Her legs were about two inches long, her torso about the size of a peanut in the shell, and her head was recognizable only as an odd bump on her shoulders. He wondered how anybody that small could possibly exist. The sea on her left side at any moment would wash her away; the dunes on her right were towering mountains that seemed fearfully about to fall upon and bury her forever. Harrison almost felt like yelling out to her to beware for her life. But would she hear me? he thought, and smiled sadly. Are people reachable when their lives are in danger?

Now she reversed her doomful course and started walking back toward Harrison lying under the big beach umbrella. A sand fly boldly attacked his fine serenity, a bite on the leg, and Harrison slaughtered it with a blow of his hand. He squinted his eyes almost to closing and resumed his observations of his wife. Everything abetted his distorted view: the heat waves vibrating crazily off the sand denied the scene its customary reality; the surf, its sovereignty awesome, refused to yield entrance to any other sound, and thus cut him off from the world outside this moment; and his squinting, through trembling, enlarged eyelash filaments, revealed things in their microscopic hugeness (as if he were somehow a bug looking on). Edith thus gradually became bigger and bigger as she got closer, and in another few moments (can such time be measured?) a giant hand was reaching down to him with a terrifying object in it. He jerked away in fright.

"What's the matter?" Edith asked, annoyed and surprised. "It's only a baby hermit crab. It washed up on the beach."

"And you naturally picked it up," he said, recovered now.

She remained standing, hands now resting on hips, and by doing this, rather than dropping down in a beach pose beside him, she made it clear, quite clear, that she was not, at least for this jarred moment, in harmony with the rhythms here. "I thought it would interest you," she said. The surf noise battered her words in mid-air, bruising their tender surface, making them sound weak instead of merely soft, giving them an unjust quality of supplication.

"A baby monster," he said. "Sure. What could be a more fascinating present!" He was coming up now from his microscopic vantage point and feeling, the grotesque aura was giving way to a more or less normal one; he swung into a squatting position on the blanket.

Edith sat down now on the sand, not on the blanket, and looked down the beach, instead of at her husband. "It seems that everything I give you turns into a monster," she said, and threw a pebble into the foaming surf near her feet.

Well, now, I guess maybe you're right, Harrison thought. I wonder why that is. Am I responsible for such mid-air mismagic? These things must start out as gifts, of some kind or other, but when they arrive at my threshold, something awful has happened to their shape and chemistry. Why? "All right," he said, getting up. "I'm sorry."

"I think you want them to become monsters," Edith suggested, her back to the raging surf, arms jutting geometrically from her hips, hair curling delicately in the sea wind.

She is like a Botticelli now, rising up miraculously from the sea, Harrison thought, and for a second or two, as he stared at her, he felt they were both transfixed in timelessness, in design, in motionless thought, in stilled heart.

"We'd better be going," Edith announced deferentially, yet not so deferentially that her words did not rob Harrison of his jewel-like moment of timeless isolation. He nearly winced as she ceased, simply by opening her soft mouth, to be his Botticelli.

"That's right," Harrison murmured. "We're going to that cocktail party at what's his name's place, aren't we?"

"Mason Bowler's . . ."

"The rich queer."

". . . and remember, you promised you wouldn't drink too much and act peculiar."

They were slogging off the beach, arms wrapped around the essential scenic props—umbrella, towels, lunch basket, for they had picnicked—toward the car.

"You know," he began, "for a few minutes you looked like a dwarf. It was very remarkable."

Edith opened the car door. "So I suggest that you absolutely stay away from martinis. Drink Scotch or something. Promise?"

He sighed heavily, a stricken sigh, for a terrible loneliness had come over him again, like a soft shadow of death. "Whatever you say."

"Something awful happens to you when you drink too much," Edith continued. She got into the driver's seat quite naturally, not in the manner of a reigning queen, nor with the aplomb of the aggressor, but rather with the emotionless ease of having gotten there by default. "I think you should lay off it completely for a while. For your own good."

He listened to the meshing of the gears as Edith drove off down the narrow black tar-smelling road. He listened so raptly that the gears seemed to be inside his head. "I've thought of laying off everything for a while."

"Just what does that mean?"

"I wish I knew."

He leaned back and closed his eyes, giving himself over completely to being chauffeured by Edith, like a helpless little baby, he thought, being taken for an airing in a carriage. As he allowed himself to gradually roll down the long hill inside himself, to quiet nothingness at the bottom, he wondered if Edith would take the wrong turn at the crossroads ahead and get them lost again. But right now this possibility did not have any importance for him.

"Are you and your wife spending the summer here on the shore?"

"Just two weeks," Harrison replied, looking at a shy black mole on the man's right ear.

"Oh," the man gasped, as though Harrison's reply had been a punch in the belly. "It's a wonderful place to relax, don't you think?" he went on, apparently revived.

Harrison sipped his Scotch and soda and wondered what this man did to keep a roof over his head. "What do you mean by relax?" Harrison answered (he had made up his mind to ask into the man's occupation).

A freckled, pinkish eyelid quivered, a soft blanched hand suddenly was rubbing a cheek in sheer amazement, and a moist baby mouth, as if forming its first words of defense, was saying, "Uh, well . . . to be on the beach . . . you know, uh, swimming in the ocean . . ." The mouth closed for a second (Harrison thought of the mouth of a squid).

"Ah, that I tried, but I just became more uncomfortable." He smiled somewhat. "I guess something must be the matter with me. My wife frequently suggests that."

An eyebrow, hairy and sandy, lifted. "Really?"

"Yep." He paused. "You don't have a wife, do you?"

Mouse fear tensed the man's face. "Uh, no, as a matter of fact, I don't."

Harrison took a long satisfying drink of the cool Scotch and smiled at the man. "Well, if you did, you would know *exactly* what I mean." He is afraid now that I am going to expose him as a homosexual. But I'm not. Just look at the terror at the corners of his eyes! "You see, wives are often suggesting that something is the matter with their husbands. It probably makes them feel less inferior—that's what I might say if I were a psychoanalyst or something."

A dry, choppy sound came from the man's mouth, a forced

laugh to fill the awful void between them. But his eyes, Harrison saw, ah, there was nothing smiling about them.

We'll never see that one again, unless it's in the Sargasso Sea
with the rest of the eels. He looked around the room for the
presence of Edith. All kinds of faces were animated in various
scenes, to Harrison distressingly like the subjects in an im-
pressionist mural, their faces flushed and mottled with the
feverish colors of unreality. Voices he heard, of course, and
familiar word formations, but the largesse of meaning that
usually accompanies those two things was not now forthcoming
to Harrison. What he heard, poised as he was on the brink of
his own definition, all of it sounded quite insane. While he
was searching for Edith, his hand chilling from the highball
glass, she found him.

"Are you having a good time?" she inquired, appearing
abruptly at his left side (he always thought of it as his weak
side) like a secret agent.

"I'm certainly trying to, sweetie." He held up his highball
glass to show that his drink was on a comparatively rational
level: no disintegrating gin fluids. He felt he could have been
holding up a scrap of the Constitution.

No somersaults of joy, or appreciation, came from Edith at
this; a gentle nod, that's what she responded with, plus a patient look in her eyes. "That's fine," she said. "I met a rather
nice couple, named Andrews. He's a furniture designer."

Between them now sprang up a pure greensward, an absolute pause of tentative exploration, and upon it, like children
suddenly in a foreign country, they stalked each other, ma-
neuvered this way and that, each utterly permeated with the
need to hear the other's song first, whatever its words: I won't
hurt you, please don't misunderstand me. So they listened,
listened and watched.

"Do you know of him?" Edith finally continued, returned,
both of them, from that other land.

"I think I've heard his name," Harrison replied. He finished
the rest of his Scotch. Now he was a little high, but this was
not noticeable. "Why do you say they were nice? Did he say
surprising and amusing things? Was she sexy without being
vulgar? Or do you just mean that they smelled clean? Which?"

All of the gentle signs of female resignation, those incalculable changes of interior costume, showed upon Edith after his words were out. She allowed her attention, as if to rest it, to wander to strangers' faces in the room before answering her husband. "Why do you hate the human race so much?"

Harrison thought for a moment before answering this challenge. "I don't really know."

"Maybe you should try to find out."

"How? By going to a doctor?"

"That's one way."

His face untensed and he smiled at Edith. "Is it really so bad to hate the human race?"

It seemed to Harrison, in reflection, that the reply came from the air rather than from the mouth of his wife, for she responded as she was drifting away from his side, in flight almost, and the words thus became, as in the thin hours of the night, disembodied Ariels. "It must be," the words whispered, "because it makes you feel so terrible."

Then he himself was traveling, in the other direction, for a refilling of his Scotch-and-soda highball. He felt more at bay than before: There was absolutely no defense, worthy of him, to Edith's gentle thrust.

At the bar in this fashionable house, what had sounded to him before like zithers of mutual hysteria had now become, from those drinkers and talkers clustered there, a music of rancor counterpointed oh, so impressively, with chords of vilification. In fact, Harrison, sloshing Scotch and soda inadvertently over his fingers, felt, heard and saw it as a Renaissance horror opera; shivs flashed, garrotes twisted—what screams, what dark denunciations, what bleats of outraged innocence! The thuds of bodies falling off stage, these chilling sounds could be heard most clearly by Harrison. So he put his lonely mouth to the Scotch business at hand.

"Have you had any experience with the restaurants around here?" he heard a large-eyed blonde woman asking of him. Harrison gazed into those eyes and very nearly drowned in their self-pity.

"You mean have I been a bus boy in them or something?"

She looked at him as if he were crazy, or as if he had not

quite understood her seemingly harmless question. "Oh, no,
no," she blurted, her face wanting to escape. "I meant had you
tried eating in any of them. You know, found any, uh, good
food."

The words just had to come out of him. "I'm not going to
hurt you, so please don't look so scared. I am not crazy or violent or even real drunk yet." (Her mouth was partly open now
in readiness for something, like an oxygen mask.) "But, honestly, I take the word experience seriously, and I feel it shouldn't
be misused for purposes of chic. See what I mean?"

The woman regained herself in a split pause—apparently he
really did not mean to assassinate her—her mouth smiled somewhat patiently, and she said, "Well I suppose so, but I don't
see why you have to be so goddam rude about it. After all . . ."

He did not let her go on. The Scotch was allowing him too
much freedom inside. "Now as for good food, why, last night
I ate some incredibly delicious sea squabs. I had four of them,
all for myself. My wife had only two, but that's because two is
enough of anything for her. Anyway, they had been rolled in a
perfectly divine egg-and-flour batter, then fried in deep fat. Mm!
Yummy! Well, I was so impressed by these delicacies that I
spoke to the waitress about it. I said that I was not familiar with
sea pigeons and their young, and were they members, perhaps,
of the albatross family. Well, you can imagine my surprise
when this young lady, she couldn't have been over nineteen, informed me that they were plain ordinary blowfish and you could
catch them by the millions swimming around Fire Island."

The lady's large brown eyes blinked slowly at Harrison, who,
by now, had drunk nearly all his Scotch. "Sounds like *quite* an
experience," she said, and with the cruel deliberateness of a
guillotine in slow motion, turned her face away from him and
toward the others like herself at the bar there.

I'm getting a bit drunk and aggressive, Harrison whispered to
himself—though audibly if you were standing very close to
him—and he charted a course toward a crowded sun porch
where he saw Edith talking in a group of four or five men and
women very smartly garmented in summer styles. He felt now
that the scene around him was a thriving insane asylum, filled
with strangers, among them somewhere himself, whom he

should try to find and help to escape as soon as possible. How and through what special unguarded aperture in the scene the two of them were going to slip free, this he wasn't sure of at the moment, as he moved thoughtfully across the large living room that was jiggling with gabbling bodies, toward his wife and others intertwined there on the sun porch. But he knew, quite beyond any question, that this escape must absolutely take place. Or else.

"Do you know that you won't be able to recognize New York in five years?" he overheard a woman say. "They're tearing down so many buildings."

The place they lived in was a converted barn; about a hundred yards in front of the barn was the original old farmhouse. This, too, had been wrenched from its self-enclosed and indisputably deserved grave and forced to serve generations more, except that these were not connected in any way with the warmth and the cold, the inscrutable breathing, of the soil. But what part of nature's body *are* they connected with? Harrison asked not only himself but Edith and whoever else of the human race might be tuned in to him at this moment as he sat in the un-self-effacing early American living room of the barn, looking out at the shy, green, and gently swollen Connecticut landscape.

"They're scavengers," he said aloud. "They leave scars and holes and garbage piles wherever they go." He looked at a wastebasket that was cleverly decorated with *Vanity Fair* drawings. "And I'm one of them."

Edith came in from the bedroom, where she had been napping. "What on earth *are* you talking about?" she asked, and then stifled a baby of a yawn with the soft back of her left hand.

"Me. Us."

"Oh, we're doing that again. Please count me out. I came up here to get a rest." She sat down, one leg nestling secretly under the other, and struck a match to a Pall Mall. Persian tapestry was her natural design; she seemed to contain no straight lines whatsoever. Even the faint sleepiness and dark femininity encasing her felt almond-shaped to Harrison. Then I must be a bomb fragment in shape, he decided.

"What would you like to talk about then?" he asked, looking at the hoarded beauty of her bare legs. Edith made the long cigarette her companion rather than her husband, in that moment, and did not reply. Instead of words, thick sets of smoke streamed from her mouth. "Let's talk about sex," he continued.

Edith sucked in and exhaled a ferocious quantity of smoke. "What's there to say about it?"

Harrison smiled wolfishly. "Oh, lots and lots. Just oodles, in fact. Let's take you and sex. [Edith slowly mashed her cigarette to death in a saucer.] Just what is there with you and sex, Mrs. Harrison? Does it make your little tummy just a wee bit sick? Does it make you want to grab your Teddy bear and cry yourself to sleep?"

"You're being very cute," Edith said, and put her hand to her throat as if to comfort it.

"Oh? I'm sorry, because I'm really trying to be very scientific about all this—in the interests of enlightenment." He tried to bring off an ironic smile, but it failed, and an unhappy compromise of a sneer appeared. "For instance, this afternoon when I came in as you were lying down . . ."

"I explained to you that I was very tired and not in the mood."

He felt thousands of pricklings inside his body and mind now, as though he were a huge bar of metal being tortured for stress resistance in a factory. "Now which was it: fatigue or not in the mood? I'd like to be exact about these things."

Edith lit another cigarette and, as was her custom during strenuous conversations, presented him—as one, turning away, gives a beggar in the market place a stained coin—with her profile as she looked away at the blank wall to maintain an idea of her dignity. "All right, then. I simply wasn't in the mood to make love. Does that make me a criminal or something?"

"No," Harrison replied. "It makes me feel like one."

"Well, I'm sorry, but that's your problem. If you want to feel like a criminal, that's up to you."

Harrison shook his head at the floor. "You're never in the mood. Even when you do have sex, you do it reluctantly. I can't remember when you have ever made me feel you wanted me." He made a noise like a snort, of both anger and amazement. "You ought to be in the Metropolitan Museum. You just lie there with your eyes closed like an Egyptian princess mummy. Tell me," he went on, hoping she would turn her head toward him just for a moment, which she didn't, "do you feel that you are dying or that it is really happening to somebody else?"

He wasn't really waiting for a reply; for some minutes, like a lost explorer, he had been wandering, stumbling about, in the vast caverns of her being. He had never experienced so irrevocably such desolation, such hopelessness; each time he put his hand against a wall for comfort, it repelled his hand with dankness or cut it cruelly with sharp edges; the paths that promised to take him somewhere ended abruptly at sheer drops; he shouted for help and then had to suffer the mockery of hearing his own voice, distorted by distance and fatigue, thrown back at him. He felt that he would eventually just disintegrate there.

"If you wanted a sexpot for a wife, why didn't you marry one?" Edith said, gliding toward the kitchen to make coffee.

"That isn't the point," he replied, and reached out for his highball glass. "What interests me is why did you marry me if you didn't want to share yourself? I suspect," he continued, the soothing loveliness of the Scotch sluicing intimately down his throat, "that fundamentally you must dislike the hell out of me." He paused for sounds from her. "Come on, 'fess up."

That was the thing about his work these past few months— like Edith, it had become deaf, mute, so unresponsive and deathlike as to make him utterly despair having to engage in it every day or grapple suffocatingly with it every second. Each new project was an insidious challenge to his sanity.

"Don't you feel well?" Evans had inquired one day at the office.

"To tell you the truth, Ev baby," he had confessed, "I don't feel at all."

Ha! Ha! That was Evans' reaction, but oh, Harrison knew that Evans was not really collapsing with humor; what he really thought, and Harrison could tell this by the patronizing tenseness at the corners of his field-mouse lips, was that something was a bit flibberty with Harrison. It was not at all unusual for him to be approaching the heart of a matter, there in his cubicle, and suddenly, instead of driving full speed ahead as other rational humans would have done, find himself floating abstractly in mid-air, like a balloon that a child has abruptly grown weary of. When this happened, he pushed his chair far away from his desk and went out to a movie.

Somewhat later, as he sipped a fresh Scotch and water, he was listening to the sounds of his wife getting dressed in the bedroom. They were intimate and exciting, and forbidding, sounds: He wondered, very hazily, because he was drunk now, if women themselves were aware, in their way, of the world of unique sounds they created. A rustling of stiff material and then a snap, snap of a brassière created Edith's opulent but indifferent breasts; a stretching of sheer nylon against fingernails and there was an elegantly outstretched naked leg; a pulling of tight elastic, a stress of breathing, the running of hands down the mesh surface of her girdle, and into view came Edith's completed underclothed body. Harrison held her there, like a connoisseur holding a china figurine, turned her this way and that, then, overcome with futility, let her crash to small pieces. Harrison's hand for stricken seconds ached; then he put it back around the chill of his glass.

"I'll be ready in ten minutes," she called to him.

"Wonderful," he murmured to the sweet glass as though it were Edith. "I promise I won't run away." He felt somewhat crazy now; the old watchman who usually guarded the impervious border line between the self of today and that other older self of childhood, this ancient had abandoned his post, and the two Harrisons began racing back and forth across this unguarded sacred terrain, mockingly almost. The two of them alternately howled and whispered recklessly to each other.

Edith came in from the bedroom. "Well, are you all set to go?" She plucked a wanton thread from her dress. "We're supposed to meet John and his girl friend in front of the theater at eight-fifteen." She smoothed the dress over her hips. "Have you ever heard of the author of the play?"

Both selves in him stopped in their fevered roaming in that special country, looked questioningly at each other, observed her words in wingless flight across their land, then together, holding hands and staring into each other's fugitive eyes, worked on an answer to lift back into space to her.

"We played lacrosse together in San Marino," Harrison said, smiling.

Edith seemed to recoil into a huge blazing question mark. "You did *what?*"

His two selves grinned at each other. "He was the toast of the Andes. And I was the English muffin."

Not disgust, really, but rather a blend of irritation and hopelessness tinged with slight fear showed itself in Edith's reaction as she stared at him, before saying, "Oh, I see. It's going to be like that, is it?" She walked partly across the room and turned around. "Why don't you just stay here and I'll go alone? You'll only wreck the evening—and I'm in no mood for another social disaster." She snatched her pocketbook from a table top and headed for the door, where she paused after wrenching it open. "I hope one of these days you decide what you're going to do about and with yourself. Because I can't stand it any more."

"Sir Isaac *Newton!*" he said just as Edith was disappearing and the door was being slammed.

Harrison was very concerned, for the trembling moments that followed, with the possibility that she might have hurt the door, in the way that you would surely hurt a person if you were to slam him shut. Who can prove that a door doesn't have feelings? he asked the other Harrison. This other self, recovered from his boyhood, was sitting on a large rock now, resting from some furious activity. He gently nodded his head at Harrison's question and said, I very much agree with you. Harrison was very pleased to hear this, and he smiled sweetly to show his pleasure. He drank off the remainder of his highball; then he walked, quite uncertainly, over to examine the abused door. He touched it gingerly here and there, as if he were a doctor and the door his patient, and strained his being to receive its vibrations. He was quite sure he could hear it crying, oh, so softly, in such bewilderment. "There was absolutely no need to do this," he said, almost to comfort the door, and his other self, who was pacing restlessly, replied, Most people are dirty brutes. Take my word for it.

It was clear to Harrison that the other was anxious for them

to go somewhere. "All right, all right," he said. "I'm coming."
He turned away from the door, which was down to its last tears
of injury, and looked around the living room before leaving.
The invisible nerve that before had held it all together as a
recognizable unity, a design of purpose, had apparently snapped,
for what lay before Harrison now, as he prepared to depart, was
an abstract of fierce isolation; the pieces of furniture seemed
angry and abandoned in space, and the enclosing room, bereft
of its previous property, emptied, was hungry and menacing.
Harrison shook his head in sadness; then, responding to the
bidding of the other one, left.

He and his other self walked around to the back of the building; he was being led by the hand, and the impeccable inside
terrain, where he had first caught sight of and then gamboled
with the other, had now become fused with the outside terrain.
Gentle conspiracy was in the air. The grass beneath his somewhat stumbling feet refused to allow any sound of his escape to
be heard; the long stone field wall, like a member of the family,
firmly stated that no stranger should intrude upon this utmost
privacy. As they walked toward the large pond which lay patiently waiting across the field at the edge of the woods, the
other began whispering fabulous things to him, things that
Harrison had never heard from any other human being. Each
thing had the dazzling wonder of a secret that had been kept
from him all his life. And with each awesome revelation Harrison became more and more aware of another world opening
for him, one that had oh, *absolutely* nothing to do with any
other.

At the edge of the pond Harrison bent over and plucked a
handful of small white flowers growing there; then, still listening
to the stream of revelations, he followed the other (whose young
boy face was beaming beautifully) into the cool water.

THOMAS PYNCHON

Entropy

Boris has just given me a summary of his views. He is a weather prophet. The weather will continue bad, he says. There will be more calamities, more death, more despair. Not the slightest indication of a change anywhere. . . . We must get into step, a lockstep toward the prison of death. There is no escape. The weather will not change.
Tropic of Cancer

Downstairs, Meatball Mulligan's lease-breaking party was moving into its fortieth hour. On the kitchen floor, amid a litter of empty champagne fifths, were Sandor Rojas and three friends, playing spit in the ocean and staying awake on Heidsieck and Benzedrine pills. In the living room Duke, Vincent, Krinkles and Paco sat crouched over a fifteen-inch speaker, which had been bolted into the top of a wastepaper basket, listening to twenty-seven watts worth of *The Heroes' Gate at Kiev*. They all wore horn-rimmed sunglasses and rapt expressions, and smoked funny-looking cigarettes that contained not, as you might expect, tobacco, but an adulterated form of *cannibis sativa*. This group was the Duke di Angelis quartet. They recorded for a local label called Tambú and had to their credit

one ten-inch LP entitled *Songs of Outer Space*. From time to
time one of them would flick the ashes from his cigarette into
the speaker cone to watch them dance around. Meatball himself
was sleeping over by the window, holding an empty magnum
to his chest as if it were a Teddy bear. Several government girls,
who worked for people like the State Department and NSA, had
passed out on couches, chairs and, in one case, the bathroom
sink.

This was in early February of '57, and back then there were
a lot of American expatriates around Washington, D.C., who
would talk, every time they met you, about how someday they
were going to go over to Europe for real, but right now it
seemed they were working for the government. Everyone saw a
fine irony in this. They would stage, for instance, polyglot
parties where the newcomer was sort of ignored if he couldn't
carry on simultaneous conversations in three or four languages.
They would haunt Armenian delicatessens for weeks at a stretch
and invite you over for bulghour and lamb in tiny kitchens
whose walls were covered with bullfight posters. They would
have affairs with sultry girls from Andalucía or the Midi who
studied economics at Georgetown. Their Dôme was a collegiate
Rathskeller out on Wisconsin Avenue called the Old Heidelberg, and they had to settle for cherry blossoms instead of lime
trees when spring came, but in its lethargic way their life provided, as they said, kicks.

At the moment, Meatball's party seemed to be gathering its
second wind. Outside there was rain. Rain splattered against the
tar paper on the roof and was fractured into a fine spray off the
noses, eyebrows and lips of wooden gargoyles under the eaves
and ran like drool down the windowpanes. The day before, it
had snowed, and the day before that there had been winds of
gale force, and before that the sun had made the city glitter
bright as April, though the calendar read early February. It is a
curious season in Washington, this false spring. Somewhere in
it are Lincoln's Birthday and the Chinese New Year, and a for-
lornness in the streets because cherry blossoms are weeks away
still and, as Sarah Vaughan has put it, spring will be a little late
this year. Generally, crowds like the one that would gather in
the Old Heidelberg on weekday afternoons to drink Würtz-

burger and to sing "Lili Marlene" (not to mention "The Sweetheart of Sigma Chi") are inevitably and incorrigibly Romantic. And as every good Romantic knows, the soul (*spiritus, ruach, penuma*) is nothing, substantially, but air; it is only natural that warpings in the atmosphere should be recapitulated in those who breathe it. So that over and above the public components—holidays, tourist attractions—there are private meanderings, linked to the climate as if this spell were a stretto passage in the year's fugue: haphazard weather, aimless loves, unpredicted commitments; months one can easily spend *in* fugue, because oddly enough, later on, winds, rains, passions of February and March are never remembered in that city; it is as if they had never been.

The last bass notes of *The Heroes' Gate* boomed up through the floor and woke Callisto from an uneasy sleep. The first thing he became aware of was a small bird he had been holding gently between his hands, against his body. He turned his head sidewise on the pillow to smile down at it, at its blue hunched-down head and sick, lidded eyes, wondering how many more nights he would have to give it warmth before it was well again. He had been holding the bird like that for three days: it was the only way he knew to restore its health. Next to him the girl stirred and whimpered, her arm thrown across her face. Mingled with the sounds of the rain came the first tentative, querulous morning voices of the other birds, hidden in philodendrons and small fan palms: patches of scarlet, yellow and blue laced through this Rousseau-like fantasy, this hothouse jungle it had taken him seven years to weave together. Hermetically sealed, it was a tiny enclave of regularity in the city's chaos, alien to the vagaries of the weather, of national politics, of any civil disorder. Through trial-and-error Callisto had perfected its ecological balance, with the help of the girl, its artistic harmony, so that the swayings of its plant life, the stirrings of its birds and human inhabitants were all as integral as the rhythms of a perfectly executed mobile. He and the girl could no longer, of course, be omitted from that sanctuary; they had become necessary to its unity. What they needed from outside was delivered. They did not go out.

"Is he all right?" she whispered. She lay like a tawny question mark facing him, her eyes suddenly huge and dark and blinking slowly. Callisto ran a finger beneath the feathers at the base of the bird's neck, caressed it gently. "He's going to be well, I think. See: he hears his friends beginning to wake up." The girl had heard the rain and the birds even before she was fully awake. Her name was Aubade; she was part French and part Annamese, and she lived on her own curious and lonely planet, where the clouds and the odor of poincianas, the bitterness of wine and the accidental fingers at the small of her back or feathery against her breasts came to her reduced inevitably to the terms of sound, of music which emerged at intervals from a howling darkness of discordancy. "Aubade," he said, "go see." Obedient, she arose, padded to the window, pulled aside the drapes, and after a moment said: "It is thirty-seven. Still thirty-seven."

Callisto frowned. "Since Tuesday, then," he said, "no change." Henry Adams, three generations before his own, had stared aghast at Power; Calisto found himself now in much the same state over Thermodynamics, the inner life of that power, realizing like his predecessor that the Virgin and the dynamo stand as much for love as for power, that the two are indeed identical, and that love therefore not only makes the world go round but also makes the boccie ball spin, the nebula process. It was this latter or sidereal element which disturbed him. The cosmologists had predicted an eventual heat-death for the universe (something like Limbo: form and motion abolished, heat-energy identical at every point in it); the meterorologists, day-to-day, staved it off by contradicting with a reassuring array of varied temperatures.

But for three days now, despite the changeful weather, the mercury had stayed at thirty-seven degrees Fahrenheit. Leery at omens of apocalypse, Callisto shifted beneath the covers. His fingers pressed the bird more firmly, as if needing some pulsing or suffering assurance of an early break in the temperature.

It was that last cymbal crash that did it. Meatball was hurled wincing into consciousness as the synchronized wagging of heads over the wastebasket stopped. The final hiss remained for an instant in the room, then melted into the whisper of rain outside. "Aarrgghh," announced Meatball in the silence, looking at the empty magnum. Krinkles, in slow motion, turned, smiled and held out a cigarette. "Tea time, man," he said. "No, no," said Meatball. "How many times I got to tell you guys? Not at my place. You ought to know. Washington is lousy with Feds." Krinkles looked wistful. "Jeez, Meatball," he said, "you don't want to do nothing no more." "Hair of dog," said Meatball. "Only hope. Any juice left?" He began to crawl toward the kitchen. "No champagne, I don't think," Duke said. "Case of tequila behind the icebox." They put on an Earl Bostic side. Meatball paused at the kitchen door, glowering at Sandor Rojas. "Lemons," he said after some thought. He crawled to the refrigerator and got out three lemons and some cubes, found the tequila and set about restoring order to his nervous system. He drew blood once cutting the lemons and had to use two hands squeezing them and his foot to crack the ice tray, but after about ten minutes he found himself, through some miracle, beaming down into a monster tequila sour. "That looks yummy," Sandor Rojas said. "How about you make me one?" Meatball blinked at him. "*Kitchi lofass a shegitbe*," he replied automatically, and wandered away into the bathroom. "I say," he called out a moment later to no one in particular. "I say, there seems to be a girl or something sleeping in the sink." He took her by the shoulders and shook. "Wha," she said. "You don't look too comfortable," Meatball said. "Well," she agreed. She stumbled to the shower, turned on the cold water, and sat down cross-legged in the spray. "That's better," she smiled.

"Meatball," Sandor Rojas yelled from the kitchen, "somebody is trying to come in the window. A burglar, I think. A second-story man." "What are you worrying about?" Meatball said. "We're on the third floor." He loped back into the kitchen. A shaggy woebegone figure stood out on the fire escape, raking his fingernails down the windowpane. Meatball opened the window. "Saul," he said.

"Sort of wet out," Saul said. He climbed in, dripping. "You heard, I guess."

"Miriam left you," Meatball said, "or something, is all I heard."

There was a sudden flurry of knocking at the front door.

"Do come in," Sandor Rojas called. The door opened and there were three coeds from George Washington, all of whom were majoring in philosophy. They were each holding a gallon of Chianti. Sandor leaped up and dashed into the living room. "We heard there was a party," one blonde said. "Young blood," Sandor shouted. He was an ex-Hungarian freedom fighter who had easily the worst chronic case of what certain critics of the middle class have called Don Giovannism in the District of Columbia. *Purche porti la gonnella, voi sapete quel che fa.* Like Pavlov's dog: a contralto voice or a whiff of Arpège and Sandor would begin to salivate. Meatball regarded the trio blearily as they filed into the kitchen; he shrugged. "Put the wine in the icebox," he said, "and good morning."

Aubade's neck made a golden bow as she bent over the sheets of foolscap, scribbling away in the green murk of the room. "As a young man at Princeton," Callisto was dictating, nestling the bird against the gray hairs of his chest, "Callisto had learned a mnemonic device for remembering the Laws of Thermodynamics: you can't win; things are going to get worse before they get better; who says they're going to get better? At the age of 54, confronted with Gibbs' notion of the universe, he suddenly realized that undergraduate cant had been oracle, after all. That spindly maze of equations became, for him, a vision of ultimate cosmic heat-death. He had known all along, of course, that nothing but a theoretical engine or system ever runs at one hundred per cent efficiency; and about the theorem of Clausius, which states that the entropy of an isolated system always continually increases. It was not, however, until Gibbs and Boltzmann brought to this principle the methods of statistical mechanics that the horrible significance of it all dawned on him: only then did he realize that the isolated system—galaxy, engine, human being, culture, whatever—must evolve spontaneously toward the Condition of the More Probable. He was forced, therefore, in the sad dying fall of middle age, to a radical re-evaluation of everything he had learned up to then; all the cities and seasons and casual passions of his days had now to be looked at in a new and elusive light. He did not know if he was equal to the task. He was aware of the dangers of the reductive fallacy and, he hoped, strong enough not to drift into the graceful decadence of an enervated fatalism. His had always been a vigorous, Italian sort of pessimism: like Machiavelli, he allowed the forces of *virtú* and *fortuna* to be about 50/50; but the equations now introduced a random factor which pushed the odds to some unutterable and indeterminate ratio which he found himself afraid to calculate." Around him loomed vague hothouse shapes; the pitifully small heart fluttered against his own. Counterpointed against his words the girl heard the chatter of birds and fitful car honkings scattered along the wet morning and Earl Bostic's alto rising in occasional wild peaks through the floor. The architectonic purity of her world was constantly threatened by such hints of anarchy: gaps and excrescences and skew lines, and a shifting or tilting of planes to which she had continually to readjust lest the whole structure shiver into disarray of discrete and meaningless signals. Callisto had described the process once as a kind of "feedback": she crawled into dreams each night with a sense of exhaustion and a desperate resolve never to relax that vigilance. Even in the brief periods when Callisto made love to her, soaring above the bowing of taut nerves in haphazard double-stops would be the one singing string of her determination.

"Nevertheless," continued Callisto, "he found in entropy or the measure of disorganization for a closed system an adequate metaphor to apply to certain phenomena in his own world. He saw, for example, the younger generation responding to Madison Avenue with the same spleen his own had once reserved for Wall Street, and in American 'consumerism' discovered a similar tendency from the least to the most probable, from differentiation to sameness, from ordered individuality to a kind of chaos. He found himself, in short, restating Gibbs' prediction in social terms, and envisioned a heat-death for his culture in which ideas, like heat-energy, would no longer be transferred, since each point in it would ultimately have the same quantity of energy, and intellectual motion would, accordingly, cease." He glanced up suddenly. "Check it now," he said. Again she rose and peered out at the thermometer. "Thirty-seven," she said. "The rain has stopped." He bent his head quickly and held his lips against a quivering wing. "Then it will change soon," he said, trying to keep his voice firm.

Sitting on the stove, Saul was like any big rag doll that a kid has been taking out some incomprehensible rage on. "What happened?" Meatball said. "If you feel like talking, I mean."

"Of course I feel like talking," Saul said. "One thing I did, I slugged her."

"Discipline must be maintained."

"Ha, ha. I wish you'd been there. Oh, Meatball, it was a lovely fight. She ended up throwing a *Handbook of Chemistry and Physics* at me, only it missed and went through the window, and when the glass broke, I reckon something in her broke too. She stormed out of the house crying, out in the rain. No raincoat or anything."

"She'll be back."

"No."

"Well." Soon Meatball said: "It was something earth-shattering, no doubt. Like who is better, Sal Mineo or Ricky Nelson."

"What it was about," Saul said, "was communication theory. Which of course makes it very hilarious."

"I don't know anything about communication theory."

"Neither does my wife. Come right down to it, who does? That's the joke."

When Meatball saw the kind of smile Saul had on his face, he said: "Maybe you would like tequila or something."

"No. I mean, I'm sorry. It's a field you can go off the deep end in, is all. You get where you're watching all the time for security cops: behind bushes, around corners. MUFFET is top secret."

"Wha?"

"Multi-unit factorial field electronic tabulator."

"You were fighting about that?"

"Miriam has been reading science-fiction again. That and *Scientific American*. It seems she is, as we say, bugged at this idea of computers acting like people. I made the mistake of saying you can just as well turn that around and talk about human behavior like a program fed into an IBM machine."

"Why not?" Meatball said.

"Indeed, why not? In fact, it is sort of crucial to communication, not to mention information theory. Only, when I said that, she hit the roof. Up went the balloon. And I can't figure out *why*. If anybody should know why, I should. I refuse to believe the government is wasting taxpayers' money on me, when it has so many bigger and better things to waste it on."

Meatball made a *moue*. "Maybe she thought you were acting like a cold, dehumanized, amoral scientist type."

"My god," Saul flung up an arm. "Dehumanized? How much more human can I get? I worry, Meatball, I do. There are Europeans wandering around North Africa these days with their tongues torn out of their heads because those tongues have spoken the wrong words. Only the Europeans thought they were the right words."

"Language barrier," Meatball suggested.

Saul jumped down off the stove. "That," he said, angry, "is a good candidate for sick joke of the year. No, ace, it is *not* a barrier. If it is anything, it's a kind of leakage. Tell a girl: 'I love you.' No trouble with two-thirds of that, it's a closed circuit. Just you and she. But that nasty four-letter word in the middle, *that's* the one you have to look out for. Ambiguity. Redundance. Irrelevance, even. Leakage. All this is noise. Noise screws up your signal, makes for disorganization in the circuit."

Meatball shuffled around. "Well, now, Saul," he muttered, "you're sort of, I don't know, expecting a lot from people. I mean, you know. What it is is, most of the things we say, I guess, are mostly noise."

"Ha! Half of what you just said, for example."

"Well, you do it too."

"I know." Saul smiled grimly. "It's a bitch, ain't it?"

"I bet that's what keeps divorce lawyers in business. Whoops."

"Oh, I'm not sensitive. Besides," frowning, "you're right. You find, I think, that most 'successful' marriages—Miriam and me, up to last night—are sort of founded on compromises. You never run at top efficiency; usually all you have is a minimum basis for a workable thing. I believe the phrase is Togetherness."

"Aarrgghh."

"Exactly. You find that one a bit noisy, don't you? But the

noise content is different for each of us because you're a bachelor and I'm not. Or wasn't. The hell with it."

"Well sure," Meatball said, trying to be helpful, "you were
using different words. By 'human being' you meant something
that you can look at like it was a computer. It helps you think
better on the job or something. But Miriam meant something
entirely—"

"The hell with it."

Meatball fell silent. "I'll take that drink," Saul said after a
while.

The card game had been abandoned and Sandor's friends
were slowly getting wasted on tequila. On the living room
couch one of the coeds and Krinkles were engaged in amorous
conversation. "No," Krinkles was saying, "no, I can't put Dave
down. In fact I give Dave a lot of credit, man. Especially considering his accident and all." The girl's smile faded. "How
terrible," she said. "What accident?" "Hadn't you heard?"
Krinkles said. "When Dave was in the army, just a private E-2,
they sent him down to Oak Ridge on special duty. Something
to do with the Manhattan Project. He was handling hot stuff
one day and got an overdose of radiation. So now he's got to
wear lead gloves all the time." She shook her head sympatheti-
cally. "What an awful break for a piano-player."

Meatball had abandoned Saul to a bottle of tequila and was
about to go to sleep in a closet when the front door flew open
and the place was invaded by five enlisted personnel of the
U.S. Navy, all in varying stages of abomination. "This is the
place," shouted a fat, pimply seaman apprentice who had lost
his white hat. "This here is the hoorhouse that chief was telling
us about." A stringy-looking third-class boatswain's mate pushed
him aside and cased the living room. "You're right, Slab," he
said. "But it don't look like much, even for Stateside. I seen
better tail in Naples, Italy." "How much, hey?" boomed a large
seaman with adenoids, who was holding a Mason jar full of
white lightning. "Oh, my god," said Meatball.

Outside the temperature remained constant at thirty-seven
degrees Fahrenheit. In the hothouse Aubade stood absently
caressing the branches of a young mimosa, hearing a motif of

sap-rising, the rough and unresolved anticipatory theme of those fragile pink blossoms which, it is said, insure fertility. That music rose in a tangled tracery: arabesques of order competing fugally with the improvised discords of the party downstairs, which peaked sometimes in cusps and ogees of noise. That precious signal-to-noise ratio, whose delicate balance required every calorie of her strength, seesawed inside the small tenuous skull as she watched Callisto, sheltering the bird. Callisto was trying to confront any idea of the heat-death now, as he nuzzled the feathery lump in his hands. He sought correspondences. Sade, of course. And Temple Darake, gaunt and hopeless in her little park in Paris, at the end of *Sanctuary*. Final equilibrium. *Nightwood*. And the tango. Any tango, but more than any perhaps the sad sick dance in Stravinsky's *L'Histoire du Soldat*. He thought back: what had tango music been for them after the war, what meanings had he missed in all the stately coupled automatons in the *cafés-dansants*, or in the metronomes which had ticked behind the eyes of his own partners? Not even the clean constant winds of Switzerland could cure the *grippe espagnole*: Stravinsky had had it, they all had had it. And how many musicians were left after Passchendaele, after the Marne? It came down in this case to seven: violin, double-bass. Clarinet, bassoon, cornet, trombone, tympani. Almost as if any tiny troupe of saltimbanques had set about conveying the same information as a full pit-orchestra. There was hardly a full complement left in Europe. Yet with violin and tympani Stravinsky had managed to communicate in that tango the same exhaustion, the same airlessness one saw in the slicked-down youths who were trying to imitate Vernon Castle, and in their mistresses, who simply did not care. *Ma maîtresse*. Celeste. Returning to Nice after the second war, he had found that café replaced by a perfume shop which catered to American tourists. And no secret vestige of her in the cobblestones or in the old pension next door; no perfume to match her breath heavy with the sweet Spanish wine she always drank. And so instead he had purchased a Henry Miller novel and left Paris, and read the book on the train so that when he arrived he had been given at least a little forewarning. And saw that Celeste and the others and even Temple Drake were not all that had changed.

"Aubade," he said, "my head aches." The sound of his voice generated in the girl an answering scrap of melody. Her movement toward the kitchen, the towel, the cold water, and his eyes following her formed a weird and intricate canon; as she placed the compress on his forehead, his sigh of gratitude seemed to signal a new subject, another series of modulations.

"No," Meatball was still saying, "no, I'm afraid not. This is not a house of ill repute. I'm sorry, really I am." Slab was adamant. "But the chief said," he kept repeating. The seaman offered to swap the moonshine for a good piece. Meatball looked around frantically, as if seeking assistance. In the middle of the room the Duke di Angelis quartet was engaged in a historic moment. Vincent was seated and the others standing: they were going through the emotions of a group having a session, only without instruments. "I say," Meatball said. Duke moved his head a few times, smiled faintly, lit a cigarette, and eventually caught sight of Meatball. "Quiet, man," he whispered. Vincent began to fling his arms around, his fists clenched; then, abruptly, was still, then repeated the performance. This went on for a few minutes while Meatball sipped his drink moodily. The navy had withdrawn to the kitchen. Finally, at some invisible signal the group stopped tapping their feet and Duke grinned and said, "At least we ended together."

Meatball glared at him. "I say," he said. "I have this new conception, man," Duke said. "You remember your namesake. You remember Gerry."

"No," said Meatball. "I'll remember April, if that's any help."

"As a matter of fact," Duke said, "it was 'Love for Sale.' Which shows how much you know. The point is, it was Mulligan, Chet Baker and that crew, way back then, out yonder. You dig?"

"Baritone sax," Meatball said. "Something about a baritone sax."

"But no piano, man. No guitar. Or accordion. You know what that means."

"Not exactly," Meatball said.

"Well, first let me just say that I am no Mingus, no John

Lewis. Theory was never my strong point. I mean things like reading were always difficult for me and all—"

"I know," Meatball said drily. "You got your card taken away because you changed key on "Happy Birthday" at a Kiwanis Club picnic."

"Rotarian. But it occurred to me, in one of these flashes of insight, that if that first quartet of Mulligan's had no piano, it could only mean one thing."

"No chords," said Paco, the baby-faced bass.

"What he is trying to say," Duke said, "is no root chords. Nothing to listen to while you blow a horizontal line. What one does in such a case is, one *thinks* the roots."

A horrified awareness was dawning on Meatball. "And the next logical extension," he said.

"Is to think everything," Duke announced with simple dignity. "Roots, line, everything."

Meatball looked at Duke, awed. "But," he said.

"Well," Duke said modestly, "there are a few bugs to work out."

"But," Meatball said.

"Just listen," Duke said. "You'll catch on." And off they went again into orbit, presumably somewhere around the asteroid belt. After a while Krinkles made an embouchure and started moving his fingers, and Duke clapped his hand to his forehead. "Oaf!" he roared. "The new head we're using, you remember, I wrote last night?" "Sure," Krinkles said, "the new head. I come in on the bridge. All your heads I come in then." "Right," Duke said. "So why—" "Wha," said Krinkles, "sixteen bars, I wait, I come in—" "Sixteen?" Duke said. "No. No, Krinkles. Eight you waited. You want me to sing it? 'A cigarette that bears a lipstick's traces, an airline ticket to romantic places.'" Krinkles scratched his head. "'These Foolish Things,' you mean." "Yes," Duke said, "yes, Krinkles. Bravo." "Not 'I'll Remember April,'" Krinkles said. "*Minghe morte*," said Duke. "I *figured* we were playing it a little slow," Krinkles said. Meatball chuckled. "Back to the old drawing board," he said. "No, man," Duke said, "back to the airless void." And they took off again, only it seemed Paco was playing in G sharp while the rest were in E flat, so they had to start all over.

In the kitchen two of the girls from George Washington and the sailors were singing "Let's All Go Down and Piss on the *Forrestal*." There was a two-handed, bilingual *mura* game on over by the icebox. Saul had filled several paper bags with water and was sitting on the fire escape, dropping them on passers-by in the street. A fat government girl in a Bennington sweatshirt, recently engaged to an ensign attached to the *Forrestal*, came charging into the kitchen, head lowered, and butted Slab in the stomach. Figuring this was as good an excuse for a fight as any, Slab's buddies piled in. The *mura* players were nose-to-nose, screaming *trois*, *sette* at the tops of their lungs. From the shower the girl Meatball had taken out of the sink announced that she was drowning. She had apparently sat on the drain and the water was now up to her neck. The noise in Meatball's apartment had reached a sustained, ungodly crescendo.

Meatball stood and watched, scratching his stomach lazily. The way he figured, there were only about two ways he could cope: (a) lock himself in the closet and maybe eventually they would all go away, or (b) try to calm everybody down, one by one. (a) was certainly the more attractive alternative. But then he started thinking about that closet. It was dark and stuffy and he would be alone. He did not feature being alone. And then this crew off the good ship Lollipop or whatever it was might take it upon themselves to kick down the closet door, for a lark. And if that happened, he would be, at the very least, embarrassed. The other way was more a pain in the neck, but probably better in the long run.

So he decided to try to keep his lease-breaking party from deteriorating into total chaos: he gave wine to the sailors and separated the *mura* players; he introduced the fat government girl to Sandor Rojas, who would keep her out of trouble; he helped the girl in the shower to dry off and get into bed; he had another talk with Saul; he called a repairman for the refrigerator, which someone had discovered was on the blink. This is what he did until nightfall, when most of the revelers had passed out and the party trembled on the threshold of its third day.

Upstairs, Callisto, helpless in the past, did not feel the faint rhythm inside the bird begin to slacken and fail. Aubade was by the window, wandering the ashes of her own lovely world; the temperature held steady, the sky had become a uniform darkening gray. Then something from downstairs—a girl's scream, an overturned chair, a glass dropped on the floor, he would never know what exactly—pierced that private time-warp and he became aware of the faltering, the constriction of muscles, the tiny tossings of the bird's head; and his own pulse began to pound more fiercely, as if trying to compensate. "Aubade," he called weakly, "he's dying." The girl, flowing and rapt, crossed the hothouse to gaze down at Callisto's hands. The two remained like that, poised, for one minute, and two, while the heartbeat ticked a graceful diminuendo down at last into stillness. Callisto raised his head slowly. "I held him," he protested, impotent with the wonder of it, "to give him the warmth of my body. Almost as if I were communicating life to him, or a sense of life. What has happened? Has the transfer of heat ceased to work? Is there no more . . ." He did not finish.

"I was just at the window," she said. He sank back, terrified. She stood a moment more, irresolute; she had sensed his obsession long ago, realized somehow that that constant thirty-seven was now decisive. Suddenly then, as if seeing the single and unavoidable conclusion to all this, she moved swiftly to the window before Callisto could speak, tore away the drapes, and smashed out the glass with two exquisite hands which came away bleeding and glistening with splinters; and turned to face the man on the bed and wait with him until the moment of equilibrium was reached, when thirty-seven degrees Fahrenheit should prevail both outside and inside, and forever, and the hovering, curious dominant of their separate lives should resolve into a tonic of darkness and the final absence of all motion.

NELSON ALGREN

The House of the Hundred Grassfires

I<small>T WAS</small> during that rumorous dappled hour when evening spreads like the latest scandal, before the night's true traffic starts. When such whore's foliage as vermilion bras and chartreuse panties still hang, in the airless heat of back-yard lines, between G-strings that once were silver. A joint-tog jungle festooned by garments of such bright shame as stay washable. Above a vegetation of contraceptives lying in puddles of gray decay.

This is the early-buyers' hour when women dust their navels for afternoon bugs who can't wait till evening to fly: all those hurrying from loneliness in order to preserve their solitude later. The city was full of lonesome monsters who couldn't get drunk any more.

At The Hundred Grassfires the night's first girl stood in the night's first door, feeling sweat molding her pink pajama to her thighs.

The whole street felt molded, thigh to thigh. Perdido Street was a basement valet shop with both irons working. In the round of her armpits the girl felt sweat creeping in the down.

She did not solicit; it was too hot for that. She had lived fifteen years in Chicago without once feeling warm; now she had lived almost ten in New Orleans without once feeling cool.

It was so hot that at sight of a man she could feel both watery navels stick. So she merely crooked her small finger now and then and let it go at that.

The courts were against these cork-heeled puppets, the police were against them as well. Politicians used them, editors mocked them. Doctors disdained them. Judges and Ministers were sustained by them. Daughters, sisters and wives were perpetually outraged by them. So mothers organized against them. Their own pimps conspired regularly against them.

Now a man wearing a shadow for a cap marched up and down, across the street, below a curious sign—

BEWARE THE WRATH TO COME

The missions were dispatching mercenaries announcing that Christ Himself had decided against them.

The man under the sign cut slantwise across the street to give the girl full benefit of his warning. She turned her hip to give him a bit of her backside, simply to show how little she needed him. Like all the women who kept the doors, Chicago Kitty knew that, like the police, the columnists, the courts, the doctors, the preachers and the pimps, he wanted to save her only to have her. For all the indignation these women provoked, no one ever wanted them to be anything but whores.

The prostitute never sent for anyone's husband. Husbands came to her. She never sent for a brother or son; sons and brothers came to her.

In the parlor behind Kitty sat other outlaws, eight nine ten, who had died of uselessness one by one. Yet now they lived on, behind veritable prairie-fires of wishes, while prying salt-water taffy from between their teeth. Envy and ennui divided each.

"A light drizzle would be good for trade," Kitty heard a man's voice say behind her, "but a heavy fall would ruin it."

That would be that appleknocker, an apprentice pimp calling himself Big Stingaree, recently arrived from nowhere in a red shirt and high-heeled Spanish boots; who'd be gone once more before the heels ran down.

The juke began complaining about everybody—

> *It isn't fair for you to taunt me*
> *You only want me for today*

A small man wearing a clerical collar, under a face favoring a raccoon's, skipped up—he was built like a bag of sand and somewhat favored a badger too. As Kitty stepped aside to let him pass, she caught a whiff of violet talc. The juke went on complaining—

> *It isn't fair for you to want me*
> *You only want me for today.*

A moment later she followed him inside just to see what he really wanted.

He was pulling off his collar—then flinging it across the room, then challenging the house:

"*Bring on your beasts of the wild!*"

"Are you sure you're in the right place, mister?" the apple-knocker pimp, standing a full head higher, inquired.

"Oh, I know what you people do here," Bag of Sand lowered his voice confidentially—"*I* know what you do."

"One of the things we do," a girl holding a poodle dyed pink remarked, "is pitch people out on their heads."

Bag of Sand laughed into the palm of his hand.

"*Exactly* what do you think you're geared to, mister?" the apprentice pimp wanted to know, stepping closer.

"Exactly what am I *geared* to?" Bag of Sand glanced up. "My dear young man, I'm exactly geared to the girlies, exactly. Otherwise why would I be here *exactly*? Or is this a hardware store?" And turning his back on the slow-witted macker, he began an explanation of the Immaculate Conception that not even Mama, the mulatto madam of The Hundred Grassfires, had ever heard before.

"Parthenogenesis is scientifically possible," he explained, as though the question had been troubling him for some time, "but it can only occur in the haploid chromosomes. As these are only half the size of the somatic chromosomes, they result in dwarfism. *That* was what happened to Mary."

"The hell with all that," the apprentice pimp decided. "How about some action?"

"Let him speak," Mama overruled the apprentice. "I know I'll never die sanctified. But I *do* hope at least to die blessed."

Bag of Sand began pacing up and down, in a sweat from more than the climate, one hand on his belly and one on his head— "and furthermore I'll tell you how the Church covered up the scientific truth that Jesus Christ *was* a dwarf. Every time the church fathers came to a biblical reference to Jesus as 'tiny,' 'little,' 'undersized,' or 'small,' they changed it to 'humble,' 'meek,' 'gentle,' 'modest,' or 'sweet.' I've done research all over the world on this and I can tell you: The Church has perpetuated a hoax!"

"Are you for action or aren't you, buddy?" Big Stingaree wanted to know.

"Well, in May, 1929, I wrote C-U-N-T on a convent wall in red chalk—how's *that* for action?"

Big Stingaree clapped his hand to his forehead and staggered backward to show that the mind boggled at the very thought.

"Not only *that*"—Bag of Sand seemed anxious to paint as black a picture of himself as possible—"*I was wearing the cloth at the time!*"

"No matter how you look at it," Mama deliberated solemnly, "it's a bad situation. I hope you've confessed, young man."

"Not formally," Bag of Sand explained, "but later in the same year, while passing the same convent, I wrote *Jesus Saves* where I'd written that other."

"What were you wearing," Mama wanted to know, "when you wrote *Jesus Saves* where you'd written that other?"

"A sports jacket and huarachos."

"I see," Mama said sorrowfully. "You write something like *that* while wearing the cloth and then come back six months later dressed like Bing Crosby, scribble *Jesus Saves*, and think you've missed Purgatory. It isn't as easy as all that, young man."

"The Pope himself couldn't get you off," Big Stingaree decided. "How about a bit of action as long as you're sunk anyhow?"

Bag of Sand agreed. For he was geared to the girlies just as he'd said. In fact, this ghee could scarcely remember one day to the next where he'd lain the night before. And as often as not, he wound up on the very same sack as he had at noon disheveled.

Twitched-struck and pussy-simple, snatch-mad and skirt-sick, he was a side-street solitary who had nothing but a petticoat with seven ruffles on it in his mind. One who dreamed by night of nothing but what he'd do to the girls tomorrow. This was a sinner whose family had once had him committed because he had decided he didn't want to be a priest after all. Any man who didn't want to be a priest was obviously out of his mind. There had been simply nothing left to do but to commit him.

What had thereafter emerged, obsessed by myths, was no longer of either the church or the world, but the ghost of a ghost who roamed a curious twilit land between the world and the church.

A land where the thousand images of sex stood transfixed like stone ruins in a desert place. Lost in a world where sex had gone blind, deaf, mute, cold and alone as a seaward stone.

"So long as I'm sunk I might as well have some fun out of sinking," he reasoned Jesuitically. Then, turning to the girl holding the poodle dyed pink, he inquired, "What may your little friend's name be, miss?"

"Heavensent," the girl assured him.

"Why, then Heaven must have sent him," Bag of Sand deduced. And offering the girl his arm, all three, girl, poodle and defrocked priest, proceeded up the unsanctified stair.

Now the blinds, drawn fast, held the room in a dappled gloom where dimly fell the shadows, one by one, of bars. And in this dusk like a jailhouse dusk the juke sang on and on.

> *Didn't have nobody*
> *To teach me right from wrong—*

The moment the song stopped, the creaking of the overhead fans began, regular and slow. The women shifted restlessly from doorway to divan, lighting fresh cigarettes or opening fresh Dr. Peppers at each new post; yet never finishing either a drink or a cigarette.

"You never know when a trick is a cop or somebody missing one bubble," the Chicago girl complained.

"When he starts in to strangle you, chances are he ain't a cop," Kitty explained. "It's why I keep saying it would be best if every trick took two girls. Then when he got your neck in his hands, your buddy could holler for you."

They never finished anything. Restlessness was their common affliction. Reba was sure the fan was giving her a chill, Floralee wanted to sing, and Kitty had to know why she wasn't permitted to spike a Coke with gin. While Mama worried lest she should die unblessed.

The girls crowded forward in their watery gloom, shading their eyes against the street: No one had seen the cab drive up.

It came out of nowhere. Like a cab that wheels all night through a misting dream.

All saw step forth in the greenish light a naval lieutenant in full regalia, a seagoing executive in rimless glasses: A hero of sea fights yet unfought. Bearing like a rainbow across his sky-blue breast all the honors a peacetime navy could pin.

Bag of Sand, wherever he'd gone, was immediately forgotten when this sight stepped out on Perdido Street.

Mama simply *scuttled* to the curb. Mama had never captured a prospect so glorious to behold.

Yet he seemed reluctant of capture. For he held Mama there in some earnest discussion, speaking low so as to keep his driver from hearing.

"Mammy-freak," Mama *thought* she heard him saying, "stick out so fah behind she hahdly got time to make a child behave."

Mama took one step closer. "I don't quite catch what you're saying, Officer."

He cupped his lips, leaning toward her—"*Made a lemon pie. Made me a lemon pie, little lemon pie all my own.*"

Mama took a step back. "Lemon?" she asked. "All your own?"

"The very day I broke the churn."

"Then I have just the girl for you," Mama decided. For whatever this rascal had in mind, she couldn't afford to lose a customer so prosperous. "Every man likes a little change now and then. I know exactly how you feel."

He drew himself up. "*Nobody* knows how a mammy-freak feels," he informed her point-blank. "How could anyone but another mammy-freak know how a mammy-freak feels?"

If it was an organization, he was the president. Mama simply turned to go, but he held her back with a wheedling touch. "You know yourself," he cajoled her, "how they stick out in back."

"*Who* stick out in back?"

"Why, all of them, especially when they get in a hurry. Now, *admit* it."

Mama shook off his hand. "Who stick out? Who get in a hurry? Admit *what*?" Mama was getting angry but she didn't know at what.

"Why, old black mammies of course," he told her as though everyone knew old black mammies were the coming thing.

"Maybe you ought to come inside before it rains," Mama invited him, suddenly feeling she'd be safer in the parlor.

"It isn't going to rain." Navy sounded certain as God and began unfolding a little apron from under his coat. He bent to tie it about her waist. It was striped green and white like peppermint, and as he tied it, Mama plucked without strength at the apron's price-tag. He picked the tag off himself and the cab dusted off in disgust.

"A good many black-mammy freaks visit you, I presume?" the officer assumed.

"It's been several days since one called," Mama told him. Standing in her Aunt Jemima apron, she now felt as if *she* had become the prospect.

"My men call me 'Commander,' " he announced.

"That," Mama decided inwardly, "isn't what my chicks are going to call you."

And led him inside The Hundred Grassfires like leading a child home.

Inside the parlor the six-year-old boy with the mind of a forty-year-old pimp, the one his grandmother called Warren Gameliel but whom the women called the King of the Indoor Thieves, stood on a divan wearing shoes that belonged to a grown man and nothing else but a shirt.

A shirt that barely reached his navel, revealing a hide not

exactly high yellow. The King was in fact closer to high brown. He was even closer to dark brown. As a matter of fact, let us face it—Warren Gameliel was black as a kettle in hell.

Truth to tell, the King looked to be a cross between a Black Angus calf and something fished out of the Mississippi on a moonless night. One shade darker and this kid would have disappeared.

"Meet my grandson," Mama introduced him to the Commander. "Ain't he jest *fine?*"

Turning his head proudly upon his iron-colored throat, the King fluttered his lashes modestly at the woman's flattery.

"Age six years, waist 32½, weight one hundred and two, and she asks is he fine," the woman called Hallie Dear mocked Mama fondly. The big overdressed man saluted the small naked one.

"Pledge allegiance, Boy-Baby," Mama encouraged the King to perform his single accomplishment. But the King simply planted his black toes wider, as though saying he'd have to know more about this gold-braid wheeler-dealer before he'd pledge his teething ring.

Then Reba honked with hollow glee: under the shirt the boy was reacting to the scent of the half-naked woman like a baby bull.

"I do it *back*," the King made his intention known.

"Ain't you *shamed*," Mama reproved him in a voice that simply *donged* with pride, "gettin' a upper right in front of ladies?"

"He'll be a pimp like everyone else," Kitty prophesied.

"I worked for loryers," Reba entered the stakes. "We specialized in tort'n'seizure."

These women regarded Hallie with an intermixture of admiration and pity. They felt she held herself aloof because she'd once taught school. At the same time they perceived that she was defenseless. Floralee alone loved and trusted the older woman.

But was there anyone Floralee didn't trust? If this pale lost blonde wasn't down the stairs by the time street-lamps came on, somebody went up and fetched her down. For should lamps come on or lamps stay dark, all was one to this pale lost blonde.

Nobody had counted, since nobody cared, how many lamps had gone down since the night she had stood where marquee lights flickered in an uncertain rain; and a cabbie had held a door wide for her. She had gotten in and offered him a pressed flower for her fare.

"I sing just *ever* so purty, mister," she assured the officer now. "Only modesty songs, of course, for I don't know vulgary words. May I recite a modesty poem?"

"Wait till you hear this loony holler," Kitty warned him. "I think all they did in them hills was bury their dead."

"Don't begrudge the child," Mama put her arm about Floralee's shoulder to indicate *she* wasn't one to begrudge *any* child, "she got the innocence God protects."

"He's got a strange notion of protection then, that's *my* opinion," Kitty told how she felt about everything.

And turned her back on the parlor.

What must I do to win a diadem

Floralee burst into song strung on a silver string—

When I reach that shining strand?

"*Shh*, honey," Mama tried to quiet the demented girl, and turning apologetically to the naval prospect, explained, "This one is a regular angel."

"She's a whore like everyone else," Kitty announced with her back still turned. Floralee cupped her face in her hands to hide her blush of shame.

"Anybody can be a whore," added Kitty.

"Is that true?" the Commander asked Mama seriously. "Can any one woman become a whore? Any woman at all?"

"Anyone at all," Mama seemed optimistic. "Aren't we all created free and equal?"

"Where do you keep your submarines?" Kitty turned abruptly on the officer.

"Why ask me a thing like that?"

"It would help me in my work—I'm a spy on the side." Nobody laughed when Kitty turned to the juke.

"I feel rotten about everybody but myself," she said aloud.

"I got half my choppers out 'n no ovalries," Reba remembered. "The doctor said he never seen nothin' like it. So what? I can still be a practical nurse without ovalries, can't I? Hey! How'd you like all the cigarettes you can smoke, General? Just go down to American Tobacco 'n give my name; they'll give you all you can haul in one trip."

"Baby," the girl called Big Five marveled, "I don't know what you're on, but *I* never heard nothing like it either."

"I do it back," the King insisted, but Mama yanked the gold-braid cap, which he had taken off the Commander's head, far down over his eyes. As if by shutting off his vision she might improve his manners.

"I *do* it," the infant insisted, warning everyone of what would happen the second he got this damned hat out of his eyes.

Somebody got the juke going, somebody said, Make mine a double, and somebody else called for gin—

> *Mama don't 'low no gee-tar playin' here*

the juke cried in dread—

> *Mama don't 'low no banjo-playin' here—*

"Oh, I can sing purtier *far* than that," Floralee boasted amid pleas, claims, threats, and tiny squeals. For now the women vied openly for the Commander's attention. While the King worked his thighs in a rage of blinded love but still couldn't get that cap out of his eyes.

"I want you girls to respect our guest!" Mama began shouting, though nobody had yet gotten around to insulting him. "Look *up* to this man. Hear this! Hear this! Warren Gameliel, you little black fool, get the Commander's hat off your head this *instant!*"

"Mama!" Hallie began scolding Mama. "Stop giving orders! We're not in a battle!"

"This man represents the entire Atlantic fleet combined!" Mama cried out. "Warren Gameliel! Pledge allegiance!"

"She's just being carried away," Hallie explained to the officer. Brushing the other girls aside, she framed his face in her hands until he returned the look she gave.

"If you don't behave, I'll send you to the nigger school," Mama threatened the King.

Outside the drunks were coming out of the country's last speakeasies and the street-lamps began to move like the breasts of a young girl under the hands of a man who has bought too many. Warren Gameliel reached out blindly and secured a black strangle-hold on the officer's neck.

And in an odd little silence a girl's voice said, "I was drunk, the jukebox was playing; I began to cry." All the air felt troubled by cheap cologne.

"Our guest wants to say hello," Hallie guessed, and pulled Navy's head right against her breast. He nodded strengthless assent.

She helped him to rise and he rose: more like a sick man than one drunk.

"Send two double-gins to my room," Hallie ordered Mama. "The rest of you drink whatever you want."

A kerosene lamp lit Hallie's room—one that might have served a whore of old Babylon: a narrow bed in hope of bread, a basin in hope of purity. A beaded portiere to keep mosquitoes out yet let a little music in. A scent of punk from an incense stick to burn off odors of whiskey or tobacco. A calendar from the year before and an image above it of something or other in hope of forgiveness for this or that. A whole world to millions since the first girl sold and a world to millions yet.

The lamp's brown glow on her amber gown made of Hallie a golden woman. For her eyes burned with a gray-green fire, and about her throat she wore a yellow band. Her gown fell off one shoulder but was kept from falling farther by the rise of her breast.

"No matter how often I trick," she murmured aloud, "as soon as I'm with a man, I get shaky."

"No need of even taking off your clothes," he told her. "Nothing is going to happen."

Hallie, always defensive about her darkness, was ready to be hurt. "Some men like dark girls best."

"Nothing to do with it," he explained. "I was brought up in

a special way. Yet I'll pay you for your time. I don't mean charity."

"I never turn down charity," Hallie told him candidly. "I have too much pride for that. What kind of whore would I be *then?*" She held herself proudly upon her dishonored bed.

"I'm from Virginia," he now thought she should know. "We go back to the Old Dominion."

"It's nice to have two homes, I'm sure," she congratulated him.

He smiled gently, then cupped her ear to confide something —"*It's where Old Black Mammy come by with a broom 'n 'most knock you down—'Stay outa mah way when ah'm cleanin', boy!'—but when you stay out of the way here, she come with bucket 'n mop 'n 'most knock you down again—'Boy, when you gonna learn to behave?'—'n when you start behavin' here, she come right at you—'Boy! You got nuthin' to do all day but stand in mah way?'*" His voice took on a secret excitement. "*Wham! She give it to you good, Old Black Mammy got a heavy hand—'Boy, you fixin' to git yourself soaked?'*"

He composed himself.

"Mister," Hallie asked at last, "how long you been in this condition?"

The big flushed man, boylike yet strangely aged, ran his hand across his hair to be sure its part was in place. He was one of those men whose teeth are so well-kept and whose hair is so well-groomed that both appear to be false.

"Black Mammy's been dead nineteen years," he told Hallie, returning to his white pronunciation. "Hand and foot that woman waited on us, and when the day came that found her crippled, who was there left to wait on her? 'Mammy,' I told her, 'you waited on me, now it's my turn to wait on you.'" A mischievous light came into his eyes: "That wasn't *all* I told her."

"All *right*—what else?"

"I told her, 'You made *me* behave, now it's my turn to make *you* behave.'"

"Mister," Hallie told him, "I really don't take your meaning —couldn't you get to the point?"

He crossed his large hands and looked at her evenly.

"I was working the churn when the handle snapped. The water from it was flooding the porch. When Black Mammy saw what I'd done, she aimed her hand at me. I slipped and fell trying to get away, so she paddled me face down. I started hollering, pretending she was half killing me, when it really hardly hurt at all. That was the first time she made me *behave.*"

Hallie saw light however faintly.

"What happened *exactly?*"

"*Exactly?* Exactly what happens when a man is having a girl, exactly. And I've never been able to make it any other way since." He laughed in the watery light. "Exactly."

Hallie waited.

"That was when I was ten. She died when I was twenty-one. And the day she died, the last motion she made was to give me a backhanded slap on my bottom. To let me know she had understood all along." He put his hand to his forehead. "I'm terribly tired, I don't know why."

"She must have been grateful for your care," was all Hallie could think to say. For it came to her that this wasn't a monster of the nastier sort but only a boy playing Commander with his nose still running.

"She was. As I'm grateful today for hers. Who else but Mammy ever felt I was worth human care?"

"Mister," Hallie told him quietly, "you don't need a girl. You need a doctor."

"There aren't any doctors for Black-Mammy freaks," he explained dryly, as though he'd tried looking one up in the City Directory.

"Then just try to rest," Hallie told him. "I'll do what I can."

"There's money in my wallet. It's in my coat," he instructed.

She took the coat off the chair and found the wallet. "I won't take it all," she assured him.

He didn't look interested in her count.

He looked stricken.

Fast as she could pin, Hallie began preparing Mama for a great impersonation.

"You don't think he stole his ship's money, do you?" Mama had to know. "He isn't going to get us all in trouble, is he?"

"You never made an easier dollar your whole enduring life," Hallie reassured her. "He's just a green boy kept on black titty too long. All you got to remember is he keeps getting in your way. Don't hit him too hard—just hard enough. Make it look good. Getting whupped by his old black mammy is what he come here for—turn around so I can pin you." She began stuffing a small pillow into Mama's bosom. "The more you stick out in front the more you stick out behind. I'll have you sticking out so far you'll look like Madam Queen."

"Girl, I was *born* in this country. You won't catch *me* hitting no member of our armed forces."

It was plain Mama hadn't caught the play.

"*Mama,*" Hallie pleaded, "*forget* the man's uniform. I'm trying to tell you he isn't like other men."

Mama stiffened like a retriever. "Honey, he ain't one of them O-verts? I won't cater to *them.* Not for *no* amount."

"If he were, he'd be better off," Hallie reassured her. "Now turn around," and pinned skirt over skirt till Mama, weighted down, sank heavily into a chair.

"Honey, I'm starting to sweat," she complained.

"Sweat till you shine," Hallie encouraged her, "but don't show your face till I give you the sign." And stepped through the portiere.

Beneath the ruin of the Commander's gold-braid hat, the King of the Indoor Thieves had collapsed at last, his undershirt tangled about his throat as if someone had tried to improve his manners by finishing him off altogether. He snored till his toes were spread; he stretched till he creaked in dreams. Dreams of some final assault for an earth about to be his for keeps.

"All of you stop talking out of the corners of your mouth like you were Edgar G. Robinson and everybody was in the can," Hallie quieted the women. "You've got a guest tonight that means gold from way back. Try to show manners."

For down the stair with an admiral's tread came the hero of sea fights as good as won. Looking like the dogs had had him under the house. With a gin glass latched to his hand.

Hallie crooked one finger toward the portiere and Mama came

forth with forehead shining, bandanna and broom, all sweat and Aunt Jemima in a peppermint apron that hung like candy.

The second he saw her, Commander dropped his glass. "I didn't *mean* to do that," he apologized immediately, and began trying to clean the floor with his sleeve, glass, splinters, and all, immediately making a worse mess than before.

Mama seated herself across from him in her preposterous gear. The girls exchanged looks, part fear and part wonder.

"I'm a Protestant by birth but a Catholic by descent." Mama felt it was time to explain the curious no-man's land of her faith. "I've shod the horse all around." Meaning she had had four husbands. "So I'm not acceptable to the Church. But if I can't die sanctified, I *do* hope to die blessed."

His elbow touched Floralee's glass. It tottered; he reached as if to keep it from tipping and knocked it over instead. The girl pushed back her chair and he began mopping it up with a silk handkerchief, although all he was doing actually was swishing the handkerchief around in it. "Go on with your story," he told Mama. "I'm *sorry* to be so clumsy."

Mama had lost the thread. All she could remember was that she'd shod the horse all around.

"Three of them were thieves and one was a legit man—I'd never marry another legit man. Do you know that you're safer living with a man who kills for hire than with a man who has never killed? That's because one knows what killing is; the other don't."

"Why," Commander remarked, "in that case, ill-fame women ought to make better wives than legitimate girls."

Nobody knew what to say to that.

"Navy, I think that's the nicest thing I've heard anyone say since I've been in the trade," Hallie said at last.

His elbow tipped Mama's glass into her lap.

"Now don't tell me *that* 'just happen,'" Mama scolded him in earnest now. "Mister, my frank opinion is you done that a-purpose."

"Honest, I didn't, Mammy," he lied patently.

"*Don't* whup him, Mama," Floralee pleaded for him.

"I'm *sure* he won't do it again," Hallie defended him too.

"Give me *one* more chance, Mama," he whimpered.

"Only out of respect for your uniform," Mama issued final warning, "and one more is *all* you gets." She turned to shake out her skirts, somebody tittered and somebody honked and she whirled just in time to catch the Commander with two fingers to his nose. Mama scarcely knew what to feel.

"Why, that isn't the least *bit* nice, a man of your background to have such manners—"

"He didn't *mean* anything, Mama," Hallie was sure.

"*Don't* whup him," Floralee begged.

"*Cross my heart* I didn't mean anything," Commander swore in that same unbearable small-boy whine that in itself entitled him to a thrashing.

"Oh, he *meant* it all right," Kitty informed. "I seen him with my naked eye. And I have a *very* naked eye."

"I *will* try to do better, Mammy," he promised too humbly. "Oh, I *will* try to behave, Oh, I *will* be a good boy, cross my heart 'n hope—" Standing up to cross himself, his hand caught the tablecloth and brought cloth, bottles, decanters, ash trays, Cokes and a centerpiece of artificial pansies crashing to the floor.

In the silence everyone heard a small clock saying "sick-sick-sick."

Then Mammy went even blacker with rage as he went whiter with fright. Now she went at him with no pretending, and he flung his two hundred and fourteen pounds under the table in true fear.

"*Don't* whup me, Mammy," they heard him pleading. "*Please* don't whup me just this *one* time."

Hallie tried to hold her and Floralee helped, because Mama *could* murder when out of control. Reba fastened onto Mama's waist to hold her back. Kitty stood to one side not caring particularly who got killed so long as blood was spilled.

"Beat him blue!" Big Five joined Mama's forces. "If you can't do it, I will!" and dove right for him.

"He's *Mama's* date, not yours," Hallie hauled Big Five back and held her until she calmed down—holding a strip of gold-braided blue serge in her hand ripped from the officer's sleeve.

"I'm just a little boy," they heard somebody under the table whine, "*please* don't hurt me."

"Now he's *really* asking for it," Kitty commented.

Just as the apprentice pimp showed up at last, complete in sombrero and boots newly shined. He was the only one capable of holding Mama in a true rage and Mama herself knew this. When he got both arms around her, she ceased to struggle and began to cry. He and Hallie got Mama into a chair, where she daubed at her eyes with his big bandanna.

Big Five got hold of one of the Commander's silken ankles and Floralee the other. Between them they succeeded in pulling him forth.

He lay on his stomach, rump elevated to invite kicks, eyes closed with rapture. Big Five pushed him onto his side, then by inserting one toe underneath him, rolled him over like lifting a great drugged cat, onto the flat of his back.

He lay face up, his eyes still shut.

"He got no right to lay around so loose, without being drunk or sick, either one," Big Five expressed her disgust. "Somebody get some water."

"I don't have any *water*," Floralee reported in her light sweet voice and a white pitcher in her hand—"Wouldn't beer do as well?"—and emptied it full in the officer's face.

Then, looking down into her pitcher, the girl saddened, "Now it's empty." She looked ready to cry.

"You could use Cokes," Hallie told her.

Now who but Hallie would have thought of *that?* Floralee gathered the half-finished bottles standing on ledge and divan, and in no time at all had her pitcher refilled. But this time she poured it down the front of the Commander's shirt.

"That *was* fun," she reported hopefully to Hallie, and lifting his legs and holding them, began to sing—

> Don't throw bouquets at me
> Don't laugh at my jokes too much—

while all the while the Commander lay licking his big ox-tongue like a Coke-dripping Lazarus too languid to rise.

"I've been everywhere God got land," Hallie told him, "but you are the *most* disgusting sight yet seen—you can drop his legs any time," she told Floralee. Who promptly let both legs fall at once.

"I had a very strong hankering to go to sea at one time myself," the apprentice pimp recalled, kicking the big man lightly: "Get up, officer."

But nobody really knew what to do with this hero of sea fights yet unfought.

Except the King of the Indoor Thieves. *He* always knew what to do.

"I do it *back*," he announced. And with no further ado, straddled the fallen leader and began urinating upon him with solemn delight. "I'm a sonofabitch," he explained, "I *do* do it back!" And fluttered his lashes above the torrent.

"Why!" Mama came suddenly to herself in a burst of sunrisen pride, "Why! Listen to *that*! A child of six using the language of a child of ten! Hear this! Hear this! Salute the Atlantic fleet!"

"Mama," Hallie sought to calm the older woman, "I respect the Atlantic fleet as much as the next person, but I do feel this child is going too far."

Mama came to attention, eyes straight forward, put her palm to her forehead in the hand-salute and began the Pledge of Allegiance. The King brought his own hand up to his forehead and stood at attention as well as he could while continuing to urinate.

The big man on the floor looked up. He opened his eyes so blue, so commanding. "That was the nicest party I've had in eleven years," he announced, rising at last.

Someone handed him his crushed hat and his soiled coat.

At the door he smiled but no one smiled back.

Mama lowered herself, inch by inch in all her finery, onto a divan. She felt like the real thing in black mammies. But all she did was sigh. Just sigh.

Outside, she heard the night's last drunk pause as if listening for a friendly voice, then cry out "God forgive me for my sins! Empty saddles in the old corral!"

And passed on toward the breaking day.

Half in wake and half in sleeping, Mama heard the jukebox weeping—

> *Let your tears fall, Baby*
> *If you really want to cry—*

When the juke began to bark, she wakened. Down the stairs the poodle dyed pink came bounding and barking all the way. Behind him came the girl who owned him, crying to Heaven: "Heavensent! Heavensent!"

And behind her, holding the banister with one hand, Bag of Sand came feeling his way down.

If he'd been out of shape when he went upstairs, he was really disheveled now. He came down like a man fearing to break his neck every step. And when he made it all the way down, he found himself facing the apprentice pimp, who seemed to have grown in size somehow.

"Are you for action or *aren't* you, buddy?" the would-be pimp wanted to know.

Bag of Sand got past him and stood in the middle of the parlor boggling blindly about.

"I can sing like a damned bird," Floralee told him. "Only how did I fly in here?"

Bag of Sand turned slowly away. But at the door he turned.

"Goodnight, girls," he told them. "Someday I'll tell you about the time I reviled the Virgin for fifteen minutes."

And he passed, like the Commander had passed, through a dark doorway into a darker dream.

"Go out and get the morning papers," Mama instructed Floralee. "I want to see what the white folks are up to."

The Authors

NELSON ALGREN lives in Chicago. Among his works are *The Man with the Golden Arm*, for which he received the first National Book Award, and *A Walk on the Wild Side*. His writing has received both critical and popular acclaim, and Hemingway named him, after Faulkner, as one of America's first writers.

SAUL BELLOW is Canadian born, grew up in Chicago, and was educated at Midwestern universities. As a recipient of a Guggenheim Fellowship, he has also spent some time abroad. In addition to five books, Saul Bellow has written critical pieces for *The New York Times*, the *New Republic*, and *The New Leader*, and he has contributed fiction to *The New Yorker*, *Harper's Bazaar*, *Partisan Review*, *Esquire* and numerous literary quarterlies. He is a member of the National Institute of Arts and Letters.

JAMES BLAKE writes: "Born Edinburgh—education interrupted by somnolent sojourns at University of Illinois, Northwestern. Left to resume education as night club pianist—nine years of graduate work at Florida State Prison—appeared in *Les Temps Modernes* and *The Paris Review*—now working on a novel in Connecticut."

CHANDLER BROSSARD is the author of *Who Walk in Darkness*, *The Bold Saboteurs*, *The Double View* and editor of several anthologies, among them *The Scene Before You: A New Approach to American Culture*. Born in Idaho in 1922, he has lived in New York City for the past twenty years and has been in publishing for twenty-three years. He has lived in France, Spain, and Italy.

BROCK BROWER is a writer of short stories, articles, and plays. An assistant editor of *Esquire*, to which he frequently contributes, and an associate editor of *Transatlantic Review,* he lives in Princeton, New Jersey, with his wife and three children. He wrote "Peacetime" while on duty with the U.S. Army at Fort Bragg, North Carolina, working on matters of guerrilla warfare strategy. He was born in 1931 and was a Rhodes Scholar.

HAROLD EDWARD FRANCIS DONOHUE, born and raised in Trenton, New Jersey, spent one year at William and Mary and then ten years in and around the University of Chicago, successfully avoiding teaching jobs and graduate degrees. He now lives in New York. At 39 he has finally finished his first novel (*The Higher Animals,* to be published by Viking), and is completing a connected series of short stories, *Life in the Movies,* about his home town. Married; three children. Beginning to go bald. Chews gum. Always wanted to win the Boston Marathon. Feels he is a failure as a writer because he is not anti-American. Strums the guitar when glum. Laughs too loudly for fun. Still likes women. A square.

GEORGE P. ELLIOTT writes: "I was born in Indiana in 1918 on a farm. When I was ten my family moved to the Southern California desert, where there was nothing half so good to do as to read; we had no money. I studied English in junior college and at the University of California in Berkeley, where I got my M.A. in 1941. I have had a variety of jobs—shipfitter, taxi driver, engineer's helper, filling station attendant, real estate broker, labor union official, reporter—but since 1947 I have worked at the job I like best, teaching college English, with three years off to write on fellowships. I am now professor of English at Syracuse University, teaching great books and fiction writing. My wife is an editor of *The Hudson Review.* We have one child."

BERNARD FARBAR has lived and worked in France, Spain, and Mexico and is now an editor in New York. He reports: "Am finishing a long awaited (by me, at any rate) first novel. Born in 1935 and have been fighting main events ever since."

BRUCE JAY FRIEDMAN was born in 1930 in New York City, attended De Witt Clinton High School, and received a Bachelor of Journalism degree from the University of Missouri. He served several years as an officer in the U.S. Air Force. His stories have appeared in numerous magazines, including *Mademoiselle, The New Yorker, Commentary, Playboy,* and in the literary quarterlies. His first novel, *Stern,* was published in 1962. A collection of his short stories called *Far from the City of Glass* will be published in mid-1963. He lives with his wife and three children in Glen Cove, New York.

JOSEPH HELLER lives and works in New York City. He attended New York University, Columbia University, and Oxford University, the last on a Fulbright Scholarship, and has taught at Pennsylvania State College. In recent years he has worked as a promotion executive. His first published novel, with Simon and Schuster, is *Catch-22*.

JAMES LEO HERLIHY was born in Detroit, studied at the Yale University Drama Department, and is the co-author of the highly successful play, *Blue Denim*. His stories have appeared in such magazines as *The Paris Review, Eve*, and Pocket Books' *Discovery #2*. Aside from writing, his chief occupation has been acting.

JOAN BALLARD KERCKHOFF, who was born in St. Louis, Missouri, in 1935, attributes the fact that she cannot eat chicken in any form to the circumstance that she was raised too close to chickens. *Talk to Me, Talk to Me* is a section from her longer work *Paid Friends and Good Companions*.

THOMAS PYNCHON was born on Long Island and is a graduate of Cornell University. His stories have been published in the *Kenyon Review, The Noble Savage*, and *New World Writing*. His first novel, V., was recently published by Lippincott.

HUGHES RUDD grew up in Waco, Texas. He attended the Universities of Missouri and Minnesota, was an air force pilot in World War II, and after that attended Stanford. Currently a CBS News correspondent covering the southeastern United States and the Caribbean area, he has also been a newspaper reporter, editor, industrial motion picture writer and director. Mr. Rudd has published short stories, articles and a novella. His work has appeared in *Harper's Magazine, Esquire, New World Writing, New Campus Writing, Southwest Review, Stanford Short Story Collections, University of Kansas City Review*, and *The Paris Review*. In 1961 he won the Gertrude Vanderbilt Prize for Humor offered by *The Paris Review*. His novel in progress will be published by Dutton.

TERRY SOUTHERN was born in Alvarado, Texas. His first short stories were published in Paris, in *New-Story* and *The Paris Review*; a novel, *Flash and Filigree* was published in England in 1958; and his short stories have been anthologized by David Burnett. He was awarded the Vanderbilt Prize for Humorous Fiction for a portion of his novel *The Magic Christian*, published by Random House in 1960. Mr. Southern is married and lives in Connecticut.